Death in October

LOWELL GREEN

Published by

GENERAL STORE
PUBLISHING HOUSE

1 Main Street Burnstown, Ontario, Canada K0J 1G0
Telephone 1-800-465-6072 Fax (613) 432-7184

ISBN 1-896182-68-2
Printed and bound in Canada

General Store Publishing House gratefully acknowledges the assistance of the Ontario Arts Council and the Canada Council.

This is a work of fiction; all characters are products of the author's imagination.

Canadian Cataloguing in Publication Data

Green, Lowell E., 1936-
Death in October

ISBN 1-896182-68-2

    I. Title.

PS8563.R41665D42 1996   C813'.54   C96-990109-7
PR9199.3.G73D42 1996

First Printing October 1996

Canada is not a real country.
— Lucien Bouchard, 1996

DAY ONE

Through the blurred windshield it looked like a large white rag streaked with red dangling on the gate. It wasn't until he stepped from his car into the rain and the night that he was sure it was Niki. His cry was filled with anguish and fear.

"No!"

A large spike had been driven through the dog's neck, pinning her to the top bar of the wooden gate. Most of the blood had been flushed away by the rain, but her once-beautiful snowy coat was streaked with red.

Niki, Dog of the North (as her registration papers identified her), had been a much loved member of the family since she arrived nine years ago as a present for Lee Henry's third birthday, a tiny ball of bouncing, whirling, tumbling, fluffy white Samoyed.

Listeners to the nightly Grant Henry syndicated open line radio talk show were often amused by the stories he related and invented about her, but horrified as he was at the sight of the sad, limp bundle dangling grotesquely on the gate, the terror exploding inside him, sucking the breath from his lungs, had nothing to do with the family pet.

Frantically, he lifted the metal latch and threw his shoulder into the gate, jolting it partially open. The limp torso swung violently on the spike. Grant had jogged that gravel lane countless times and knew it was almost half a kilometre to the house. Driving would have been faster, but for reasons he would later have difficulty explaining, he abandoned the car, motor idling, door flung open, lights blazing, and ran.

As he approached the corner of the sprawling building faintly discernable in the loom of the distant car lights, his heart racing, lungs on fire, he began shouting.

"Lee! Lee! Madame Gratton!"

He wrenched open the kitchen door and plunged into thick darkness.

"Lee! Honey, where are you? Madame Gratton are you all right?" Moving from memory now, in suffocating blackness, room to room; breath, sobs of desperation.

At first he thought the electricity was out again, something which occurred with maddening frequency in these Quebec hills a few kilometres north of Ottawa. The crunch of broken glass beneath his feet revealed the truth. Every light in the house had been smashed – except one. A faint sliver of light splashed the carpet beneath the door to his office. Cautiously, he pushed the door open and recoiled in horror. A blood-soaked cloth had been draped over his office desk lamp, which projected a narrow rectangle of light. Centred in the grisly, muted spotlight was a familiar piece of metal. Its numbers had been very carefully painted over, but clearly visible was the *fleur-de-lis* and the word *Quebec* across the top. Along the bottom was the provincial slogan: *Je me souviens*.

He recognized it immediately: the licence plate which had disappeared from his New Yorker two nights ago, removed from the car sitting in his driveway as he slept only a few metres away.

But of his twelve-year-old daughter, Lee Tracy Henry, and their housekeeper, good friend and neighbour Thérèse Gratton, there was not a trace. They had disappeared into the rainy October night.

Ottawa 12:14 AM – Day One

Jack (Jake) Barr would not have been on duty that night if he hadn't broken his staff sergeant's arm. As the chief complained bitterly during the subsequent disciplinary hearing, it wasn't so much the broken arm as the fact that it happened during a charity hockey game. "Did it ever occur to you to take it easy, to slow down a bit for Chrissakes?" the chief had asked, shaking his head in exasperation. Jake only stared at him. After cleaning pig pens on a prairie farm for most of the first twenty years of his life, Jake Barr had a lot of living to catch up on. The thought of taking it easy, of slowing down for anything, never entered his mind.

The price was paid. Jake was yanked from the youth services section where he had been the bright (if not so young) rising star, and ordered back into uniform. He was behind the wheel of an unmarked Dodge, cruising the market area on hooker patrol when he got the call.

"Jake, your buddy, Grant Henry, the radio man? He just phoned. . . frantic. . . looking for you. Sounded like he'd just had the shit kicked out of him. . . wants you to phone him at home right away. Geeze Jake, sounds like he's got one big problem. I don't like the smell of this one at all. Think I should give the boys across the river a call?"

Jake's response was emphatic. "Don't say anything to anybody until I find out what the hell is going on up there. Hear me?"

"Yeah, yeah, okay Jake, whatever you say. Just let me know what happens and listen, if you get yourself into a pack of shit up there in froggy land don't say I didn't warn you."

Pay phones were not hard to find in the market. Grant answered the first ring.

"The bastards got Lee, Jake. Madame Gratton too it looks like." He sounded frightened and angry. "They killed Niki. Nailed her to the gate!" He was almost shouting now. "For God sakes, get up here as fast as you can and Jake. . . listen, whatever you do, be careful. I think they're still out there! And," his voice calmer now, almost a whisper. . . " let's keep the Quebec police out of this as long as we can. Right now, I'm telling you, I don't trust a goddamn soul. . . especially not on this side of the river!"

12:21 AM – Day One

The rain pounded down harder than ever as the Dodge crossed the Ottawa River, left Ottawa and Ontario and climbed into Quebec's Gatineau Hills. It was four lanes most of the way, traffic was light and twenty five minutes later Jake whipped in behind Grant's still-idling car and braked.

"What the hell. . . !"

He'd been at a desk for most of the past eight months, but his reflexes were still good. He dove out the car door onto the gravel and in the same motion, yanked his service revolver from its holster. For just the briefest of moments, he'd caught a glimpse of what he was almost certain was a rifle barrel glinting dully in the headlights.

Jake was rolling in the mud and the gravel away from the car and its lights, when he saw the gun again. This time there was no mistaking it. There, no more than twenty metres away, at the top of the knoll which guarded the laneway.

He saw the flash, heard the crack, jumped to his feet and darted to the rear of his cruiser where he crouched, his heart flip flopping wildly. He couldn't return fire without revealing his position and had no idea how many were out there anxious to put a drain in him, or where they were. He was trying to quiet his breathing when, from the direction of the house, he heard Grant shouting.

"Jesus, Grant," Jake muttered to himself under his breath, "freeze your ass just where she is. These sonsabitches mean business."

He was about to vacate his position of safety and make a dash for the house when, from the knoll almost directly to his left, someone shouted in a deeply accented voice.

"Fucking anglais."

Jake whirled and snapped off three quick shots at the sound. In the same motion, he dove to the ground, rolled several times to his right and skidded down a small embankment onto Grant's front lawn where he lay as still as his heavy breathing would allow, listening. For what seemed an eternity, but was really no more than two or three minutes, he heard nothing but the murmur of the idling cars just above and the rain spattering the trees ringing the lawn as their tops tossed in the wind. From somewhere on the far side of the knoll a car door slammed, and for a brief instant headlights shot overhead into the sky before disappearing into the night.

Jake lay on the edge of the lawn, immobile, straining to hear every sound until, soaked to the skin and covered in mud, he slowly pulled himself to his knees. Hearing nothing but the idling cars, the wind and the rain, he scrambled back up the to the laneway.

'Got to get those lights out,' he told himself, 'or I'm a sitting duck.' Crouched low, he slipped to the rear of his car, paused to listen, then edged his way along the driver's side to the open door. Reaching inside, he switched off the headlights, slammed the door shut and dropped to the ground. If they were still out there, now was when they would shoot. They would have seen him silhouetted momentarily against the car's interior light.

Hugging the ground, he could see the outline of the knoll from where the rifle had been fired. Nothing. The only sound was Grant's car idling a few feet away. The rain had stopped.

Alert to any sound or movement, bent almost double, he crab-walked his way to the driver's door of Grant's vehicle and without pausing, vaulted into the seat, slammed the door shut and jammed the gearshift down. In a spray of gravel and mud, the car shot down the driveway towards the house. Jake tucked his head so low he could barely see over the dash.

The gate, with the dog still pinned to it, was only partially open. The car's left fender slammed into it, shattering the headlight and splintering wood. Something on the seat beside him slithered off the leather onto the floor. He was too preoccupied to notice.

The house was in pitch blackness, but Jake had been there often enough to know where he was. Turning sharply right as the tires hit the edge of the bricked patio, he braked and ducked even lower behind the dash, ready to fire. For an instant, the single headlight caught a man lying on the floor of the house, sprawled halfway out the kitchen door. A shotgun was aimed directly at the car. Jake recognized him.

"Grant," he shouted, "it's me, Jake. For Chrissakes point that thing someplace else. We're okay. I think they've gone."

To the south he could hear sirens coming closer.

* * *

The friendship between the radio broadcaster and the rookie cop began more than a decade earlier in the handball courts of Ottawa's Argyle Street "Y".

Beale Broadcasting had just begun feeding Grant's show to its seventeen radio stations across the country. Money was pouring in. Everything he touched seemed to turn instantly to gold. He began to consider himself more or less invincible.

Jake, on the other hand, had just joined the Ottawa police force and was walking one of the toughest beats in the city. He was just getting over a very messy and costly divorce, and if anyone had bothered to ask, he'd have admitted to feeling about as bad as it gets. The one level playing field he could find was the handball court, and anyone who tried to beat him there was sure as hell going to pay for it. Especially some rich asshole radio personality!

They were ready for each other.

Their battles in the handball court bordered on the vicious. They shouted obscenities, usually only partly in jest, and more than once they hammered the ball so hard at each other that Grant's wife Carol playfully asked him who the bony broad was he was screwing on the side.

"Get one with some meat on her," she giggled, "this one's going to beat you to death."

It was Grant who first suggested that they extend the relationship beyond the handball courts. When Grant called to change the time of a game, Jake sounded more dejected than usual. With alimony and child support on a rookie cop's pay, Grant knew handball was about the only luxury (if you could call it that) he could afford. Small wonder he hammered the ball so hard!

"Jake," said Grant, "I've got an idea. My wife's away, my daughter's off on a school trip; what say you and I suck back a beer and a steak at Al's tonight?"

There was a pause.

"Geeze, I'd love to," groaned Jake, "but you know I can't afford that kind of shit."

"Make you a deal," said Grant. "Let's you and me screw the government. Got anything against that?"

"Not so's you'd notice."

"Okay then, join me for dinner tonight and I'll tell Revenue Canada I was interviewing the Prime Minister so it's fully tax deductible. But Jake. . . one thing."

"Yeah, what?"

"No sob stories okay. . . ? We get shit faced, but none of your boring sob stories."

Jake chuckled. "Works both ways pal. Works both ways!"

They did invade sob story territory however, and they didn't do badly on the beer either. Grant, for the first time since university, didn't care to stop knocking it back. At some point in the evening, he was astonished to find himself admitting that his marriage was falling apart and he was devastated. "Jake," he said, as the beer began to short circuit inhibition, "you've been through it, does the pain ever really let up?" Jake gave him a look of startled disbelief.

"Wait a minute," said Jake. "Wait just a minute. You're rich and you're famous, it's true you can't play handball worth a fiddler's fart, but you're still in pretty good shape for an old guy of forty or so. Some women, God knows why, think you're kind of sexy with the Paul Newman eyes and the blond hair and big brain and all, and you're telling me you're hurting! Man, you have no idea what hurting is! Let me tell you what it's really all about. Pain is when your wife walks out on you with a guy you thought was your friend, takes your house, your car, your kid and more than half your salary. Pain is living in a little bachelor apartment so your wife and her new boyfriend can keep the fridge, which used to be yours, filled with beer which isn't even your brand. Pain is. . . " Jake stopped abruptly and peered at Grant with a wry look that danced back and forth between puzzlement and suspicion. "Sorry about that handball remark. I guess I always thought guys like you had it made. Silver spoon and all that."

"Silver spoon! Silver spoon!" Grant exploded with laughter. "You've got to be kidding! Silver spoon my ass! Jake, we were so goddamn poor when I was a kid, my mother used to send me along the railway tracks to pick up unburned coal so we wouldn't freeze to death. And in northern Ontario, believe me, that wasn't impossible. I played soccer wearing an old pair of ski boots. It was all we could afford. You can imagine what that did to my social standing in school. Hell's bells, I played high school football one year without a jock. Belly flops at practice were a lot of fun, let me assure you. You want to try it some time! Jake, every Goddamn thing I ever got in this life I earned with no help from anybody. Even when my old lady inherited a bundle, she was too damn mean to drop a dime on me. My old man was too lost in his dreams and crazy schemes to notice if I had pants, let alone a jockstrap. I went without eating for one full week in Sudbury once; my mother wouldn't loan me ten bucks even though she was loaded by then. I arrived there for a new TV job without a dime in my pocket, too young and stupid to realize I wouldn't be paid for a week. There was no silver spoon anywhere near me, believe you me. I swore a long time ago that no kid of mine would ever have to scrounge coal or anything else, but I'm telling you Jake, with all the shit I've been through, nothing hurts as much as my marriage breaking up, absolutely nothing."

In the end, Jake had to drive him home, Grant with his head out the window, puking his guts out for the better part of thirty kilometres. 'Like some stupid high school kid,' Grant told himself in one of his more lucid moments.

It had been raining that night too; pouring.

After that, their handball games remained as hard fought as ever. The shouted obscenities continued, but the bruising, save for the occasional "miss," ended.

Hull 1:08 AM – Day One

Chief Superintendent Marcel Charron of the Quebec Provincial Police (Sûreté du Quebec, Hull District) was, above everything else, a Montreal Canadiens fan. Along with almost every male raised in Quebec, he had dreamed about playing for them when he was a boy. Charron's affinity for the Canadiens was common knowledge in the department, the subject of countless jokes. What wasn't as well known was that Superintendent Marcel Charron was a separatist. Not a rabid and vocal one, as were some of his wife's university friends, but he had been convinced for some time that Quebec's independence from the rest of Canada would be the best for all concerned; the only thing which would ever resolve the differences driving many Canadians crazy.

Fluently bilingual, he often listened to Grant Henry's two hour week-night talk show. It was broadcast from just across the river in Ottawa, but as one of his wife's friends remarked, "Only a few meters from here, but like the rest of this crazy place, we're light-years apart!"

In recent months, Grant, along with most of his anglophone callers from across the country, had been complaining bitterly about the manner in which English speaking Quebeckers were being treated following the second referendum defeat for the separatists in fifteen years. He shared a growing belief with many that the separatist government was intent on driving the anglophones out of the province in order to assure themselves of a victory in a third referendum.

The inspector didn't believe a word of it, and was convinced that the growing threats of partitioning off federalist strongholds and Indian lands in Quebec after a separatist victory were nonsense.

A few weeks ago Grant had launched a campaign to, in his words, "expose a campaign of calculated discrimination against the English minority in Quebec."

"Great for the ratings," the superintendent had grumped grimly to his wife one night, "but a long way from the truth." As far as Charron was concerned, the English in Quebec were still the most pampered minority to be found in any jurisdiction in the world. "The English sure as hell get a lot less discrimination here in Quebec than the French do in Ontario!" he had shouted at his radio one night, as a particularily bigoted caller began ranting and raving about Quebec's sign laws.

Charron's sentiment was shared by many who lived in Quebec, including some whose mother tongue was English.

Tonight though, the superintendent was in an especially good mood. The Canadiens had pounded the Buffalo Sabres and he'd tuned in to the last part of the Grant Henry show just in time to hear an obviously very well educated separatist present his case very skilfully, refusing to back down from the host's biting, satirical wit.

"It's not often," Charron told his wife, "that anyone beats up on that son of a bitch Henry the way that caller did tonight. Hot damn! I'd sure like to know who he was." Charron was still chuckling about it when he fell asleep.

It would be a long time before Superintendent Marcel Charron felt like laughing again.

His sleep, and although he had no way of knowing it, his life, was interrupted by the phone. It was the desk sergeant speaking rapidly in French.

"Sorry to wake you superintendent, but the shit is in the fan. Looks like someone's kidnapped that radio broadcaster Grant Henry's daughter up in Poisson Blanc. The housekeeper, Therese Gratton is missing too. There's apparently been some shots fired. I've already dispatched Charlebois and Lamare. They should be half-way up there by now. Pichè just pulled out of the yard here. I sent Ryde with him. Do you want me to call in some off-duties?"

Charron, with a spryness belying his fifty six years, sprang to his feet beside the bed.

"Who kidnapped his daughter? Who's shooting? What the hell is going on here?"

There was a pause as the sergeant checked his notes. "Sir, we received the call at 1:03 this morning from Mr. Henry himself. He told us that when he returned home from work early this morning, someone had broken into his house, his daughter and their housekeeper were missing and he'd heard shots only a moment before he called us. He said he believed someone was shooting at him, or possibly at Constable Jack Barr of the Ottawa City Police, a friend he'd called for help. He started to say something else but the phone went dead. The operator says a wire must be down."

"Did he say if he knew who was shooting? Does he have any idea how many there are? What were they shooting at? Why are the Ottawa Police involved? This isn't their jurisdiction."

"No sir. I didn't have time to ask him anything. All he said was that his daughter and Madame Gratton were snatched and someone was shooting. Constable Barr is a friend of his sir," said the Sergeant. "I've played a couple old timers games against their hockey team." He couldn't resist adding, "neither one of them can play worth a shit."

The superintendent's mind was racing.

"Do any of our off-duty men live in that area?"

"Stapley, sir. He's at Ste Rose des Peche, maybe ten minutes to the north of the Henry residence."

"Get him to set up a roadblock at Ste Marie right away," instructed Charron. "Get another one up immediately at Domville too, that will cover us to the north. Down here to the south, let's see, set one up at the Meech Road. Tell them to be very careful. We don't know what we're dealing with. Everybody gets checked at the roadblocks you understand? No drivers licence, no identification, anything strange, they don't get through. Tell all our men to be very very careful. Don't take any chances. We have no idea what we've got going here, but we must assume that we are dealing with armed and very dangerous people.

"Call in all off duty officers and have them assemble at the Chelsea intersection and await further orders. And sergeant, tell your men not to be taking pot shots in the dark unless someone's shooting at them and they have a damn good look at who's doing it.

"Oh yes, be sure to tell them to make sure Henry knows who they are when they approach his house. He may be scared shitless but I understand he's no pattycake and living in the country he probably has a gun and may be spooked enough to shoot at anything. Let's not be having any stupid accidents. I'm on my way right now; should be there in less than half an hour."

Charron was about to hang up when another thought struck him. "Sergeant?"

"Yes sir."

"The media doesn't get this. Not a peep, do you hear me?"

"Absolutely, sir. Not a peep!"

1:22 AM – Day One

Charron was just climbing into his car when Sergeant Albert Lamare and Constable Eugene Charlebois skidded their cruiser into the Henry laneway, almost ploughing into the car blocking their way. Suspecting an ambush, both men dropped down behind the reinforced metal doors of their vehicle and pulled their weapons. Hearing and seeing nothing suspicious, they cautiously climbed out and carefully examined the abandoned car, its engine still running.

"Hey," said Lamare, "this thing belongs to the Ottawa Police Department. What the hell is going on?"

A moment later two more cruisers, sirens blaring, lights flashing, spilled into the laneway.

4:12 AM – Day One

Aside from two men parked in a cruiser at the end of the laneway, they were all gathered in the Henry garage which had been hurriedly converted into a temporary command post. Charron had used his cellular to make several calls to his office in Hull and to Montreal. The missing girl's mother had been tracked down in Vancouver and would now be on her way to the airport. Thus far no one had been able to locate Madame Gratton's only relative, a son living in Windsor.

For several minutes they sat in silence, except for Grant, who grimly paced back and forth across the garage entrance, staring at the black outline of his home a few metres away. A rooster began to crow from the small chicken coop at the rear of the garage, then another. Golden Pencilled Hamburgs, colourful, exotic chickens raised from eggs by Lee. It would soon be dawn.

Charron glanced at his watch then turned to look closely at Grant who had stopped his pacing for a moment and stood slumped against the garage door frame. Earlier, he had raged at the superintendent. "Why the hell aren't you out looking for my daughter? Why are we just sitting around?"

Charron gently explained that he'd called Montreal for assistance. Two detectives, including the province's leading investigator were already on their way and he didn't want his men trampling around in the dark, destroying God knows what evidence. Bell Telephone was already repairing the phone line which had been cut at the end of the laneway and someone was on his way from Hull to put a tap on Grant's phone. An APB had been issued with the descriptions of both his daughter and Madame Gratton to all police forces in Quebec. Both the RCMP and the Ontario Provincial Police had been notified.

Stepping forward, Charron touched Grant lightly on the shoulder.

"It's almost 4:30," he said kindly, "can I have one of my men get you a coffee or anything?"

Grant shook his head and said grimly, "Look, sorry for the blow-up, but are you certain there isn't something else we could be doing? I just can't stand this sitting around waiting. It doesn't make any sense when. . . "

"But we aren't just sitting around," insisted Charron. "Our people will be here very soon from Montreal. There's only one highway in and out of here, as you know, and we've got roadblocks up everywhere. Until we get some daylight, there isn't much else we can do." He paused, then turned to look directly at Jake sprawled on the floor, his head propped on a feed bag. "And as for the Ottawa Police, they have no business up here at all in any kind of official capacity."

There was no response from Jake whose mind was on something else.

Constable Stapley had managed to round up a few light bulbs, but Charron had instructed that nothing in the house was to be touched until the special investigators arrived from Montreal. Shortly after his arrival, the superintendent, alone, careful not to disturb anything, had gone from room to room with a flashlight to insure there was no obvious evidence, or so he told Grant. What he really wanted to be certain of was that a body, or perhaps even two, had not been left somewhere inside. From what he could see however, there was nothing amiss other than the broken lights, the gruesome desk lamp and the licence plate. There was not the slightest sign of a struggle.

He spent a long time staring at the licence plate still lying on the desk in the eerie light.

"Damn," he whispered into the shadows, "has it come to this?"

4:33 AM – Day One

It was Jake who found Lee's hair. His nerves were screaming at him; he found the waiting intolerable, but there was something else, something poking around at the edges of his consciousness. What had he seen during his wild ride down the laneway? A movement of some kind. Where? Puzzled, he slouched to his feet and, ignoring Charron's glare and admonition not to touch anything, borrowed Stapley's flashlight and stepped outside.

The rain had stopped, a few stars were out, and to the east across the Gatineau River, a faint glow indicated the roosters' instincts were correct. Dawn was just on the other side of the mountain.

Jake began to explore the patio, casting the cone of light from side to side. Something drew him to Grant's car, the empty socket of its smashed headlight faintly visible in the growing light. He opened the driver's side door and augmenting the overhead light with his flash, explored first the front seat and floor then the back. Nothing. Slowly he withdrew and closed the door. His heart was pounding. What was it? And then the veil dissolved. He saw it clearly. Something moving beside him on the seat. Running around to the passenger side, he threw open the door.

He didn't need the flashlight to see it. There it was, almost under the seat, tight against the gearshift hump where it had fallen during his wild ride down the laneway. A clump of blond hair, maybe five inches long, tightly tied with a blue ribbon. Lee's.

* * *

The pregnancy had been a delightful surprise and the cause of considerable concern. Only three months into their marriage, Carol had suffered a traumatic miscarriage late in the second trimester, and her doctor was not at all sure if she could become pregnant again, let alone carry a child to term. But aside from the fact the birth had to be induced ten days late, the pregnancy was absolutely normal. Lee could not have been a happier, more lovable child.

Her great-great paternal grandfather had been a Danish sea captain from whom she had inherited, as had all his descendants, the blond hair and blue eyes which once prompted someone to remark that Henry family reunions, with their ever-increasing swarms of children swooping about, were beginning to look a lot like gatherings of little Viking munchkins!

The fact she was an only child occasionally concerned both Grant and Carol. They discussed adoption several times, but while neither would ever admit it, even to themselves, they sensed their own relationship was too fragile to risk another ingredient. If Lee missed the company of siblings, she gave no indication of it.

Carol was determined Lee was going to be raised, not as she had been, like one of a large brood of cute, rough and tumble puppies, but by the book. Any book it seemed, so long as it dealt with child development or psychology. From Spock to Burton-White, Lee was guinea pig to it all, and none of it appeared to make the slightest difference. No matter what school of psychology Carol was avidly devoted to that particular month, Lee just kept doing what she had done since birth, what just seemed to come naturally: smiling, laughing, singing, exploring and bouncing about.

Their home movies and videos were an endless montage of Lee mugging for the camera, Lee opening Christmas presents with big smiles, Lee singing at the school concert, Lee playing with Niki, Lee coming up laughing after taking a tumble on her new bike. The only variant was one shot which they used to play over and over, to great guffaws every time, of Lee, aged about five, carefully feeding her beloved Golden Pencilled Hamburg chickens. To shouts of "watch this, watch this," every time they screened it, one of the roosters, not much bigger than Grant's fist, marched boldly up to Lee's leg, and without warning, landed a vigorous peck. You could see Lee's look of astonishment, only inches from the camera, then the eyes crinkling into tears, not of pain, but of absolute shock and disbelief at the discovery that the world held anything but kindness and love for her.

Grant remembered thinking more than once, while watching that scene, that Lee was destined for a few more shocks in her life.

The decision to move to the Gatineau hills of Quebec shortly after Grant and Carol were married had been easy. House prices were about a third less than on the Ontario side of the Ottawa River and the spectacularly rugged mountain terrain entranced them both, but it was the house which the moment they saw it, convinced them this was where they wanted to live.

Built originally as a large and ornate summer cottage, bits and pieces had been tacked on over the years, until now it sprawled and rambled so much neighbours began calling it Chateau Henri as a local joke.

That first winter they almost froze to death, the oil furnace and huge fireplace no match for the arctic winds which whistled merrily through the walls and floor. Residents of the tiny nearby village of Poisson Blanc were obviously more than a little amused at the crazy anglais who dared spend a Gatineau winter in a summer cottage, chateau or not.

A local wit suggested to his buddies one day that his wife was so upset with him over a weekend drunk, she had become *frois comme le Chateau Henri*, as cold as the Chateau Henry. And so was born a bit of local folklore.

Separatism was not an issue most Canadians gave much thought to when Grant and Carol first moved to Quebec.

For Grant, the first inkling of what lay ahead occurred one evening in that bastion of the ruling Westmount class at the time, the Ritz Café, on the lower floor of Montreal's Ritz Carleton Hotel. They were there to celebrate the launch of his talk show in Ottawa.

As was the custom at the Ritz, seating was in concentric circles, according to power and wealth. The richest and most powerful were carefully placed in the booths circling the outer edges of the dining room. Everyone else was pretty well relegated to the centre of the room. "Just a little," Grant told Carol as they were seated, "like the good old days, when all we sinners had to sit in the back rows of my grandfather's church, except here at the Ritz it's not the back rows for those of us not among the chosen few, it's the middle of the room!"

The evening was about half over when the tempo of the Café suddenly changed; a quickening of its pulse, a subtle shift to a higher gear. Voices switched from English to French, a decibel louder, then up another notch. Waiters, almost torpid with servitude and acquiescence, began bustling with excitement and purpose. All eyes, including those which otherwise would have been focused on the outer circle to detect the slightest arched eyebrow, or raised finger, snapped to the front entrance where a beautiful ash blond woman, dressed entirely in black leather, swept in. Amazingly, she was virtually ignored. The excitement was generated, not by her, but by the little wizened bantam rooster of a guy, hair carelessly thrown over to one side, stained fingers clutching a cigarette, strutting cockily behind her.

René Levesque, recently elected leader of the separatist Parti Quebecois, was greeted and escorted across the room with great ceremony by the head waiter, then immediately surrounded by a small bubbling army of waiters and bus boys at the table furthest from the centre.

Thick black clouds of hostility, precursors of the gathering storm, drifted up from the English power booths of the outer circle.

The reaction in the dining room was so fascinating, Grant discussed it the following Monday on his show, and issued what was probably English Canada's first warning of what lay smouldering on the horizon. Most of the diners were anglophone, the majority old Montreal money from upper Westmount, with a sprinkling of the nouveau riche here and there, also English speaking. The waiters and bus boys were all working class French Canadians.

"What you have to remember," Grant told his listeners, "is that for every English speaking Quebecker, there are about eight whose mother tongue is French." And judging from what he had seen, there was absolutely no question of where French Canada stood on René Levesque and the Parti Quebecois!

The P.Q. victory at the polls less than a year later, which shocked most Canadians, and scared the hell out of English speaking residents of the province, came as no surprise to Grant. Unlike thousands of other Quebec anglos who fled Quebec, frightened or frustrated, or both, the Henrys decided to stay. At no time did they feel anything but total acceptance by their neighbours, the majority of whom were francophone.

Grant was surprised to learn how much common experience he shared with the hard-working farmers who scraped a bare existence from the thin, mean soil of the Gatineau Hills. Growing up poor in Ontario in English he decided, was pretty much like growing up poor in Quebec in French. One day, not long before his thirty-first birthday, he found himself rolling around in the dirt, flailing away at an Irish tough who'd been heckling a couple of the younger members of his Poisson Blanc softball team.

"Hey," whined the tough, through bloodied lips, "you're English, what in hell ya doin' cuddlin' wit da frogs?"

Grant belted him again, having learned very early in life that when something important had to be done he'd best get on with it himself.

But as the years progressed, Grant became more and more disenchanted with what he was seeing and hearing. The election of the Bloc Quebecois to official opposition status in the House of Commons several years ago disturbed him deeply but he had no intention of leaving. Quebec was his home.

The decision to stay became extremely difficult for him during the divorce two years ago. It was Lee, actually, who made up Grant's mind for him. He was helping her feed her chickens one evening not long after the final split with Carol, when his daughter very solemnly announced that since they wouldn't be able to live together as a family anymore, she had decided she wanted to live with him here in the chateau, where she could keep her friends and her chickens.

Afraid she might try legal action to remove Lee, Grant had not told Carol about the telephone threats which had begun about three months ago. Not until he found one of Lee's chickens nailed to the garage door with a note scrawled in English saying, "fuck off anglais," had he even bothered to tell Jake.

"I have no idea who's doing this," he told a very concerned Jake, "but it's really starting to worry me. These days you really don't know what's happening. From what I understand, half the Quebec police force has turned separatist and I don't imagine they're exactly too crazy about me, with what I've had to say about their speed traps for anglos."

Jake had made no bones about what he thought of it.

"Lay off the Quebec stuff for awhile," he warned Grant. "Some of the kooks out there today will shoot you for a dollar, let alone an insult. And you're right about the Quebec coppers. They hate your guts."

But, with only the slightest twinge of worry, Grant continued with a series of broadcasts exposing discriminatory practices against the English speaking minority in Quebec by government officials and the Quebec bureaucracy. Most of the recent information came from an anonymous source who obviously had access to government files. The material, which had begun arriving about six weeks before, was well researched and documented, always arriving by mail postmarked Quebec City. Thus far the information had been accurate.

Two days ago he had received a tape cassette, apparently from the same source. It was accompanied by a scrawled note which claimed it had been recorded during a meeting of the Quebec cabinet the day previous. If it was authentic, and Grant would soon know, the recording provided him with his best ammunition yet. It was a piece of dynamite which, if made public, would cause tremendous embarrassment to the separatist government.

The tape was badly muffled, as though recorded from a distance, but someone, presumably a cabinet minister, could be heard quite clearly making outrageously racist statements about anglophones, and in one case, native Indians.

Jake had warned him the tape could be dangerous stuff but Grant, accustomed to warnings and even death threats over the years, from various sources for various reasons, had only laughed and said, "Come on Jake, you've been watching too much Robocop. This is Canada!"

5:12 AM – Day One

Grant watched in horror as Quebec's most famous detective, rumpled from his three-hour drive from Montreal, carefully placed some of Lee's beautiful golden hair in a plastic pouch, sealed it with a large piece of masking tape and handed it to his assistant.

Inspector Paul Boisvert, Chief of Detectives, Sûreté du Quebec, Montreal District, brushed the palms of both hands down the sides of his raincoat, as if to rid them of something distasteful, and said in impeccable English, "Monsieur Henri, there are some things here I am having extreme difficulty understanding." He was staring thoughtfully at the plastic pouch holding Lee's hair. "For example, how did that hair get in your car? Very strange wouldn't you say?"

Grant jerked his head back in surprise at the tone and content of the inspector's question.

"How the hell should I know how it got into my car?" he bristled. "What do you mean, strange? Presumably someone was hiding in the dark near the entrance to the laneway, probably the same person Jake fired at. When I ran to the house. . . " He stopped, and peered intently at the odd looking detective. "Wait just a minute here. What do you mean something strange? What are you suggesting? That I somehow know how her hair got into my car?" His voice rising: "Or that I put it there? Is that it? Are you seriously suggesting that I'm involved?" Almost shouting: "Are you crazy?"

Boisvert stared at him for a moment through narrowed eyes, then snorted in derision, "Well we shall soon see won't we? You and I sir," he said, jabbing a finger almost in Grant's face, "have a great deal to talk about when I'm finished examining your house. Stay out of our way now but don't leave the premises." He made no attempt to conceal his hostility.

Under normal circumstances Grant would have silently seethed. You either learned to handle public insults when you were in the talk show business or ended up on assault charges every other week. But this morning, disoriented from shock and lack of sleep, already enraged at what he believed to be inaction and incompetence, he exploded from his chair.

"You Goddamn son of a bitch," he screamed, "get off my property. It's bastards like you who cause all the trouble!" The little detective whirled about and clenching his fists, took a step towards Grant. Then, with a glare of pure malevolence, he jammed his hands into his coat pockets and with a curt nod to his assistant, turned and walked towards the house.

Grant was about to charge after him when Jake grabbed him

roughly by the shoulders. "Don't even think about tangling with that mother," said Jake. "Get it under control man, under control."

* * *

Paul Boisvert had learned his hatred of English-speaking Canadians early and well. Growing up in north end Montreal's St. Leonard district was, for most, a desperate struggle. The streets, playgrounds and school yards were battlegrounds, with English and Italian speaking children, boys and girls, pitted against their French Canadian counterparts. No one was ever sure why. Mutual hatred was just part of the air you breathed in St. Leonard; an inherited disease passed from one generation to the next. Newcomers acquired it quickly through osmosis.

If life was difficult, as it was for even the strongest, fleetest and most attractive, then for Paul Boisvert it was a nightmare.

On some obscure twig of some long-forgotten branch of his ancestral tree, a gene had gone awry; recessive for generations, but ever-present. It lurked, lying in wait for the opportune moment to pounce, needing only to mate with a comparable genetic misprint to initiate an ambush of the innocent. Or, as a family friend reputed to possess powerful psychic abilities claimed, maybe it was only because his mother had eaten chokecherries the day she conceived him!

Errant genes or chokecherry consumption, Paul Boisvert had been born with a face which looked as though someone had taken forceps and yanked his nose so violently forward it hadn't been able to snap back, but remained frozen there; a large and pointed beak, spliced onto the top half of his face.

Paul had no idea there was anything different or odd about him until, at the age of four, a group of young children, all speaking English, passed him and his mother on the street. One of the children turned suddenly and pointed to Paul, shrieking in badly accented French, "*La petite poule, la petite poule.*" It was a name he had to endure, usually accompanied by loud clucking noises and the flapping of elbows, well into adolescence. It ended only after he was rescued by a sympathetic Montreal cop from a frightful beating at the hands of a gang of English speaking ruffians. It was the cop who introduced him to the St. Hubert Boxing Club.

Paul's small size was more than compensated for by a deep seated rage, which within a few weeks had so frightened most of the young fighters at the club, that only a few, more experienced and stronger than he, dared enter the ring with him. Within a year he had won the Montreal championship in his weight class and had offers to turn professional. The little chicken had become a fighting cock!

All but the most foolhardy of St. Leonard's dwindling English speaking population now gave him a wide birth. Any who dared offer a challenge were savagely beaten.

Paul's technique was to poke and jab, bruise and cut. In and out like lightning. To the eye, the nose, the cheek, the ear. Hardly ever to the body. "Makes them quit too soon," he sometimes explained to the crowds that gathered to watch and applaud English defeat. "There's nothing I enjoy more than blood on an English face."

He was tempted to turn professional but could see no real future in it.

One of the few acts of kindness he had experienced from a stranger was his rescue by a Montreal cop in that alley off Jean Talon Street, so the day after he graduated from high school, he applied to join Quebec's Provincial Police force. Having no inkling of the rage which boiled just beneath the surface, they accepted him.

6:13 AM – Day One

At first light, Charron's men cordoned off the areas immediately surrounding the chateau and the scene of the early morning gunfire. Charron removed the dog's corpse from the gate as Boisvert watched silently. Grant had been instructed to remain inside the house on the pretext of assisting in the search for clues there. Jake offered to join in the inch-by-inch search of the knoll from where the rifle had been fired, but was cooly rebuffed by both Charron and Boisvert. All he could do was watch, curious that Boisvert seemed intent on searching the ground around where Grant's car had been parked, despite the fact the rain had obliterated even the tiremarks.

Their first success was discovering the spent rifle bullet buried in a dead elm tree, at least five metres from where Jake had spilled from his car.

Boisvert was visibly puzzled by the discovery. He motioned to Jake. "Constable Barr," he said, "would you come here? I need some help with this." Jake ambled over to the detective. "Yes, yes, that's fine," said Boisvert, giving Jake a strange look. "Now then, would you please show us exactly where you were this morning when the shots were fired. If you don't mind please re-enact for us everything you did. Make sure you are exactly where you were this morning when all this happened." When Jake complied he repeated," You're absolutely sure, Mr. Barr, this is where you were lying when the shot was fired?"

Jake had little difficulty in pinpointing the spot some two car lengths from the now shattered gate. Finally satisfied, Boisvert and Charron walked to the base of the tree struck by the bullet and conversed briefly with each other in French. Both nodded several times in apparent agreement.

It was Charron who now approached Jake. Boisvert, his hands plunged deeply into his pockets, was a half step behind, listening intently.

"Mr. Barr, how long was it, would you say, from the time the shot was fired until you heard Mr. Henry shouting? Are you absolutely sure the shouting came from the house?"

A bolt of alarm raced up Jake's spine.

"Now wait a minute, what the hell are you guys getting at? I heard Grant shouting only a few seconds after the shot was fired and there's absolutely no question he was inside the house or certainly very close to it when he yelled at me. And, as you can plainly see, that house is a hell of a long way from where that shot was fired. Geeze Murphy, what are you thinking? Grant's dog has been killed, his daughter, whom I assure you he loves deeply, has been abducted, their housekeeper, who's a very good friend, is missing, and you're standing there, hinting all over the place that maybe he had something to do with it! Kidnapping his own daughter! Killing his own dog! Is that really what you guys are thinking? Come on. Get serious!"

Charron paused for a moment, collecting his thoughts, glancing briefly at Boisvert. "Oui, oui," he muttered to himself in French, then said in English. "You are probably right, but then again some things puzzle us. You are police, you put some pieces together for us." He stopped, waiting for a response, then continued when there was none. "Okay, first off, by the time you heard that car pull away, we had already been alerted and were setting up road blocks. We figure the one at Ste Rose de Peche went up no more than twenty minutes after the shots were fired and probably only about fifteen minutes after you heard the car drive away. Speeding like a crazy man, you could clear Ste Rose in less time than that, but ten minutes later we had another roadblock at

Domville. That's a good forty-five kilometres to the north of Ste Rose. The kidnapper's car couldn't possibly have made it that far in that time.

"That's to the north. To the south, we had a roadblock up at the Meech Road intersection long before any car could have made it from here according to your timetable. There's only one road, as you know, up through these hills, which means they're either still in this area or a helicopter popped down and lifted them out. That's possible I suppose, but dangerous as hell in these mountains in the dark. The other thing is, we've checked, and air traffic control, both at Macdonald Cartier International in Ottawa and the local airport at Gatineau report nothing. The Macdonald Cartier radar definitely would have spotted a helicopter."

"They could have parked a car on this side of a roadblock," said Jake, "walked around it through the hills, then been picked up by another car on the other side. Hell, they could be holed up someplace right around here."

It was Boisvert who responded. "Yes they could have stayed in this area, although it's not likely, but as for walking around the roadblocks, where's the car? Our men have checked every side road and every field large enough to park a car within walking distance of the roadblocks and have found nothing, but even so, if that's all that was puzzling about this we wouldn't be as concerned. The fact is, there are a few other things hard to explain. The hair in Mr. Henry's car. That means someone. . . excuse me. . . whoever kidnapped the daughter must have hung around waiting until the father arrived. . . knowing he would abandon his car and run to the house!" The little detective shot both eyebrows skyward, dangerously close to his hairline. "And. . . you really have to ask yourself, why would anyone leave a car and run a good half kilometre instead of drive? And how could the kidnappers have possibly known he was going to do that? Getting back to your friend's little jog down the laneway, you must have asked yourself why he would leave his car here at the gate and run all the way to the house, keeping in mind, of course, he was in a great hurry."

He shot Jake a quizzical look, and continued without providing a chance for a reply. "There is also the matter of the licence plate we found in the house. . . from Mr. Henry's car let's not forget. . . and there's something else." He peered intently at Jake. "You say the person with the rifle was only up there." He gestured towards the knoll. "Whoever it was must have seen you in that car. They could hardly miss you could they, with all the lights and everything? They must have known you couldn't be far away from the car when they fired. How could that shot. . ." Here he stepped closer and pointed his finger directly at Jake's head then away towards the tree which had been hit. "How could that shot have missed you by so much?"

Jake snapped the answer off in a rapid burst of anger. "How the hell should I know? Maybe he was blind. Maybe he shot high on purpose. Maybe he was a fucking separatist and lucky he didn't shoot himself!" He knew it was a mistake and was sorry before the words were half out, but the bastards had asked for it. "Besides which," he added hastily, "how about the guy who yelled at me?"

Both Charron and Boisvert looked at him coldly, a slight flush creeping up Boisvert's extraordinary face. "Aah oui," he said, "we believe there is more than one person involved in this all right!"

He began to walk away, then turned around suddenly.

"Oh," in his precise English, "Constable Barr, in discussing this situation with your superiors a few moments ago, they were distressed that you had abandoned your post in Ottawa to attend a situation out of your jurisdiction without their knowledge or approval. They indicated they would very much appreciate hearing from you at your earliest possible convenience with an explanation!"

Boisvert wheeled and walked briskly away towards the Henry house. He was startled for an instant as the windows appeared to fill with flames, then realized they had caught the ball of fire just now cresting Mt. Cascade to the east.

* * *

The outburst between Grant and Boisvert at the garage command post had shocked and puzzled Superintendent Charron.

At the first opportunity, he cornered Boisvert alone. "What are you up to?" he asked. "What have we got here? Some kind of Simon and Garfunkle? Good cop-bad cop? Why? Henry doesn't have anything to do with this. Better clue me in." He peered intently at Boisvert over the Henry kitchen table and had to stifle a sudden desire to giggle. "My God," he thought, "this guy looks like a chicken!"

It was the fighting cock who replied. "You're probably right, but I smell something very funny going on here. This guy's in the entertainment business isn't he? Any idea what this kind of publicity would do for him? This is the kind of thing which could pump him right into the great U.S. of A., and can you just imagine what the TV or movie rights for something like this would be worth. The guy just got a divorce didn't he? Any idea what that must have cost him? Listen, I learned a long time ago that people will do almost anything for money, and there's nothing they won't do for money and fame. Besides which," he added, speaking softly, "you forget the most important part of all." He paused and stared intently into Charron's eyes.

Charron broke the silence.

"Which is?"

"If this English son of a bitch gets too much sympathy here it could really hurt us."

There was no mistaking what Boisvert meant by "us". For a moment, Charron found himself back in that room just overhead, staring at a licence plate beneath a blood-stained cloth, wondering where it was all going to end. It filled him with a terrible sense of foreboding.

They discussed the case for a few more moments before Charron reluctantly agreed to a strategy he didn't fully understand and had grave doubts about.

He didn't know it, but he didn't stand a chance against Boisvert, who would never allow himself to lose a battle of wills, particularly against an opponent he considered far inferior. The master of the jab, cut and bruise had no intention of losing this fight, which he sensed might become the most important of his life.

As part of the strategy, Grant was instructed to remain in the house while they quizzed Jake alone at the laneway entrance.

"We're going to dust for fingerprints," Charron explained to Grant. "We'll photograph every room, especially your daughter's bedroom, and we'll vacuum every surface. We can DNA even a single hair. I want you to show my men through the house. Make sure they hit every room and closet. Please pay very close attention to everything you see. If there's anything, anything at all you think is out of the ordinary, stop everything and call me. I'll be at the gate with your friend Barr and Detective Boisvert, seeing what we can learn there."

7:32 AM – Day One

Grant was having trouble concentrating. Boisvert's face flickered in and out of his vision. At times he could recall events with great clarity then, without warning, his mind would play tricks and even the simplest information escaped him. Half way through a sentence he would forget what he had set out to say. And most disconcerting, despite his intense antipathy towards the little weasel-faced bastard, he found himself unable to stop apologizing to him. Several times he was on the verge of tears when his inability to recall every detail seemed to disappoint the detective.

Early in his career, Boisvert had acquired a secret Scotland Yard report which very thoroughly documented experiments with sleep and sensory deprivation carried out on IRA prisoners during the 1950s. Over the years, he had added certain refinements of his own. During one interrogation, deep in the bowels of Montreal's Atwater Police Station, well concealed from his fellow officers, he had managed, with ice water and a pair of needle nosed pliers, to keep a suspect awake and more or less conscious for seventy eight hours. His problem now was that this English bastard, as exhausted as he was, was not stupid. Push too hard and he was likely to have enough smarts left to clam up and demand his lawyer, something Boisvert did not want just yet. To keep Grant talking, Boisvert had to do something he had little inclination for. He had to show sympathy.

"I know this is very difficult for you," he said, "but Mr. Henry, you've told me something of what happened, but only in bits and pieces. This time I want you to explain everything to me, exactly as it happened, and exactly in sequence. I don't want you to leave anything out. The timing of events is particularly important to our investigation. There may be some things I'll ask which you'll have difficulty understanding, but it is all very important if we are to find your daughter. Tell me everything you saw, heard or even thought, from the time you left the radio station after your show last night, until Superintendent Charron and his men arrived here."

Boisvert switched on his tape recorder and two officers seated behind them at the kitchen counter prepared to take notes.

Grant did not respond immediately, staring coldly at Boisvert as he pushed the mike closer.

From his experience, the detective knew that most subjects entered a stage of resistance at some time, usually fairly early in the process. He also knew the most effective manner of inspiring co-operation.

Very slowly Boisvert extended both his hands and gently covered one of Grant's.

"I'm so sorry I spoke harshly to you before," he said in a voice approximating solicitude. "To tell you the truth, I find this very difficult. I have a daughter not much older than yours. I understand perfectly how terrible you must feel." Here he paused and clasped Grant's hand more tightly. "And I can imagine how terrified your daughter must be right now. . . God help me, I hope they haven't hurt her."

The act and the lies produced the desired effect. Grant sank his head to the table and once more began to relate the events from the time he pulled into his driveway early that morning and confronted horror.

Superintendent Charron, who was standing at the kitchen door, had to stifle his anger as he watched Boisvert's performance. Boisvert did not have a daughter, he was not even married. For the second time that day the superintendent found himself enveloped in a terrible melancholy.

Boisvert stopped Grant when he began to describe leaving the car behind and running towards the house.

"I know we've discussed this before, Mr. Henry," Boisvert said, making a pretence at patience, "but taking into account the fact there was great urgency for you to reach your home, why do you think you left the car behind, when it would have been much faster driving than running?"

"As I told you before," replied Grant wearily, "I'm not sure myself. For some reason all I could think about was getting to the house to see if Lee was all right. The thought of going back to the car just seemed impossible at the time. I know it doesn't make much sense. If I had to do it again, I'm sure I'd take the car. It certainly would have been faster, but I suppose I wasn't thinking too clearly. Maybe I just panicked." It was essentially the same reply he'd given before.

At the word panicked, Boisvert looked up sharply and stopped him.

"Panicked. . . you never used that word before, but you know, it makes me wonder. You told us someone nailed a chicken to your garage door a few weeks ago, did you panic then?"

"It certainly worried me," said Grant, "but no, I didn't panic."

"In fact," said Boisvert, "I believe you told me you didn't even report it to police, other than your friend Constable Barr in an unofficial manner. No official report about the affair was ever filed with any police department. Why did that incident bother you so little, but a few weeks later, the same thing is done to your dog and you panic so badly you decide to run almost half a kilometre in the dark with your car sitting right there?"

As exhausted and dazed as he was, familiar alarm bells began to go off. Danger! He could hear his mother's voice screaming. "Don't lie to me Grant," her face twisted and red with rage. "I can tell you're lying to me," her hand drawn back, ready to strike. Danger! Long ago, he had promised himself never again!

"Wait a minute," said Grant, "I don't have to put up with anymore of this crap. You can take a flying. . ."

Boisvert knew immediately there was nothing more to be learned here. He dropped the mask.

"To tell you the truth sir," he snarled, "I don't believe you are telling me everything. There's something else going on around here. Something you're holding back. I can feel it." He waved off an attempted denial from Grant. "Listen, whatever it is you aren't telling us, you can be certain I will find out. For your sake, I hope your refusal to tell me everything doesn't place your daughter in more danger!" Jab, jab, cut and bruise. Blood on the face. English blood!

11:24 AM – Day One

Despite his determination to stay awake, Grant had fallen into a fitful sleep which was interrupted after less than two hours by one of Charron's detectives shaking him violently, and shouting in broken English into his ear. "Madame Gratton, Messieur Henri. Messieur Henri, Madame Gratton; they got her okay."

Grant bolted from the bed.

"What happened? Where is she? Is there any word of Lee? What about Lee? Can I talk with Madame Gratton? Does she know where Lee is?"

"Unfortunately," explained Charron calmly, as he entered the room, "the housekeeper knows very little. She was found wandering near the abandoned railway tracks east of Poisson Blanc only about an hour ago. She was pretty badly disoriented, but otherwise unhurt. I'm sorry to say," sighed Charron, "she seems to know virtually nothing of what happened, either to her or your daughter. According to her. . ." He checked some notes. "Shortly before ten last night (she remembered that the CBC news was just starting), she responded to the doorbell and stepped outside when no one appeared to be there. Something, a bag or a large cloth or a blanket, was dropped over her head. She remembers a brief instant of a very strong smell but nothing more until awakening sometime this morning lying at the side of the railway tracks."

He went on to explain that she was in hospital for observation but Inspector Boisvert, who had questioned her for some time, was confident she would be of no assistance in their investigation. She hadn't seen anyone, nor heard a thing other than the doorbell.

Charron's recital of events was interrupted by the ring of the phone which sent a shot of adrenalin rushing up from the pit of Grant's stomach. The kidnappers? No. Carol, just arrived at the airport, a twenty-minute drive south of Ottawa. As reassuringly as he could, Grant explained that Lee still had not been found. "No," he told her, "the kidnappers have not been heard from and yes, you are welcome to come and stay in the chateau for the time being."

A moment later it was Jake on the phone.

"The chief gave me a twenty-minute lecture about not sticking my nose into someone else's business and tacked on a two-week suspension," he told Grant. "Hey don't worry about it pal, I need the holiday, besides which, in good old public service style, the suspension is with pay. Not too shabby eh? Listen, I'm packing a few things. I'm coming up and I'm moving in. Any objections?" Before Grant had a chance to reply, Jake continued, "I didn't get a chance to talk to you earlier, but whatever you do, don't say anything to that little chicken faced bastard. He seems to believe we've got something to do with this, which indicates, along with everything else, he's got the I.Q. of a gerbil. I hope you didn't tell him about that tape recording."

"No," said Grant thoughtfully, "but the little cock-face knows I'm holding something back. I don't think he's dumb at all."

"Just ugly," said Jake.

"No," said Grant, "ugly and mean."

12:00 Noon – Day One

The house was strangely still. Charron had acquired use of the RCMP crime lab in Ottawa on the assumption that international terrorism might be involved. Both he and Boisvert were probably already at the lab with the evidence they had been able to collect; the licence plate, the blood-stained cloth, the badly mangled bullet, Niki's body and Lee's hair. They also had the photographs they had taken and the contents of the vacuum used in Lee's bedroom. Grant was not aware of it, but they had also vacuumed and photographed the interior of his car.

The two detectives who remained were idly smoking in the dining room, glancing from time to time towards a small battery of tape recorders and phones scattered along the floor. Wires ran every in a tangle to the telephone box in the basement.

In the odd stillness which had settled over the house, Grant found himself straining to hear Lee's happy, excited voice. He almost expected to see her skipping through the kitchen door or down the stairs. Once, he had to stop himself from calling excitedly out to her when a partridge she had faithfully fed during the past two winters fluttered down to the base of the crab apple tree whose branches caressed the living room window on windy days.

For the past half hour he had wandered aimlessly through the house, absently opening doors, staring blindly into rooms. Alone in the bathroom, he was shocked by the drawn, weary face in the mirror, eyes puffy and red, older than he remembered. And frightened.

Without warning, he burst into uncontrollable sobs as the unspeakable grief and pain knifed into him. He stumbled into Lee's room, numbed and disconsolate, peering with tear-filled eyes into a closet, the clothes ghostly suggestions of her on their hangers, the carefully made bed with its sprinkling of teddy bears. He picked up the book she had been reading when he left for the studio yesterday. Emily Bronte's *Wuthering Heights*. Was it only last night that she had breathlessly confessed to him that she was falling desperately in love with Heathcliffe?

The room filled with a kind of thick and heavy darkness, dangerous and threatening. He was seized by an overwhelming urge to plunge down the stairs and escape into the bright sunlight, to run and run until exhausted. Charron though, had been insistent.

"You've got to stay in the house at all times. You can expect a phone call at any time from those who took your daughter. Whoever has done this terrible thing obviously knows the police will be here, and their conversations are being recorded, so you can expect them to disguise their voices on the phone and speak very briefly. There are devices available now which will distort the voice. Let them talk as much as possible. Agree to everything they say. Make sure you understand any instructions they give you, and whatever you do, don't lose your cool. Stay calm, don't get angry. You can ask if Lee is all right, they will expect that, but don't demand to speak with her. No matter where Inspector Boisvert and I are, we'll be notified immediately any contact is made with the kidnappers. We can be here in half an hour. But listen, whatever you do, don't take any action of any kind without us. And remember: keep your friend Barr out of this. This is a Quebec matter."

Grant had no intention of keeping Jake out of it. Boisvert's obvious malice, and in particular his suspicion that he and Jake knew more than they were saying confirmed what Grant's instincts had told him all along. Involving the Quebec police was a mistake. God only knew where their sympathies lay. They could not be trusted. A long buried fear was worming its way back to the surface. Who could be trusted?

Foreboding swept over him like a giant wave. Unable to escape the feeling, he paced from one side of the kitchen to the other, waiting for the call; dreading it, and praying for it.

1:19 PM – Day One

When the call finally did come, they were all there. Grant still pacing, Jake unpacking in the basement bedroom and Carol weeping quietly at the kitchen table.

As instructed, Grant answered, trying to stay calm but unable to breathe properly. The voice was muffled, the French-Canadian accent unmistakable.

"Listen carefully anglais. If you want to see your daughter alive again, you do exactly what I say. In front of 64 Torbolton Street in Hull is one of those big mail boxes with lots of little ones in it. 1B is not locked. Inside you will find a tape cassette. You big fucking hot shot Henry, you get it." Then malicious and taunting. . ." Hey Mr. Big Mouth, nice young stuff eh?" A click, and the voice was gone.

The colour drained from Grant's face. His hand shook so violently he had difficulty replacing the receiver. Carol, pale and trembling beside him, had been unable to hear the conversation but was horrified at Grant's reaction. Grasping him by both shoulders she shook him and shouted, "What did they say? Where is Lee? Is she all right?"

As calmly as possible, Grant explained.

Hull 1:32 PM – Day One

Superintendent Charron was in precisely the same spot he had been when the first call to the Henry household arrived more than twelve hours before. This time it was his wife who awakened him. She had removed the phone from the bedroom, hoping he would be able to get at least a couple of hours sleep. It wasn't to be.

"The kidnappers' call just came in," she told him. "There's a tape recording with instructions in a mail box in front of 64 Torbolton. It's Sergeant Tremblay on the line."

Charron listened intently to a recording of the call then began issuing instructions.

"We're going to do what they tell us. You remain in the chateau. Have Ryde bring Grant to. . ." the inspector paused a moment, fixing the location in his mind. ". . .Torbolton and Tache. That's about two blocks from the mail box. Tell Inspector Boisvert I'll meet him there in about fifteen minutes, as soon as I can get the area cordoned off."

"God knows why I'm sealing off the area," he admitted to his wife a few minutes later, as she hovered over him insisting he eat some toast. "You can be sure the bastards are long gone, but you never know for sure do you?"

Boisvert was waiting for Charron at the intersection. They briefly debated the wisdom of having Grant retrieve the recording, but agreed it was probably best to follow the caller's instructions. "Besides," added Boisvert, "I'm still convinced this radio son of a bitch knows something more than he's telling us. I want to watch every move he makes."

2:01 PM – Day One

There was nothing to distinguish the rack of postal boxes which stood in front of 64 Torbolton, except one of them, 1B had its lock broken. The heavy metal door swung open easily. Inside was a plain white envelope, bulky with its contents. Following Boisvert's instructions, Grant grasped it carefully by one corner, slipped it into a plastic bag and hurried away, casting nervous glances at the buildings nearby.

* * *

To Grant and Carol, the drive from the Torbolton Street mailbox to the RCMP crime lab near the prime minister's residence in Rockcliffe Park Village seemed interminable.

"It must be a cassette in the envelope," begged Carol, "why can't we play it now on the car's stereo?"

But Boisvert was adamant. "We can't risk the chance of putting even the slightest scratch on the tape. Right now this is the most important piece of evidence we have; erase some of it, or damage it in any way, Madame, and we will all very much regret it. Besides which, it must be fingerprinted."

The rest of the trip passed in silence. Boisvert sat rigid in the front seat, ignoring Grant's presence.

2:19 PM – Day One

It was a different voice on the tape. Not at all like the one on the telephone. The accent was barely discernable; strange, undefinable.

Cold, cruel and precise, the voice began to read what was obviously a carefully prepared script.

"The date is October twelve. I command the army for the independence of Quebec. We have captured the daughter of Mr. Grant Henry and are holding her hostage until the government of Canada grants freedom and independence to the sovereign state of Quebec. The recent referendum, during which the people of Quebec narrowly voted to remain within confederation, was not a true expression of the sentiment of that province, but rather the consequence of the campaign of fear and lies spread by the federal government and the monied elite of Quebec who threatened such punitive economic measures as to reduce any new republic to pauperdom. The same enemies of Quebec who bribed Canadians to attend a rally in Montreal on the eve of the referendum in their self-serving attempt to interfere with Quebec's right of self determination.

"We have informed the police and Mr. Henry that should this tape recording not be played on Mr. Henry's show this evening at exactly eight o'clock, his daughter will come to great harm."

The voice changed pitch slightly, the pace quickening.

"In our organization, as in any other of this nature, are certain individuals for whom a young, inexperienced female provokes considerable curiosity. Until now, I have been able to control their rather inquisitive and boisterous natures, but a display of anything other than zealous co-operation would make my task in this regard extremely difficult. . . perhaps impossible.

"As a sign of that co-operation and as an initial step towards Quebec independence, all foreign flags, by that I mean all Canadian flags, must be removed from federal buildings in the Province of Quebec by noon tomorrow, October thirteen.

"We will issue further instructions via this radio program each evening at eight. Should the people of Canada fail to hear from us any evening during the week in this fashion, they must know that a decision was made by the English speaking authorities to allow a twelve-year-old girl to die a very uncomfortable death. They should also know that if this should happen, other similarly unpleasant deaths will occur within the English speaking population of Quebec until independence is achieved in a fair and equitable manner.

"In the unlikely event that certain individuals should question the wisdom, or even the legality of complying with demands of this type, I draw your attention to the fact that, in an attempt to spare the lives of kidnapped hostages during October of 1970, demands of the FLQ were broadcast over a number of Quebec radio stations. A precedent has thus already been established in an attempt to spare a francophone and a British life. Surely no one would suggest that similar attempts should not be made in an effort to spare the life of an English speaking Canadian child, unless of course, the lives of English speaking Quebeckers are not deemed as important as those of a French speaking Quebecker or a British diplomat.

"Verbatim transcripts of these broadcasts will be provided to all wire services in Canada, so that all Canadians will be able to judge for themselves if any part of the recordings have been deleted or abridged.

"Now Mr. Henry, I presume you and your loyal listeners would like to hear from your daughter."

There was a pause on the tape, a few clicking noises, then a frightened little voice.

"Daddy, Daddy, they've taken all my clothes off. . . they're looking at me. Don't let them hurt me, Daddy. Please, don't let them hurt me!"

Freeport, Grand Bahama 2:44 PM – Day One

Sandra Beale was having what she usually described as a "difficult day."

It was probably the weather. A late afternoon storm had blown in from the Caribbean. As frequently happens in the Bahamas, the skies, in a matter of minutes, had mutated from bright, hot sun to ominous, black clouds. A freshening wind pounded the ocean onto the broad expanse of beach which lay a few yards away, at the foot of her lawn.

It was the kind of weather Tommy had loved. On days like this she could still see him, astride the violently pitching boat, racing joyfully out to sea to challenge an approaching hurricane. Thomas Beale, President of Beale Broadcasting Ltd., self-made millionaire, loving husband of Sandra, lord of the ocean, almost blinded by the wind, the spray and the rain, throwing his fist into the air and screaming at the top of his lungs:

"Fuck the hurricane!"

A year ago, as he lay dying, he had pulled Sandra's face down to his, clenched a fist as best he could, and whispered.

"Remember love. . . remember what we do with hurricanes."

Clara, moving almost silently despite her considerable bulk, intruded on her reveries.

"Telephone mum, they's callin you from Canada."

It was Dennis Lessing, vice president of Beale Broadcasting Ltd., trouble shooter and hatchet man for Thomas Beale when he was alive, and now for his attractive widow, who last week had toasted herself on her forty-fifth birthday. Many, when meeting Sandra Beale for the first time, were deceived by the smallness of her. The thin, almost anorexic body, the tiny gamine face. Only the eyes revealed the steel: black, intense, intelligent and dancing with life.

Most of the world credited Thomas Beale solely with building the radio empire. Sandra had never resented that misconception. She knew the truth. So did Dennis Lessing.

"Mrs. Beale," said Dennis, "we've got a major crisis on our hands, and very little time to make a decision." Carefully, Dennis explained the situation and their options. "If we air the tape and it turns out to be some kind of hoax, we could look very bad, especially with a rating period coming up. Unquestionably, some people will think we've done it only to hype the listenership. If we don't run it, and something happens to that little girl, God help us all!"

Sandra's mind was racing.

"What about the CRTC?," referring to the federal commission which controlled everything from the content of commercials to the amount and type of music every radio and TV station in Canada could broadcast.

"I've talked with the chief commissioner," said Dennis, "and got the usual runaround. You know: It's too late to call the full commission into a meeting; I can't make a decision on my own; It sounds like a matter for the federal cabinet. All the usual excuse-me-while-I-cover-my-ass stuff. The long and short of it is, they won't give us any advice. What you can be sure of is that, if the shit hits the fan, they'll be in there blowing it at us along with everyone else. The only break we'd get from that sleepy bunch is that it would probably take them a couple years to find the fan."

"What does David have to say about it?" asked Sandra, referring to David Parsons, general manager of their Ottawa station.

There was a grunt at the other end.

"You know good old Dave. 'Anything you and Mrs. Beale decide is fine by me.' He did remind me though, that this kind of thing would be great for ratings! Guy's got a lot of class."

Sandra ignored the sarcasm.

"What about Grant? How is he? He must be terribly broken up. What will his role be if we decide to air the tape?"

Dennis paused for several seconds.

"I only talked with him for a few moments. He sounded awful, as you can imagine, and absolutely desperate that we play the tape. He's obviously convinced this is no hoax. If we go to air with the tape, my suggestion is we make a simple announcement, play it, then roll music. There's no way Grant should do any kind of a program after that."

There was another pause, a longer one.

"Mrs. Beale, I must tell you something else. . . I. . . I should have at the outset. Ahh. . . the tape contains a brief appeal from the little girl. From Lee Henry. In it, she says. . . ahh. . . that they have removed her clothes and are looking at her."

He heard her sharp intake of breath at the other end of the line.

"Oh my God, Dennis, we've got to play the tape. The bastards! Oh, those bastards! Can you imagine anyone doing a thing like that? They're animals, nothing but bloody animals. Dennis I'm catching the first flight out of here. I'll be there sometime tomorrow. I'll call you when I know the arrival time. Meet me at the airport. . . in the meantime, the tape goes on tonight. Come hell or high water, don't let anyone stop you."

Not even, she said to herself, a hurricane!

Chateau Henri 4:12 PM – Day One

When they were married, a crisis of virtually any magnitude had usually resulted in an emotion-charged fight. Now, during this, the greatest crisis of their lives, Grant and Carol Henry found themselves looking to each other for comfort and support. Whatever they felt about each other, whatever their differences, they shared the common link of love for their child, and a terrible fear for her safety.

Hearing their daughter's plaintive plea for help had shattered their reserve with each other. Carol, on the verge of hysteria, began sobbing uncontrollably in the lab, and Grant found himself with his arms around her, cradling her like a child, wiping away her tears, trying to reassure her, and himself, that Lee would be found unharmed.

They were back in the chateau now, seated side by side in the screened-in porch, overlooking the broad, swiftly-flowing Gatineau River. It was here where, a million years or so ago they had all spent so many happy times. It had always been one of Lee's favourite places. As a little girl she often dragged a blanket down in the evening and pleaded to be allowed to sleep there so she could hear the peeper frogs in the spring and the birds and squirrels of summer.

Now, as the late afternoon sun drew long shadows across the lawn, her parents sat enveloped in silence, drawn deeply down into their own private thoughts. An observer would have thought them a loving couple, facing middle age at peace with each other and the world.

They were far from being at peace, but some of the tension had dissipated when they learned, shortly after arriving back from the lab, that Sandra Beale had been contacted in the Bahamas and had given her approval to air the tape on the entire network. In fact, Superintendent Charron was at that moment making the arrangements to have the lab run off a dub to be delivered to the station in plenty of time for the eight pm deadline. From there it would be fed to all network stations.

It was Charron as well who brought them up to date on the investigation. As they suspected, no strange fingerprints had been found. The blood on the cloth was animal, presumably Niki's. The lab was still running tests on Lee's hair and the sweepings from her room. The licence plate had not revealed anything, although they were following up on the type and make of paint used to cover the numbers. Essentially, to this point at least, they were at a dead end. Madame Gratton had been questioned extensively again, but was unable to reveal anything new. There was absolutely no suspicion that she had anything to do with the abduction, or was withholding any information. Whoever was responsible had been well prepared and professional.

"We aren't standing still on this though," Charron tried to assure the Henrys. "Already several people, mostly former members of the FLQ, have been rounded up across the province and are being questioned."

When Grant and Carol returned from the lab, they found that Jake had prepared lunch. It was the first food of the day for all of them and Grant was surprised to find himself hungry. Carol, still badly shaken, was able to eat only a few mouthfuls, bursting into tears at one point and shivering perceptibly.

The phone's sudden ring startled her. She let out a small scream. Everyone's heart leaped, but it was the Ottawa General Hospital calling for Jake. His mother had fallen in her kitchen and injured her back. She was asking for him. Apologizing for leaving them alone with the two detectives, Jake hurriedly left for the hospital, clearly very concerned.

4:21 PM – Day One

A sudden breeze ruffled the chateau's porch curtains. It was from the west, as it often was at this time of day, carrying with it a sound so filled with bittersweet memories that Grant's gasp of pain was audible. It was that special song that crickets sing in northern latitudes as winter approaches. Not louder than in early summer, but somehow closer, more intense. As unmistakable a portent as the red and gold exploding in the maple crowns atop the nearby mountains.

Only two days ago Grant and Lee had sat in the middle of the lawn, just over there, recording the crickets' autumn calls for a classroom science project. He remembered Lee with her head cocked to one side, bent almost into the grass, in hopes of hearing them even better. She squealed with delight when they played back the recorded songs.

He was trying to hide his tears from Carol when the phone rang again. This time it was for him.

4:23 PM – Day One

It was Boisvert, speaking in his rapid and very formal English.

"I must inform you," he said, "that the department of the solicitor general for the Province of Quebec has reviewed the situation and decided we cannot release the tape recorded threats. We are unwilling to negotiate with terrorists. There is also a question of national security. Given the political climate in the province today, we cannot be sure that hearing an appeal of this sort might not create acts of public disorder.

"We are retaining the tape recording for further investigation, but we cannot allow it to be broadcast for public consumption at this time. In the event you were to make any attempt to take to the airwaves yourself this evening, and reveal the contents of the tape, I must inform you, your stations have been notified of our decision, and warned that any contravention of our decision will result in an immediate and very strong complaint to the CRTC.

"We cannot, of course, prevent you from approaching the press with a story, but we must advise you, if you do that, we will do everything possible to blunt the effects of anything you might claim. As you are very aware, we have sufficient evidence to create doubt as to the actual events. If necessary, we are prepared to voice our suspicions concerning your role in all of this. Furthermore. . ."

A truck was roaring in Grant's head. He heard himself screaming.

"You little bastard. They'll kill my daughter. They'll rape her. You've got to let us go to air with that tape. If she was one of yours, you wouldn't think twice. You negotiated for Cross. You negotiated for Laporte. If you could negotiate with the FLQ and play their wild ramblings on the radio in 1970, why can't you do it now?" Boisvert merely grunted and hung up the phone.

"He's not going to get away with this," he stormed at Carol, after briefly explaining the conversation. He was shaking with rage. "I'm going right to the top. Right to the prime minister."

But the prime minister, well aware of what was happening, had no intentions of talking to Grant Henry. Nor, as it turned out, did members of the cabinet, all of whom had either already made arrangements to be unavailable to him and the press, or were in the process of doing so.

It was almost six pm when Grant finally gave up trying to reach someone with the authority to order release of the tape. Of the dozens of frantic calls he'd made to Ottawa and Quebec City, he had only been able to reach Superintendent Charron, who although sympathetic, regretfully explained there was nothing he could do. A decision had been made at the highest level of the Quebec government he explained, sounding sad and resigned. He was in no position to make the slightest difference.

Charron tried to placate Grant. "They aren't going to touch your daughter Mr. Henry," Charron said. "It would do too much damage to their cause." Grant had thanked him, wishing desperately he could believe him.

5:54 PM – Day One

Grant slammed the receiver down. Six minutes to six. His daughter might have only two more hours to live, and for all his contacts, and all his fame, he couldn't do a bloody thing to prevent it. He sank to his knees in the hallway and pounded the carpeted floor with his fists in rage and frustration.

He was thus occupied when Jake strode through the door and took hold of the back of his shirt, lifting him.

"Grant, it's time for you and me to take a little walk," he said. Rage barely under control, Grant followed him out the door and down the pathway to the lawn and the crickets.

Out of earshot of the house, Jake began to speak in a low, excited voice.

"Don't look around, don't do anything or say anything loud. I don't want those two Dick Tracys in the house to hear or see anything to make them suspicious. They've probably got their noses stuffed right up that little rat-faced bastard's ass. Grant. . . I have a copy of the tape!"

Despite the warning, Grant stopped abruptly and spun around to face him.

"What. . . !"

"Turn around and keep walking," Jake whispered urgently. "Nothing happened to my mother. She's fine. It was all a ruse to get me to the hospital. When I arrived, there was an envelope waiting for me with a dub of the tape and a note telling me Boisvert and his buddies had vetoed the original. The instructions are that this one is to be delivered secretly to the radio station in time for the eight pm broadcast."

Relief washed over Grant. His mind began to race as it always did just before air time. "Jake," he said glancing at his watch, "we can figure out just what kind of game is being played here later, but right now we don't have any time to waste. I've got to reach Dennis Lessing right away and persuade him to go to air with this tape despite any warnings he's had about the CRTC. Do these guys here know your mother isn't injured?"

Jake shook his head.

"They'd have no way of knowing that. What do you have in mind?"

Exhilaration began to sound in Grant's voice as he glanced at his watch again. "We're going back into the house and announce that your mother isn't well at all and I'm going with you to see her. The two cops will likely buy it. Unfortunately, we can't risk telling Carol the truth. Her nerves are so shot, I'm afraid she might blow it, so I'm going to have to convince her your mother is in such bad shape, that despite Lee, I have to see her. You play along, say I'm executor of her will, or something, then we'll get the hell out of here, and at the first pay phone call Lessing and get the tape on the air before Boisvert gets wise."

Convincing the two detectives and Carol wasn't difficult. Carol was so distraught she scarcely heard what he was saying. The detectives had found some of Grant's old Playboy magazines and could not have cared less.

Convincing Lessing was another matter. Sandra Beale had told him the tape was to be played, come hell or high water, but she had also expressed concern over the reaction of the CRTC. She couldn't be reached, having caught an early flight to Toronto and was still in the air, so the decision was all Lessing's, and with Boisvert's threat of CRTC censure hanging over his head, he was having difficulty making it. It was Jake who convinced him.

"Let me talk to him," he motioned to Grant, as Lessing continued vacillating on the phone. Shrugging his shoulders, Grant handed the receiver to Jake, who stepped into the booth, slammed the door shut, and spoke animatedly for a few moments in a voice too low for Grant to hear. It didn't take him long. Flipping the door aside, he gave Grant the thumbs up and a big smile.

"Bingo. Let's go."

As they sped south towards Ottawa Jake claimed all he'd done was assure Lessing the Ottawa police would back him in his decision to play the tape. The truth was, he'd provided Lessing with a brief but very graphic description of what was likely to happen to Lee if the tape wasn't played. His recapitulation of a gang rape and murder he'd investigated only a month ago had Lessing very close to nausea.

Jake was concerned that some of Boisvert's men might be watching the radio station, but circling the building twice they noticed nothing unusual. David Parsons, alerted by Lessing, met them at the door. The general manager was having some difficulty reconciling his obligation to express grave concern over the fate of Grant's daughter while being absolutely ecstatic at the prospect of having something like this land in his lap only a week prior to the fall ratings.

At three minutes to eight, Jake called the newly-installed private number at the chateau and briefly explained to an incredulous but relieved Carol what had happened.

"All hell is likely to break loose," Jake told her. "The press will invade the place up there as soon as this is broadcast, and Boisvert and his boys may go a little snaky. We're not going back up to the chateau tonight. Grant says to meet us at the motel where you and he used to spend your birthdays. Leave as quickly as possible. If anyone follows and you can't shake them, go to your mother's house instead, and we'll get in touch with you in the morning. And Carol. . ."

"Yes?"

"Lee is going to be all right. We're going to find her."

"Oh, Jake," she whispered in a small, tearful voice, "I'm so afraid."

8:00 PM – Day One

Precisely at eight pm, the duty announcer punched his mike on and began reading the words Grant had written:

"Ladies and Gentlemen, it is with great regret and concern that the Beale Radio Evening Network announces the temporary suspension of the Grant Henry Show. In its place we will play a tape recording received by Mr. Henry late this afternoon. The reasons for the suspension of his show will become evident during the following broadcast."

An engineer pushed a button and the tape began to play. Exactly three minutes and twenty seven seconds later when it ended and they began to roll music, the switchboards of seventeen radio stations from one Canadian coast to another began to flash frantically. So did the one in the office of the prime minister of Canada!

DAY TWO

6:00 AM

Jake had been right. All hell had broken loose! By six am the three major Canadian television networks had rolled mobile studios into location along the shoulders of the Henry laneway and were broadcasting live inserts every few minutes as their reporters obtained more information, speculation or rumour. This was interspersed with reports of concern and outrage pouring in from all parts of the country.

From their archives, the CBC had retrieved a feature, filmed two summers before for a network show entitled: "Canadians Who Make a Difference". It had some excellent footage of the chateau, including Grant's large library, Lee's beloved Golden Pencilled Hamburg chickens, and as always seemed to happen when a camera was around, Lee and Niki frolicking on the front lawn.

At one point, the camera zoomed in for a close-up of Lee's wide grin and for several moments the engineer froze her image on the television screens of the nation while Charles Whitlaw, the CBC's chief political correspondent, gravely reviewed the situation, quoting unspecified sources who were expressing concern about the effects the abduction might have on national unity.

Whitlaw pointed out that while political leaders in nine provinces, the territories, and the prime minister had been quick to express their shock and horror, nothing as yet had been forthcoming from the Quebec premier's office, or from the Quebec National Assembly, where the cabinet had been called into emergency session shortly after midnight and still had not emerged.

All networks featured a brief interview with Superintendent Marcel Charron of the Hull Detachment of the Sûreté du Quebec, second in command of the investigation which was being headed by one of the province's best known police officers, Inspector Paul Boisvert of Montreal. Inspector Boisvert was unavailable for comment, and thus far no one knew the whereabouts of either Grant Henry or his former wife.

There was a brief and rather disjointed interview with Thèrese Gratton, who was unable to add anything more than she had told police. She broke down for a moment, sobbing loudly when she explained how for the past two years she had been a "kind of mother to Lee."

The media were reporting that circumstances surrounding the abduction were not known, other than what the housekeeper had been able to tell them. Police refused to comment, but neighbours reported hearing sounds during the night, which sounded like gunshots or backfires.

Superintendent Charron would neither confirm nor deny reports of gunfire, stating only that he had been informed of an abduction shortly after midnight, had established roadblocks and rushed to the scene to find most of the lights in the house smashed and Lee Henry and the elderly housekeeper apparently abducted.

Several reporters immediately picked up on the use of the word apparently in reference to the disappearance. Charron corrected himself and halfheartedly deleted the word.

6:10 AM – Day Two

A few kilometres to the south, in a small motel tucked up against the Quebec shore of the Ottawa River, Jake was raging as he watched a hollow-eyed Charron do his television hedging. "Look at that son of a bitch slip sliding away!" he fumed. "This thing is nuts, crazy. Grant, we can't sit here in this freaking motel any longer while those bastards try to pretend this is just a little stroll in the park, maybe with you leading the stroll. We have to blow this thing apart. Let's get the hell up there and set Mr. Whitlaw and some of his parliamentary expert friggin' reporter buddies straight on what's really going down in this damn country!"

Grant, who had been watching in fascinated disbelief, grunted something which might have been assent. He was having difficulty hanging onto reality. Several times during the night he had been certain he heard Lee's voice and had snapped his eyes open, wide awake. He could still vividly recall a dream he'd had during a period of fitful sleep. Boisvert had been perched in the centre of a giant spider web, trying to entice him into it with beguiling smiles and reassuring movements of his arms. This morning as he watched fragments of his life unfolding on the tiny screen, he felt strangely disembodied. This was surely happening to someone else, in some other place, at some other time. The face they showed on the screen could not be his. The events they were describing. . . they must have happened to someone else. He had to fought a great quicksand of lethargy which threatened to swallow him.

6:41 AM – Day Two

As they turned the corner into the crowded laneway of his home, Grant was surprised. He could not remember getting into the car, or anything of the trip from the motel.

* * *

Not since the FLQ crisis of October, 1970 had Canadians been as galvanized by events in their own country. But not even the sight of troops patrolling the streets of Montreal, or the brutal murder of Pierre Laporte had angered, saddened and frightened the nation as much as the pitiful cry for help from a terrified twelve-year-old girl.

This morning, as millions of television viewers watched the drawn and weary faces of her parents, learned of the threats, the murdered family pet, the shots in the night, the abducted housekeeper, read or heard of the attempts by Quebec authorities to prevent the tape from being aired, there emerged something different across the country, a subtle shift of national mood, a low collective murmuring, angry, visceral. One astute commentator, detecting the sentiment from calls to his office, described it as a kind of warning growl from a threatened and dangerous animal.

Some wept as they watched, listened or read. Others raged in despair, but for the most part, it was a black and angry grimness which settled over the country. Or most of it. Almost every Quebecois was as horrified as those elsewhere. Many felt an added sense of shame and guilt, but for some Canadians the news could hardly have been better.

Quebec City 7:00 AM – Day Two

For five hours, the Quebec government caucus had been unable to agree on a strategy. Staunch separatists every one, but few with the stomach to gamble with the life of a young girl, or more important for some, to give the appearance of gambling with her life.

Several, headed by the highly influential Deputy Premier Mario Lefebvre, advocated providing wholehearted support to the investigation and the issuing of a statement deploring the abduction and all acts of violence in the pursuit of Quebec independence. "This is an innocent victim, a young girl," he reminded his colleagues. "To try to use this act of terrorism to advance our cause in any way would be highly immoral."

This prompted snickers in several places around the table, and an outright laugh from Marc Charbonneau, the secretary of state who turned in his chair to face his old adversary. Somewhere along the way, Charbonneau had picked up the nickname "Hawk." No one was sure whether it was in recognition of the long lean frame, hooked nose and piercing cold blue eyes, or for the viciousness of his attacks on his enemies. Those who opposed him quickly learned how sharp his talons were.

"Christ, Mario you're getting too old," said Charbonneau. "We didn't kidnap this kid, if in fact she has been kidnapped. If we go to bat for the anglais on this we're crazy. A couple more days of her yelling into a microphone and we won't have to convince our friends on Parliament Hill to let us go our own way, the rest of the country will insist on it! Let the girl do her job. No one's going to hurt her."

At this, several ministers looked at Charbonneau sharply. "What are you saying?" asked Lefebvre. "How can you be so certain she won't be hurt? Do you know something the rest of us don't?"

When the premier had restored order, Charbonneau angrily continued.

"Look," he said, "we're all here because we believe in the correctness, the nobility if you like, of our cause, the independence of Quebec. Many of us have had to endure great hardships because of our beliefs. Families have been split apart, marriages destroyed." He looked around the table, his eyes flashing a challenge, then continued bitterly. "Everyone here knows what happened when my wife decided she didn't have the stomach to continue the fight, and I'm not the only one. "Let's not be naive here. Some people have already died in the cause of independence, including innocent victims. Before this is all over, it is highly probable more will die, including more of the innocent, maybe some of us!" He paused and looked solemnly around the table before continuing. "This situation could very well save lives. If we treat this for what it is, a civilian casualty in the ongoing struggle for independence, if we do our utmost to lay the blame at the feet of an intransigent federal government which refuses to negotiate with us in good faith, we will frustrate English Canada to the point they'll begin insisting upon separate paths instead of throwing up so many obstacles. We all know the myth of economic disaster is the main impediment to our victory. If we handle this properly, shift the burden of guilt onto Ottawa's shoulders, we lessen the risk of alienating our own voters as well.

"I suggest we issue a statement expressing regret at the abduction of an innocent victim, but point out that it is the actions of Ottawa, in denying Quebec her rightful place as a separate and independent nation, which makes desperate acts such as this inevitable. Place the blame squarely at the feet of the federal government and English Canada, and make it clear this may be only the first blow by a people in such despair they are being driven to desperate acts of violence."

His powerful arguments, the force of his personality and the passing hours were beginning to have an effect; even some of the most adamant dissenters were wavering.

Mario Lefebvre however, had long since lost his fear of the Hawk's talons. The old man shook his head vigorously.

"No, no. This is wrong," he insisted. "What you are suggesting will only encourage more violence. Create the image of desperate freedom fighters, and that's what we'll have. For God sakes, let's not forget what happened when a few Mohawks took the law into their own hands."

The debate came to a sudden halt when the premier, who had been called out while Lefebvre was speaking, returned and announced:

"I have just been informed that the police are expressing grave doubts. They are actively investigating the possibility it is an elaborate hoax, perhaps perpetrated by Mr. Henry himself in order to increase his broadcast ratings and cause embarrassment to the government of Quebec. I suggest that we adjourn with a brief statement to the effect that, in light of new information now being investigated, we have decided it would be inappropriate to comment until police have completed their work." He looked around.

"Let's adjourn, but please ensure you can be reached at all times in the event we need to meet again urgently."

Ordinarily, at that point, the premier would have quickly left the chamber, the others following. This morning however, as the ministers began to rise, he remained seated until Lefebvre, angry, strode to the door and was about to exit.

In a loud, commanding voice the premier said: "Any indication, I repeat, any indication that what has been discussed here this morning has been leaked to the press will be considered as a direct and personal attack on me and this government. . . obviously by someone in this room."

There was a moment of shocked silence, before the premier rose and walked out.

Ottawa 8:24 AM – Day Two

The prime minister of Canada was watching CBC coverage of the drama as he dictated instructions to immediately remove all Canadian flags from federal buildings in Quebec. Well aware most Canadians were in no mood to take any chances with Lee Henry's life, the telephone poll of cabinet members had been swift.

Consent had been unanimous, with only two expressing concern that future demands might not be so easily acceded to. His dictation completed, the prime minister buzzed his outer office. "Get me Chief Inspector Paul Boisvert. . . on my private line."

Chateau Henri 8:25 AM – Day Two

The question, when it finally came, so shocked Grant that for one fleeting moment he abandoned almost twenty years of broadcast training. In the opinion of a few, his response was disgraceful. Most were outraged the question had been asked.

It started out innocently enough, with Charles Whitlaw broadcasting from the CBC mobile unit in the Henry driveway. He was bringing his viewers up to date on the situation, and in particular the fact the federal government had already agreed to remove Canadian flags from Quebec's federal buildings. At that point he turned to an obviously exhausted Grant Henry and said, "Mr. Henry, several sources, including some at the national assembly in Quebec City, are questioning whether you are withholding some vital information concerning the abduction of your daughter. Chief Inspector Paul Boisvert has complained that some of your actions have impeded his investigations. How do you respond to those allegations?"

Grant's head shot back as though someone had struck him a blow on the forehead. For an instant he simply stared at Whitlaw, his eyes wide.

"Whaa. . . ."

He later admitted he completely lost it, in an explosion of such violent anger that for one brief moment he was certain he was going to smash Whitlaw in the face.

Whitlaw, sensing diaster, held up his left hand, fingers spread, as though to ward off an attack, as Grant surged towards him.

Centimetres away, Grant stopped and leaned his face into Whitlaw's. Their foreheads almost touched.

"Listen you pompous ass," he snarled, "that's my daughter you're talking about. Do you really think I'd do anything to hurt her? And as for that nazi bastard Boisvert and his insinuations, he's a racist and an incompetent one at that, and. . ."

A stunned Charles Whitlaw, finally reacting to the catastrophe he had precipitated, killed his mike and bounded away, his face ashen, hoping desperately the producer had been quick enough to stop the cameras before those awful words were spoken. One glance at the mobile production booth told him the worst. All of it, every word, had gone to air. While they would never admit it to Whitlaw, the crew was beside itself with delight!

That was enough for Grant. Jake and Carol could continue talking with the press all they wanted, but as far as he was concerned, he'd said everything he was going to. They could think whatever they wanted, play whatever political games they felt like playing. None of it, as far as he could determine, was going to help find Lee. He felt a growing uneasy conviction that Lee's fate might easily become a secondary detail in the political whirlwind beginning to swirl about her.

There was another serious problem: Surrounded by the media, curious spectators and police, how would the kidnappers communicate with him? How would they get another tape to him for tonight's broadcast?

Toronto 9:22 AM – Day Two

Thomas Beale had knocked out the entire rear wall of the house and replaced it with glass to provide a magnificent view of the wooded ravine only a few metres from their back door in Toronto's wealthiest enclave.

"Everybody's got flowers in their back yard," he told Sandra, "What say you and me, love, have a whole forest?"

Sandra was sitting quietly in her living room admiring the view as she waited for Dennis Lessing who was flying in from Calgary for a ten am meeting. She'd been watching TV coverage all morning, shocked and saddened by most of it, but despite herself, chuckling with delight at Grant's outburst at Charles Whitlaw.

"Good for you, Grant," she said aloud to the TV set, "don't take shit from anybody. Tommy would be proud of you. And you're right, he is one pompous ass."

When the doorbell rang she thought it was Dennis, a little early, but it was a grubby looking little kid of ten or eleven holding a rickety bike.

"You Mrs. Beale?" He squinted up at her as she nodded.

"I gotta package here for ya. Guy gives it to me on the street. Says you'll give me ten bucks for it!" He held a small parcel tightly at his side, wary, ready to bolt at the slightest sign of trouble.

Sandra's hand flew to her throat. She was certain she knew exactly what was in the parcel.

"Who gave it to you? What did he look like? What did he say?"

"Some guy is all. Down on Bloor. Didn't say nothin'. Just deliver this here and get ten bucks is all. Lady, you gonna pay me now?"

"What did he look like?"

The boy was getting nervous, shifting from foot to foot, eyes darting from side to side. She could see he was preparing for flight.

"Jes a guy is all. Gimme my ten bucks or I'm blowin' lady, and you ain't gettin' nothin'."

She reached into her pocket, extracted several bills and jabbed a ten at him. Like a cat, he snatched it from her hand, threw the package onto the step, pounced on his bike and peddled fiercely off.

"Now I'm in for it," she muttered to herself, "I should have called the police." But she knew the boy would have been long gone with his package well before any police arrived. For a moment she stared at the object by her feet, then stooped to retrieve it, gingerly, by one corner, as Grant had explained he handled the first envelope. Placing it carefully on the hallway coffee table, she returned to her room with a view and waited for Dennis Lessing.

Quebec City 11:02 AM – Day Two

Inspector Paul Boisvert was starting to sweat. Suspecting someone had turned up the heat, he glanced around, but no one else seemed to be in any discomfort. Of the five in the room with him, he recognized only the premier and the secretary of state. The premier was doing all the talking, asking questions.

"Inspector Boisvert, we are anxious to hear from you concerning your investigations into the Henry case and in particular, we would like to hear whatever evidence you have concerning allegations you are quoted as making concerning Mr. Henry's role in it." He steepled his fingers under his chin and waited.

Boisvert could feel his shirt beginning to stick to his back.

"First Minister," he began, "thus far we have been unable to uncover any substantial leads. A thorough investigation conducted in the Henry house and car uncovered no clues. We continue to study the tape recording of the girl's plea, but aside from a slight buzz, which may be in the background or a problem with the recording device, it has revealed nothing. We have questioned," here he checked his notes, "twenty-seven people with known criminal backgrounds in this sort of thing, but intensive interrogation hasn't turned up anything of value. As is usually the case, the only thing we were able to learn from the telephone call made by the abductors to the Henry home was that it originated from a pay phone in east end Montreal. If this is a legitimate kidnapping, it appears to have been carried out by a person or persons unknown to our informants. We have talked with several former members of the FLQ who assure us they have no knowledge of the affair." He stopped, glancing around.

"And Mr. Henry's role?" asked the premier.

Boisvert cleared his throat and without thinking, pulled his handkerchief from his pocket and mopped his brow.

"Well, First Minister, I may have been somewhat misquoted in this matter. I do believe Mr. Henry is concealing information of some sort, but I have no evidence he is involved in the kidnapping of his daughter, or that he has any knowledge of the perpetrators."

The steeple bounced on the premier's lips several times.
"Inspector," he said solicitously, "perhaps we should explain ourselves more clearly here. I am certain you know we all deplore what has occurred, but on the other hand, there are certain political considerations which must be taken into account."

Boisvert blinked.

The premier continued.

"Could it be Inspector, that in your desire to protect your country, Quebec, from its enemies, you may have become overzealous? Did you in this. . . zealousness, attempt to create some doubt in the minds of some of our countrymen that this may not be the work of a separatist faction, but is instead another anglo plot to discredit our cause? To be blunt, I can find no fault with anyone whose devotion or zealousness in defence of the cause of a sovereign state takes him over the bounds of what some would describe as lawful behaviour. We must remember we are involved in a revolution here, and in a revolution there are always casualties, including, I hasten to point out, the innocent and the truth."

Incredibly, the temperature in the room seemed to have dropped several degrees. With a slight smile, Boisvert replied quietly, "To zealousness in defence of our cause I must plead guilty."

This time it was Charbonneau who spoke.

"Inspector, we have no wish that any harm come to this little girl. Nor do we wish this matter to become so inflamed that violence break out, and Ottawa find justification to send the troops across our borders, again. Make your best efforts to apprehend the abductors," here he broke into a long fit of coughing, but managed to continue. Make no arrests until we have been notified. . . and Inspector?"

"Yes?"

"Continue in your attempts to discover if in fact this is not just another anglo plot. There's one final thing."

Boisvert looked at him expectantly.

"For the time being at least, make no attempt to halt the playing of any tape recordings on English radio stations."

The premier nodded his agreement and handed Boisvert a small card with a phone number written on it.

"Contact this number at any time, day or night should you discover anything of interest, or if you require assistance of any kind. Please memorize it and return the card to Mr. Derouin before you leave this room." He canted his head towards a small bearded man who had been standing by the door throughout the meeting. A brief handshake and the premier was gone.

Chateau Henri 12:17 PM – Day Two

Grant and Jake were talking quietly in the porch. The reporters had, for the most part, departed for Ottawa, or were napping in the mobile studios still lining the driveway. The soaps and game shows had reclaimed their rightful positions on afternoon television. Radio, with the exception of the open line shows, which talked about nothing else, had returned to its duelling-jukebox mode. Although outwardly calm, Grant was still seething over his early morning encounter with Charles Whitlaw. Jake was gently trying to chide him out of his anger. "Actually," said Jake, with only the slightest of grins, "I was really disappointed in you." Grant rose to the bait. "What the hell do you mean? Geeze. . ."

"You could have done the nation a service right then and there and flattened him." Grant scowled at him for a moment, then broke into a chuckle of his own.

"Poor old Charles. He'll probably never show his face at the Press Club again. Poor bugger may die of thirst."

The two detectives, tending their equipment, were disappointed when the phone interrupted what they hoped was going to be some very interesting locker room gossip.

"Madame Beale calling from Toronto for Mr. Henry," one of them announced.

"Grant," said Sandra Beale, "I cannot describe to you how sorry I am that this has happened. You know we want to co-operate with the authorities, but our main concern right now is the safety of your daughter. Dennis and I have some ideas we would like to discuss with you. . . in person, private. I'm at Pearson Airport right now. Our flight leaves in twenty minutes. Can you meet us in an hour and a half at the radio station in Ottawa?"

"I'll be waiting for you," he said, puzzled at the urgency in her voice.

Ottawa 1:49 PM – Day Two

A worried David Parsons was waiting at the door when Grant arrived at the station and ushered him immediately into his office.

"What's happening?" he asked. "I got a call from Mrs. Beale saying she and Dennis are on their way. Are we in trouble here? Have we done something wrong? I've got to tell you, the switchboard has been going crazy since last night. I've been doing nothing but talking with the press. We've had calls from as far away as Australia. Believe it or not, even Hong Kong."

Despite himself, his enthusiasm began to overtake his well-honed political instincts which dictated a more concerned, subdued approach in the presence of the father of an abducted child. His enthusiasm quickly evaporated when Sandra Beale and Dennis Lessing arrived and without much ceremony, informed him they needed his office to speak privately with Grant.

The door was scarcely closed when Sandra leaned forward in her chair and touched Grant's hand lightly.

"Grant," she said softly, "we have another tape from the people who have your daughter. After what's happened, I couldn't risk turning it over to police."

Grant leapt to his feet.

"Where is it? What does it say? Is Lee on it? Is she all right?" Sandra was on her feet beside him.

"Grant before we play this," she said cautiously, "I want to warn you. . . there is something. . . ." She stopped for a moment. Grant's face had gone white.

"There's something very unpleasant on the tape," she plunged on, "I think maybe you should sit down while we play it for you."

It was the same voice on the tape. The same strange accent. If anything it was even more arrogant, more cruel than yesterday.

"Today is the thirteenth day of October. This is the commander of the army for an independent Quebec speaking again. As I stated yesterday, we have captured, and are holding hostage, the daughter of a man well known to you; Mr. Grant Henry. A man well known as an enemy of the people of Quebec.

"Miss Henry will be held as a hostage by our forces until the prime minister of Canada grants full and complete independence to Quebec in a manner which will allow our new republic to exist and prosper in a healthy economic and cultural climate. The first step towards this goal was accomplished this morning when all Canadian flags were removed from federal buildings in Quebec.

"As the second step towards independence, the prime minister of

Canada is to order the withdrawal of all Canadian troops from Quebec immediately. These troops will take nothing with them, except for personal belongings. All equipment, including small arms and other material, is to remain in the camps. As a sign of good faith, we will allow the removal of all fighter aircraft from Quebec bases, but only those ground vehicles required to transport the troops out of the province will be removed. All others must remain as the property of the new Republic of Quebec. We, of course, reserve the right to negotiate ownership of the planes at a later date.

"To those soldiers whose home is in Quebec and who wish to remain there following independence, let me say this. Your services will be required by our new country, but until independence occurs, you should fulfil your obligations to the Canadian government. Your right to switch allegiance to the Republic of Quebec without any loss of benefits or rank will be a key element in the negotiations required to establish our new republic.

"Should these instructions not be followed to the letter, I need not reiterate the harm which shall befall Lee Henry and other English speaking residents of Quebec.

"Removal of the troops from Quebec must begin no later than noon tomorrow, October fourteenth, with all troops to be evacuated no later than noon October fifteenth.

"Now, all of you who have been expressing so much concern over the fate of Miss Lee Henry, will no doubt be pleased to hear from her."

There was a long pause, then a little girl's voice, much calmer, more composed than was heard on the first tape recording.

"Hello Daddy. I hope the prime minister does what he's supposed to. I'm not feeling very well, I've been sick a. . ." she choked or sobbed, "sick a law. . ." more coughing, then a word sounding like "lock". She seemed to regain her composure and continued, "Daddy, please don't forget to feed my silkies."

The tape went dead for a brief moment, then the first voice returned.

"I've heard several commentators urging the government of Canada not to negotiate with us. Some have described us as kidnappers and terrorists. Others have suggested that our bluff should be called. If you listen carefully you may obtain a better idea just how serious we are and how important it is for Miss Henry, and others, that our instructions be followed."

Without warning, there was a long, horrifying scream, which Grant knew to be Lee's, several shorter ones, a loud thud, then silence.

The voice returned; a sinister whisper.

"Just remember all you anglais, those screams will go on for hours if your prime minister fails to follow our instructions, or if this radio station refuses to play this tape and the ones which will follow. Once again verbatim transcripts of this broadcast have been sent to every wire-service in the country and many in the United States. It will be impossible for Canadians not to know if one single radio station on the Beale network fails to play this tape. They will also know what happens if that should occur and. . . who to blame. Until tomorrow then. Same time, same place, as they say."

Sandra had to stop herself from throwing her arms around Grant as he sat huddled in his chair, shaking violently. His eyes were darkened hollows in a gaunt, ashen face. She blinked away tears as she grasped his shoulder.

"Grant," she whispered, "we're with you all the way on this. Whatever it is you want us to do, we'll do it." She hesitated a moment. "Money is no object here. If it will help in any way, this company, and I, personally, are prepared to spend whatever it takes to get the very best people working on this. We will use whatever influence we can. We're going to get your little girl back to you."

Lessing, mute thus far, nodded quietly. "That goes for me as well. And Grant you've got to remember one thing. I know what we've just heard sounds awful, but let's not forget they aren't going to do serious harm to your daughter. She's too important to them. In fact, right now, without Lee they don't have anything. They can carry out other acts of terrorism, but that involves a great deal of risk for them and it's doubtful if even murder would have nearly the public impact as what they're doing now. Grant, I can only imagine how badly you're feeling, but the decisions we make in the next couple of hours could be vital. Do you feel up to discussing it?"

Grant's mind was in a turmoil, unable to shut out those terrible screams and that thud. He fought back the bile rising in the back of his throat, but even as he did so, a tiny prickle of excitement began sparking up his spine.

There was something very strange about that tape, something which Lee had said which just didn't make any sense. Could it just be a mistake? No! No mistake! Lee had been very clear. Was she trying to tell him something?. . . Give him some kind of message?. . . Could she really have the presence of mind under those circumstances to try and communicate with him?

His mind was racing. Thoughts flashed in and out. Yes, that must be it! There was really no other logical explanation. . . Lee was sending him a secret message on that tape!

As terrified as she must be, as young as she was, she was fighting back with her intelligence. It was the only weapon she had. He could barely contain his excitement.

Grant picked up a phone and dialled the switchboard operator. "Bev, call my home and tell Jake Barr to get here as fast as he can. Thanks." He gave her the special emergency number and turned to Sandra.

"Before we do anything," he said, trying to suppress the excitement in his voice, "I want to hear that tape again. Not the screams, I don't want to ever hear those again. Can you advance it to the part where Lee starts to speak?"

It took her only a minute to find the spot and Grant listened again to his daughter's voice; tiny, plaintive and somehow eerie in this small room:

"Hello Daddy, I hope the prime minister does what he's supposed to. I'm sick a. . ." then a cough or sob. "Sick a law". . . another choking sound, followed by a word which sounded very much like lock. Then the strange and intriguing words. "Daddy, please don't forget to feed my silkies."

"Stop it there," said Grant, "play that part back."

There it was again.

"Daddy, please don't forget to feed my silkies."

"Do you think she's trying to tell you something?" asked Sandra. "What does she mean by her silkies?" Grant locked eyes with her for a moment, then waved his hand.

"Nah, I thought I heard something in the background. Silkies are chickens, she wants me not to forget to feed her chickens. Can you imagine! But I would like to put this tape, and last night's recording as well, on the digital voice analyzer to compare some speech patterns. Dennis, would you mind tracking Al Thompson down and asking him to make two dubs of this tape and the one we played last night. Make sure it's Thompson."

The moment Dennis left the room, Sandra turned to Grant.

"There was something on that tape wasn't there? Lee is trying to tell you something isn't she?"

He remembered her gentle touch on his hand just a moment ago, the anguish in her eyes as they listened to the tape and, without realizing it, made the decision to trust her. "I think so," he nodded, "I'm just not sure what, but I figure the fewer the people who know about it, the less chance there is that those cowardly bastards who have her will find out she's trying to communicate with us. Silkies are chickens all right, but Lee has Golden Pencilled Hamburgs. She hasn't had silkies for almost two years!"

From somewhere, probably the sales department, Dennis Lessing had rounded up a bottle of cheap scotch and three plastic glasses. "Most bars would be ashamed to serve this stuff," he admitted. "There's no ice and only tap water to mix it with, but what the hell, it's better than the coffee they serve around here! Rotten or not, I think we could all use a drink." Even Jake, when he arrived a few minutes later, didn't disagree.

The decision to air the second tape at eight that evening was easy to make, although Dennis in particular was convinced it could create serious problems, perhaps even violence, in some areas where French and English speaking Canadians were already living in a state of barely suppressed hostility.

One thing which puzzled them was the fact that the police thus far had made no attempt to determine whether a new recording had been received.

"They must know the abductors will find a way to contact us," Jake said thoughtfully. "Why isn't old Boisvert, or Charron, sticking to us like fleas on a dog's back? I'm worried that Boisvert may be doing a long slow burn after our end run on him last night. Why hasn't he come after us, demanding to know how we got the tape last night after he confiscated the orginal? Why hasn't he contacted the CRTC or anyone else to issue another warning about playing any more tapes? It's really strange. What I'm worried about is him lying low, waiting until just before airtime to show up here with a court injunction ordering us to stop playing the tapes."

"There's an easy solution to that," said Dennis. "We'll feed the tape down the line to Toronto and maybe Vancouver right now and have it supplied to the network from either of those stations if they try to stop us here. I doubt they'll think of getting injunctions in every city we have an outlet." He left to oversee the operation and swear the operators in both cities to secrecy.

"Now," said Jake, "how are we going to notify our prime minister of the little hydrogen bomb we have ticking away for him here? The decision to withdraw troops from Quebec won't be as easy to make as pulling down a few flags."

"You're right about that," said Grant. "He'll almost certainly have to summon the cabinet and maybe even the full caucus for a meeting. A telephone poll won't do for this. I think I've got the solution though. I know the PM's executive assistant very well, and I trust him. If I play the tape for him now, he can record it off the phone and immediately advise the prime minister. The House is in session, so most MPs are in Ottawa, or close by. They should be able to get the cabinet or even the entire caucus together in a couple of hours if that's what they decide to do."

"Won't parliament have to be recalled to make a decision as important as pulling out the troops?" asked Sandra.

Grant explained that it could be accomplished without parliamentary approval through an order-in-council.

"Trudeau sent the troops into Quebec in 1970 without parliament's approval," Grant reminded her, "and this guy can pull them out."

Fortunately the executive assistant was in the PMO when Grant called. After a promise that only members of cabinet and not the police would be notified of its contents, Grant played the tape down the telephone line, mumbled, "Thanks Pierre," and hung up.

The decision concerning the best way of notifying police in the various cities was much more difficult. There was one aspect which bothered them all a great deal. If the tape was played on the entire network, including Montreal, there was no telling what might happen. If hearing the broadcast and, in particular, Lee's screams, prompted some nut in Sudbury or Cornwall or God knows where to throw a rock at a car with Quebec plates, or a few local toughs on the West Island of Montreal got it in their heads it was open season on "frogs," all hell could break loose.

"Somehow," insisted Sandra, "we've got to give police in all our markets, in fact police across the country, some warning of what we're doing. We've got to let them know how dangerous this tape could be."

Reluctantly, they agreed that at seven pm, Ottawa time, the news directors of all their stations would alert police in their cities that they were going to play a tape which might inflame a few crazies.

"An hour should give them plenty of time to get prepared," said Jake, "but it probably won't give Boisvert or anyone else sufficient warning to get a court injunction to stop the broadcast."

Relieved that the decisions had been made, Grant and Jake walked down the hallway a short way to a tiny sound proof studio to listen to the tapes and watch as a computer analyzed the voices.

2:13 PM – Day Two

Al Thompson should have retired seven years ago. He could have retired comfortably with what he'd managed to sock away over the years. But as he told anyone who'd listen, "What the hell would I want to retire for? This isn't work, this is fun. Hey, they don't even have to pay me!" But they did, because at the age of seventy-two, Al Thompson knew more about how to keep a radio station on the air and sounding sweet than anyone in the country.

Four days ago, Grant had gone to Al with the smuggled recording of the Quebec caucus and asked him to identify the voice making racist statements.

"If you have a recording of the voices of every member of the Quebec cabinet for comparison, and each of those voices was identified by name, could you find a match for this?" Grant had asked, as he handed him the cassette he'd received that morning.

"Let's listen, and let's see." said Al. "First we'll punch it onto old Daisy here," indicating the computerized voice analyzer in front of him, "and see just how badly muffled it is." He played it several times, listening intently. They both watched as he flicked a switch and voice patterns began to appear on the computer screen.

"Looks like a lie detector test," said Grant.

"Which is just about what it is," nodded Al. "A lie detector test for tape recordings. What it tells me is that this tape is too muffled for us to determine whose voice it is by just listening to it, but if you get me recordings of every minister and identify each speaker, it won't take me long to tell you which one of them thinks all Englishmen and Cree Indians should be hung, strung, put into bed and the skin of their arses pulled over their heads."

Now, as Grant and Jake stepped into his tiny darkened booth, Al stepped forward and grasped Grant's hand tightly.

"Sorry what's happened Grant," he said anxiously, "I've tried reaching you, but could never get through. Do you think what you gave me the other day has anything to do with what's happening now?" He gave Jake a inquiring look.

"Thanks for your concern Al. Meet Jake Barr, a good friend of mine. He knows everything." They shook hands briefly.

"Yeah," said Grant, "I think there's a good chance that last tape I gave you does have something to do with it, although I'm not sure what. Have you been able to make a match yet?"

Al stared at him for several long moments before nodding his head slowly. "Yeah, I have. It took me a long time though, and when you see what I've got, you'll understand why. The main problem I had was the fact that the recording you got from your unknown spy friend doesn't match the voice of any cabinet minister!"

Grant frowned his puzzlement, but before he could say anything, Al waved him closer to the computer screen.

"Come here and have a look at this." He quickly fed a tape into the computer and said, "I've been able to isolate seven words which appear on two taped voices – your mystery recording, and another tape of what I believe is the same man, speaking in a situation where there can be no doubt as to his identity. Two of the words which are the same on both tapes are in English, the other five are French: *Je, mois, après, Quebec, Montréal,* English and, believe it or not, shit. I'm going to punch those seven words from the smuggled tape onto the screen now and take a hard copy of the voice patterns."

He punched a series of buttons, and squiggly lines began to appear on the screen. He hit a key and in a moment they were examining a printout of the lines, which did indeed resemble the results of a lie detector test, or as Jake suggested, a Richter scale.

"Now," said Al, "I'm going to input the same seven words from another tape recording I got from our Montreal newsroom. Before I tell you who's on this tape, I want you both to examine the results very closely and tell me if you agree they are identical. If this ever comes up in court, I want to be able to testify that both of you confirmed my findings without having any bias as to the source of the comments. Okay?"

Both Grant and Jake nodded.

In a moment they were examining another computer printout, very obviously identical to the first one.

"Now," said Al, "before I tell you whose voice that is on those two recordings, I want to know if we can all agree, for the record, that the computer printouts from both of the tapes are identical."

Grant and Jake were becoming impatient.

"Al, for Christ's sake who is it?"

Al looked steadily at them both.

"Jean Luc Menard, Premier of Quebec."

They were stunned. It was Jake who spoke first.

"Jesus H. Menard. That son of a bitch! And he's the guy goes around all the time claiming he's some fucking great moderate. The friend of all the people, defender of the little guy. Wants to build bridges to the anglos. All the time dreaming about burning wooden crosses and wearing white sheets!"

The thought hit both of them at the same instant.

"This is bloody dynamite. This could blow that slimy prick right off the face of the globe, let alone off the map of Quebec," said Grant. "Lee's kidnapping has got to have something to do with it. Good God, you don't suppose Menard's behind it all?"

The question lay ticking in their midst for a moment, till it was defused by Jake.

"Naw, couldn't be. If Menard's greasy snout was buried in this, if he suspected for a moment we'd got a pitchfork ready to stuff up his keester, the first demand we would have received would have been for us to return the tape to him. He wouldn't be fooling around with flags or troops. It's got to be just coincidence. Hey, let's not get carried away here. Just like back in the seventies, it's probably just a few patriot wing nuts running around in beat up old Chevys trying to convince us they're the French resistance, ready to come marching down Rene Levesque Boulevard, everybody throwin' roses at 'em."

Almost to himself Grant said, "You're probably right, but I just can't help thinking that somehow or other it is all tied in together."

He was having difficulty shaking the feeling of being sucked into a political maelstrom from which neither Lee nor he might ever escape. His dream of Boisvert trying to entice him onto a giant spider web flashed into his mind. He knew he had to ignore his feelings of despair. He must, at all costs, keep his mind clear and focused. Lee's life might depend upon it.

"Al," he said, trying to concentrate, "those two tapes with my daughter's voice, I want to hear them both again."

Al tilted his head slightly, eyebrows shooting up.

"No," said Grant, "not including the screams, I don't need to hear those again."

The first tape played without comment from Grant. But again, as his daughter began to talk on the cassette delivered to Sandra, Grant made Al play it over and over again, the plaintive words reverberating in the tiny room, despite the soundproof walls.

"The silkies," said Jake. "I remember them. Those crazy little chickens that looked like they were covered in fur. You haven't had those for a couple years. Didn't your neighbour's dog or a fox or something get them all?"

"A fox," said Grant. "Why would she say silkies?" Then a rush of excitement. "Could she be trying to tell us they've got her on a fox farm or something? Could there be foxes nearby? Is there a place in Quebec with a name like fox? How do you say fox in French?" He answered his own question. "Renard, is there a place called Renard?"

Al picked up the phone.

"I'll get the newsroom to check."

Grant was concentrating fiercely.

"Get them to check as well if there's any place which sounds like silk or silkie."

"You know," said Jake, "unless I'm mistaken, she may have been trying to tell us something with that bit with the coughing. Al, play that part back again would you?"

There it was again, "Daddy I'm sick a. . ." cough, "sick a law". . . coughing or crying, then the word which sounded like lock.

Jake said, "Play us just that one word Al." The tape was rolled back and cued up. The word, isolated from the coughing, was very clearly "lock".

"Maybe she's just trying to tell us they've got her locked up," suggested Al.

"Yeah, maybe, maybe," agreed Jake, "and maybe it was just a slip of the tongue, although I've got to tell you, that coughing or sobbing or choking or whatever it was, sounded kind of strange. Did it sound strange to you guys?"

Both Grant and Al nodded agreement.

"And did you notice," continued Jake, "that kind of buzzing sound in the background of both tapes? I wonder what that is? Al, what's it sound like to you? Something wrong with their tape recorder maybe, or something running in the background, a motor or something? Could it be a car?"

"It puzzles the hell out of me," admitted Al. "I noticed the buzz right away on that first tape and since then I've tried just about every test I can think of. I've put it up on the computer, tried to match the sound with motors, car engines and God knows what else, but I just can't place it. It could be a faulty tape recorder, but it doesn't sound like it. Frankly, it has me stumped, but I'm going to run some more tests this afternoon to see if I can come up with an answer."

Hours later, when Sandra knocked on the door and entered the crowded booth, there were still only questions, no answers. Al hadn't been able to identify the strange buzzing on the tape. The closest the newsroom had been able to come to Renard was Rouyn. There was nothing sounding even close to a place called silk or silkie, and the department of agriculture told them they wouldn't be able to obtain a list of all fox farms in Quebec until at least tomorrow afternoon.

Sandra's news was a little better. All police departments across the country had been alerted. With the exception of Montreal they were all extremely co-operative.

"Our Montreal news director Blake Talbot did manage to get through to Inspector Boisvert," said Sandra. "Our oh-so-polite and co-operative detective friend asked him how long we'd had the tape, then hung up when Blake told him we couldn't release that information. No attempt has been made to stop us playing the tape, although of course," she glanced at her watch, "it's only 7:15. There's still plenty of time I suppose.

"Grant, you look terrible. If nothing happens between now and eight, I want you to come with me to dinner. I've got a suite at the Chateau Laurier. You can have a long hot shower there if you like and we'll order up some food. Jake, you're more than welcome to join us. Unfortunately, Dennis has to go back to Toronto tonight."

Jake shook his head vigorously. "Thanks Mrs. Beale, but I don't think it's a good idea for any of us to remain in the chateau tonight after we air this tape. I'll pick Carol up and book into our favourite motel again. I suspect tonight and tomorrow will make this morning's circus at the Chateau Henri look like an Iraqi love-in for Stormin' Norman!"

Grant started to protest that he should go with him, but when Jake held up a hand, Grant couldn't summon the energy to argue. Besides, a hot shower and a decent meal sounded awfully good, even though it gave him a twinge of guilt to admit it to himself. He knew something else: He needed more time to think about those tapes before confronting Carol again.

"All right," he told Sandra. "It's a deal. Don't expect me to be too entertaining though," he added wryly. "And Al, guard those tapes with your life."

Montreal 7:16 PM – Day Two

Chief Superintendent Marcel Charron was more puzzled than ever. Summoned urgently to Montreal more than four hours ago, he had driven well above the speed limit all the way from Hull, only to be left waiting outside Inspector Boisvert's office for nearly half an hour. Boisvert, they informed him, had been suddenly called to Quebec City, but was expected back at any moment. Superintendent Charron should please make himself comfortable and wait.

When Boisvert finally did hurry in, he barely acknowledged Charron with a flip of the hand, and kept him cooling his heels for another fifteen minutes.

Their meeting was brief. Boisvert did most of the talking. "Superintendent Charron, some new information has come to our attention which prompts us to change tactics. From now on, the investigation into the alleged kidnapping of Lee Henry is to continue, but no attempt is to be made to stop the playing of any tape recordings which may turn up at various radio stations. As before, the position of the investigating police is that there is a very real possibility this entire affair is nothing more than a very cruel and dangerous hoax. As well, our official position is that Mr. Grant Henry remains under suspicion for withholding information."

Charron held up his hand. "What information do we believe he is withholding?" he asked. "I haven't been able to obtain a shred of evidence he's holding anything back. I have absolutely no evidence to support any theory this is anything other than a bona fide abduction."

Boisvert smiled slightly.

"My dear Superintendent Charron," he said, drawing the words out as though he were speaking to an errant and slightly stupid child, "there is a great deal more involved in all of this than you may suspect." He could not resist the boast. "In fact, I must tell you, not only have I just concluded a private meeting with the premier of Quebec, I have, as well, been speaking with the prime minister of Canada."

Charron thought to himself that if someone were to give this strange little fellow a pair of wings, he'd flap them and crow his bloody head off. What he said out loud was, "Can you tell me what they said?"

"Absolutely not," said Boisvert, drawing himself up disdainfully. "It was totally confidential, and I should warn you, all of what I have told you must be kept in the strictest of confidence. Now tell me, what new information you have been able to obtain in your investigation?"

Charron retrieved a sheaf of notes from his briefcase and laid them on the desk.

"Thus far," he said, "we have been unable to obtain any sort of lead as to who is responsible. None of the evidence we acquired at the Henry house has been of any assistance to us, but there is one thing we are now quite certain of."

Boisvert leaned forward sharply in his chair.

"What's that?"

"We believe the abductors were able to get past our roadblocks via the Gatineau River."

Boisvert cocked his head to one side.

"The river!"

"Yes," explained Charron, "we've talked to a resident who claims he heard an outboard moving quickly downstream at about the time your men arrived on the scene. We believe a car took the Henry girl and her abductors to a boat lying in wait just downstream from Poisson Blanc. There are plenty of launching sites along the river. The girl and at least one other person then boarded the boat and powered it south, well past the roadblocks to the dam at Pointe Gatineau. From there, either a second car, or more probably the first one, which would have passed safely through the roadblock to the south, picked them up and drove away."

"Unbelievable!" exclaimed Boisvert. "Ingenious! And the boat?"

"Hauled away with a trailer either attached to the car all along or, more likely, left hidden in some bushes near the dam where they pulled the boat out of the water."

Boisvert tilted back in his chair.

"And you never thought about putting up any check points or blocks along the river?"

"Virtually impossible," replied Charron shaking his head vigorously. "The water is very wide from Poisson Blanc to Pointe Gatineau. It would take several boats to mount a proper patrol, and presumably, if the abductors had spotted any kind of activity along the banks, they would simply have turned off their motor and drifted past us with the current in the dark. We don't have searchlights. There is one thing though. We took all licence numbers of cars allowed through the roadblocks. You can bet it was stolen, but we're following up on it."

They both sat silently for a moment, deep in their own thoughts.

"By the way," said Boisvert, "we were alerted just a few minutes before you entered my office that a second tape has arrived at CBBY in Ottawa, and will be played at eight this evening. Our source indicates some material on the tape may be highly inflammatory. Your people in Hull should be alerted to the possibility of trouble. You'll be able to listen to the broadcast on your way home. Please report any new findings to me immediately."

Charron had a million questions, none of which, he suspected, would ever be answered. Certainly not by this man. At eight o'clock, as he drove through the outskirts of Montreal on his way home, he turned his car radio to the proper frequency and listened. His blood ran cold at what he heard.

"My God," he said aloud, "what's going to happen to us?"

Ottawa 7:56 PM – Day Two

Grant didn't hear the broadcast. As they pulled out of the station's parking lot a few minutes before eight, Sandra quietly reached down and snapped the radio off. She said nothing and Grant didn't object. Nor did he comment when they reached her hotel suite and she extracted from her briefcase a small parcel containing toilet articles, a new white shirt and boxer shorts.

She tried to make a joke of it.

"Just remember this little gesture the next time we talk contract. Okay?"

Despite himself Grant grinned.

"Gotcha, lady!"

The hot water felt wonderful! The pain and the fear were still there, threatening to well up and overpower him, but he could feel some of the tension draining away. At least it appeared the police weren't going to try to stop them from playing any future tapes. He had a moment of panic, wondering if the federal government would co-operate in removing the troops from Quebec, but managed to reassure himself that they really didn't have much choice. Any government which didn't take every action possible to keep Lee alive would never be able to withstand the enraged public protest.

Sandra had poured them a drink as he dried himself and donned one of the hotel's thick white robes.

"Good scotch," she laughed, as he stepped out of the steamy bathroom. "In real honest-to-goodness glass glasses."

"I feel guilty sitting here like this," confessed Grant, after a moment. "I should be out doing something."

"I can imagine how you feel," said Sandra, trying to reassure him, "but a body's got to eat, you know, and more importantly, your body and your mind can only take so much stress before they begin to let you down. You've had a terrible shock and I don't suppose you've had much sleep. When I watched you shoot down our pompous ass friend this morning, I had the feeling you were very close to the edge. Before this is all over, you're going to need every ounce of energy and stamina you can dredge up. Besides which, after we've had something to eat and you've had time to unwind a bit, I want to try something with you. Something Tommy and I used to do occasionally, when he found himself with his back to the wall and in need of a brain wave."

Grant stared at her until, realizing the implications of what she had said, crimson flooded her face

"Grant, for heaven's sake, I'm talking about a technique I've learned which assists free association. I want to see if maybe we can come up with some ideas about what Lee was trying to tell you. But that's after you've eaten and relaxed a bit. That's when it works best."

Flustered, she reached for the phone.

"Now, what's for dinner?" As she leaned forward to dial, Grant could see that the flush which still had not completely receded from her face extended to the tops of her breasts.

Her eyes caught his then flicked away. The jolt made her catch her breath.

"Steak," he said. "A New York cut. Medium rare."

Montreal 8:00 PM – Day Two

Armand (Sonny) Montagano had set out that afternoon from his shabby apartment in Montreal's north end with high hopes of getting laid. He set out most afternoons with the same great expectations. As usual, he and his hopes ran aground on a shoal of beer and bravado in one of the dozen or so local taverns which dotted his neighbourhood.

Things were worse than usual today. The unfairness of it was stewing away in his gut (along with two quarts of Molson's and three chuckwagons), exacerbated, to no small degree, by a tiny bleached blond still perched at the end of the bar. Only half an hour ago she had rudely rebuffed his romantic advances with a curt, *"Mange le merde."*

"Fuckin' French cunt," said Sonny. "Don't know her pussy from page twelve."

"Fuckin' A, man," said Charles (Ducky) Drake. "Fuckin' pepsi. They're all the same. Takin' over the fuckin' world."

"Great fuckin' world," said Robert (Booby) Caswell. "Hey, Sonny boy, yer turn fer the beer."

Sonny, scowling, began rifling though his pockets, a small pile of change and bills slowly growing on the damp table in front of him. "Twenty-two bucks is all I got. Jesus, and it's three full days till pogey time!" He banged a grimy fist on the table. "Fuck!"

"Hey man, I got a boner do a fuckin' donkey proud. Let's blow this frog palace and cruise us some cunt on Ste. Catherine." It was the first original thought of the day for Ducky Drake, and the last one of his life.

Laughing, feinting and jabbing at each other, the trio piled into Sonny's 86 Bronco.

Flying out of the parking lot in a spray of stones, Booby Caswell reached inside his ragged leather jacket. "Voila, eete eese magic, no!" A quart of Molson's was firmly clutched in each hand. There were hoots of delight.

"How the fuck do you do that? You're stealing those poor bastards blind!"

"Ah," said Booby, "it is a well known fact frogs can only see orange."

"Or purple," said Ducky.

"Or pepsi," said Sonny, as he turned the radio up full blast.

Five blocks north of Ste. Catherine, the rock music suddenly died.

Ducky reached to switch stations, but Sonny stopped him. "Hey, maybe they got somethin' new on that little kid the frogs kidnapped."

They heard Lee's scream while waiting for the light at Ontario Street.

"Fuck man! You hear that?" said Sonny.

Booby looked a little scared.

"What the hell do you think they're doing to her?"

Sonny turned on him.

"You stupid son of a bitch. Those cocksuckers are fuckin' her. . . fuckin' that little girl is what they're doing." He pounded the dash. "They're all the same. Takin' all the good jobs. Lookin' down their fuckin' noses at yuh. Fuckin' little girls. . . English girls."

The light was changing as Sonny suddenly wheeled the Bronco sharply right onto Ontario Street. Several people were gathered at the corner, laughing loudly among themselves. As he sped by, Sonny, certain they were laughing at him, without warning or thinking, hurled the half-empty beer bottle into their midst. It struck one of the women in the face, exploding in a sickening crash of shattering glass, flesh and bone. She went down in a heap, blood gushing from her smashed face, and screams filled the street. Sonny, his foot jammed to the floor, threw his voice into the pandemonium.

"Fucking frogs," he screamed, oblivious to the rapidly approaching red light.

They almost made it through the intersection. A half-second would have made the difference, but a fast-moving taxi caught their right rear bumper, spinning the Bronco around. Sonny didn't have time to remove his foot from the gas pedal before they smashed head-on into one of the lamp posts lining Ontario Street.

Montreal tough guys don't wear seat belts. Charles (Ducky) Drake, travelling at close to eighty kilometres an hour, crashed into the dashboard and windshield. He died instantly, several minutes before the twenty-four-year-old mother of two, whose life-blood steadily pumped onto the sidewalk less than a block away.

News spreads more rapidly in Montreal than in most major cities. This is especially true on warm evenings when half the populace swarms the streets, or perches in comfortable chairs on outdoor balconies designed to be close enough so neighbours can easily chat with each other.

There are rules associated with the dissemination of information in this fashion. The worse the news, the faster it spreads. The more it spreads, the worse the news becomes. Within an hour, the news flying from balcony to balcony was very bad indeed, much worse than that being reported on television and radio.

A major riot on Ontario Street, at least twenty dead, maybe more. Ste. Catherine Street under seige. Shooting along Jean Talon. Troops are on their way. And so it went on the balcony telegraph.

The facts, while far less dramatic than the balcony reports, were bad enough.

Several car loads of hoodlums, having heard the rumours, and not wishing to miss the "fun," converged on Ste. Catherine Street, weaving in and out of traffic, shouting obscenities at everyone, French and English. Large crowds of the idly curious began to gather, entertained by the several fights which broke out, until police closed the street to traffic and rolled in the troops. Two cruisers per block, four officers per cruiser, all equipped with riot gear. Sensing the excitement was over, the crowd slowly began to disperse.

Another fight broke out on Crescent. Several windows were smashed, but it was quickly broken up when police waded in, clubs swinging.

An incident on Jean Talon could have been much more serious. A large blue van, owned by a small group of religious crazies, calling themselves "God's Disciples for an English Canada," began slowly driving up and down the street in north end Montreal. Its loudspeaker blared a call for all "right-thinking English speaking peoples to rise up and overcome the oppressors who surround us."

On its third swing past the intersection of St. Dennis, a group of maybe fifteen or twenty had assembled, mostly men, mostly young, some armed with baseball bats and other assorted weaponry. As the van approached, they surrounded it and began energetically beating on it.

At first it was almost in jest, but as the loudspeaker persisted in its idiocy, the attack became less of a joke, and increased in intensity. The vehicle, which could have sped away, continued to crawl along at a pace most of the attackers could sustain.

Then as one beefy fellow leapt onto the front bumper and began pounding on the roof with a large two-by-four, the van lurched to a sudden halt, throwing the bumper-rider to the ground, amid the hoots and jeers of the crowd.

The door flew open and one of the sweetest-looking people

anyone would ever want to meet emerged. White haired, plump, smiling from ear to ear, she looked for all the world like everyone's favourite granny; eighty years old, if a day. In one hand she held a microphone, but what really got the crowd's attention was the 12-gauge doubled-barrelled shotgun clutched in the other. Still smiling, looking as if she should be dusty with flour, baking up a batch of brownies in her kitchen, she held the microphone to her mouth and in a delivery style obviously borrowed from her favourite TV evangelist, began to intone:

"This is God's chariot you beat upon; this is God's work I do. Verily, verily I say unto you, if thy right hand offend thee, cut it off. Cast no more stones at this, the disciple of Christ, or I say onto you, your city, like the walls of Jerico, shall come tumbling down."

Her voice began to rise.

"Follow me, the handmaiden of the Lord, on the path of righteousness. Speak only in God's tongue and. . ."

Someone yelled in English.

"Stick your tongue up your ass lady."

Loud laughter convulsed the crowd.

"I wouldn't want it up mine," shouted someone else.

More laughter. A young man with rings in both ears, shirt sleeves rolled up to reveal tattoos from wrist to shoulder, dashed to the front of the crowd and shouted:

"Tongue this, lady," and grabbed his crotch.

Granny, who had been standing as though frozen, but still smiling broadly, dropped the microphone to the ground and in a movement so swift few saw it, slammed the shotgun's stock into her shoulder, aimed it just over the heads of the Philistines besieging her and pulled the trigger.

The results were clearly to her satisfaction. As though by a miracle, the street, in little more than a twinkling of an eye, was virtually devoid of tormentors. Only a few, who had foolishly chosen to dive to the ground rather than run, peered up at her in terror as she raised the gun with both hands over her head and shouted.

"With this, the jawbone of an ass shall God's will be done. Sodom and Ghomorra shall be destroyed. God's chosen tongue will be spoken."

She clambered back into the van, which continued its slow crawl down the street. When police caught up with her a few blocks away, she offered no resistance, other than to gently admonish one of the arresting officers for speaking French.

Two hours drive to the west, on the Ontario-Quebec border, it was one of the quietest nights on record for Hull police. The usually packed and raucous rue Principle remained virtually deserted. Under normal conditions, thousands of people, most of them young and English speaking, flocked across the bridges into Quebec when Ottawa bars closed and Hull sprang to life, thanks to its more lenient liquor laws. Not so this night. Those who did venture out, including Police Superintendent Marcel Charron, found it eerie.

There were two incidents in Toronto. A rock was thrown through the window of a well-known French restaurant on Queen Street, and two Israeli tourists, window shopping on Danforth, were attacked and beaten by a gang of young hoodlums who mistook their Hebrew for French.

There were scattered incidents across the west. Less than an hour after Lee's scream was broadcast on a Winnipeg station, a bomb threat forced the evacuation of the French language station in St. Boniface. Nothing was found. In North Vancouver, two sticks of dynamite were detonated at the transmitter site of the French language television station. Two grazing cows were killed, but little damage was done to the towers.

Phone lines on the evening talk shows across Canada, and a few in American cities hugging the border, were jammed with angry and frightened callers. A consensus was rapidly building. With very few exceptions, the callers were saying the same thing. Enough is enough. Let Quebec go if that's what it takes to bring peace and security back to the country. Many insisted the time had come to demand that the province leave confederation, and furthermore, said several, "If anything should happen to that little girl, send in the troops with all guns blazing and keep them there until hell freezes over!"

* * *

Having been alerted well in advance, most of the caucus had already assembled in room 105 of the West Block of Canada's Parliament Buildings by the eight pm broadcast.

A radio commandeered from the secretary of state's office was on the table in front of the prime minister, an extension cord snaking down and across the floor to a wall plug. The MPs sat listening in shocked silence, transfixed by the small black box in front of the prime minister. They were scarcely able to believe what they were hearing, aware, not only of the tragedy which appeared imminent, but as well, of the dreadful burden of responsibility from which they could find no escape.

The prime minister spoke first.

"Ladies and gentlemen, I don't have to tell you how terrible this is. Nor do I have to tell you how your constituents are feeling. I'm sure your offices have been flooded, as has mine, since eight o'clock last night, with callers demanding we do nothing to endanger the welfare of this little girl."

He glanced around at the glum nodding faces.

"All right then," he sighed, "let's examine our options, and the possible consequences. Please let me conclude my remarks, then I invite your comments.

"First option: We agree to the demands of the abductors, and order withdrawal of all troops from the province of Quebec. Logistically, not a difficult task. General Berger assures me that virtually all, if not all, troops could be withdrawn by noon October fifteenth, as has been demanded. So we needn't debate that aspect. We can get the troops out in time. Now let's examine what happens if we do.

"Where do we house these troops? Once again, General Berger assures me this will not be a serious problem. Sufficient space will be found, or made, at our existing bases in Ontario, preferably. . ." he glanced up from his notes and looked around the table again. "Preferably as close to the Quebec border as possible. Our main billeting location will be at Petawawa, less than thirty minutes by troop carrier from Quebec, much less by helicopter. Other accommodation can be found here in Ottawa and in Cornwall. So that poses no serious problem, at least not in the short term. Which leaves two main considerations: security and the political consequences. Let's deal with security first.

"I think we can all agree that removing our armed forces from the province does not pose any sort of risk from external forces." He paused again, collecting his thoughts, then backtracked a bit. "At least not forces external to Canada." At this, several ministers glanced uneasily at each other. Already Marcel Picard, leader of the Quebec caucus, was energetically licking his lips, the colour rising in his face – always a danger sign.

The prime minister continued. "Would removal of the troops leave Quebec vulnerable to forces from within? This is something I wish to discuss further with you this evening; in particular," here he nodded to Picard, "members from Quebec.

"As to the question of vulnerability to forces from other parts of Canada, the generals have advised me that this matter, while an extremely delicate one, is relatively easy to deal with. In the event troops are withdrawn from Quebec, sufficient numbers to discourage any troublemakers from entering the province will be stationed at key points just inside the Ontario and New Brunswick borders, carrying out 'field operations.' We do not believe there is any potential for danger along Quebec's southern border with the United States. If trouble should occur, it will be very small scale and unorganized. We will have no difficulty dealing with it.

"Before we discuss the political ramifications, your questions and comments please on aspects of security."

Marcel Picard, his lips licked almost raw, looked very much like a bright red balloon inflated to the bursting point. Anytime he opened his mouth to speak, he tended to career madly about, his escaping grandiloquence propelling him energetically from point to point, usually without pause for breath or thought, until finally, gasless and deflated, he sputtered to a halt.

"Mr. Prime Minister." He began slowly, then a quick shift of the gears and into full flight. "Mr. Prime Minister, this is outrageous. We cannot allow the province of Quebec to be stripped, denuded of its right to security. You say, Mr. Prime Minister, there is no need to fear forces from outside the country. Indeed! How can you say that? It is well known that despite the apparent collapse of communism in eastern Europe, other forces, every bit as evil, every bit as covetous, are lying in wait to challenge our sovereignty. We cannot, for one moment, even contemplate the abandonment of Quebec in this fashion. There are widely circulated reports, certainly in my province, that this whole thing may be nothing more than a carefully calculated hoax in an attempt to have Quebec lower her guard and leave herself vulnerable to whatever gypsy band decides to invite itself in."

The filibuster continued for another half hour or so, non-stop, until finally, throwing his hands into the air, he collapsed with a little sigh into his chair, sprawling there rumpled, spent and quite pleased with himself.

Despite Picard's distress, most of the members seemed satisfied with the prime minister's assessment that from a security standpoint, there was little to fear from a troop withdrawal. It was obvious most were far more concerned with the political ramifications, so very quickly they moved on.

"Politically," said the prime minister "there is far more at stake, although many Canadians, especially Quebeckers, may not agree with that.

"Let's examine what occurs if we extract our troops. Is it a victory for the separatist forces? Will the federal government be subject to criticism for appearing weak? Will the separatists use it as a pretext to advance their cause, by claiming we have abandoned them? And a very important question: Once gone, will it be difficult to re-instate the troops? And of course, we must deal with all the questions relating to ownership of federal property – materials, equipment, etc.

"All those things must be weighed against the very real possibility that if we refuse to withdraw the troops and harm comes to this little girl, the people of Canada, both anglophone and francophone, will turn on us with immense hostility. Sufficient hostility perhaps, to make our job of governing impossible. If that were to happen, would the cause of separatism be advanced? Speaking personally, I can well imagine the Quebec government and the separatists here in the house pointing their bony fingers at us, claiming our cruelty and callousness was responsible for the death of an innocent child. Should that occur, the separatists would most certainly seize the moment and ask their constituents if we are really the kind of government they wish to continue to be subject to.

"Federalism has been the choice of the majority in two referendums in that province, and I don't have to remind any of you how close the last vote was. Would federalism continue to survive in the event of Lee Henry's death? It shakes me to the core to even think about it. And we must also consider the attitudes of those outside Quebec, which may turn out to be the most dangerous lightning stick of all. There is already considerable evidence that now, only twenty-four hours since the first broadcast of the terrorists demands, the sentiments of many Canadians have begun to shift from a willingness to accommodate Quebec to outpourings of great anger. A poll conducted by Leidecker International late this afternoon indicates a dramatic increase in the number of Canadians outside Quebec who are completely fed up and want Quebec to leave. The only exception to this remains the Atlantic provinces, concerned about being cut off from the rest of Canada. I can only imagine what would happen to public opinion if any more harm should befall this little girl. And I must be frank with you, I can only imagine what would happen to this government! Ladies and gentlemen we're caught between a rock and a very hard place indeed."

In the end, which didn't arrive until well into the morning, the caucus, with only seven dissenters, voted to issue a troop withdrawal order. The official statement released to the press said that members of the Canadian Armed Forces would be temporarily withdrawn from Quebec out of compassion for the life of Lee Henry. The release made a vague reference to Quebec police authorities assuring all residents they need have no fear for their safety, and as reports of violence in Montreal and elsewhere continued to filter into the capital, the cabinet called upon all Canadians to "exercise restraint and compassion at this very difficult time in our country's history."

* * *

Less than a city block away, in a Chateau Laurier Hotel room with a magnificent view of the parliament buildings, where the cabinet was debating his daughter's fate, Grant Henry sat thinking about chickens.

The last vestiges of dinner had been cleared, the lights were dimmed, and for nearly half an hour Grant and Sandra had sat, eyes closed, listening to a tape of classical music Sandra had produced from her purse.

"As you listen," she said, "try to clear your mind of everything. You are lying on your back in the middle of a beautiful green meadow watching fluffy white clouds floating gently overhead. Bees are flitting from flower to flower. . . butterflies. . . a soft breeze in your face. . . the smell of new-mown hay and sun on your skin. In the distance you can hear a stream tumbling over rocks. A trout is lying beside an old submerged log." She stopped and for several minutes there were only the soft strains of Chopin.

"Now you are walking through a sun filled barnyard. Horses are standing asleep, switching their tails lazily under a maple tree. White geese float silently in a pond. Chickens scratch in the dust."

She stopped and turned the music down to a point where he sensed more than heard it.

"As you watch those chickens, fluffing the dust up under their wings, you see they are small and white. Instead of feathers they seem to have fur."

She paused again, shooting him a sharp glance. His eyes remained closed, his body rocking almost imperceptibly to and fro.

"Lee is with you," she went on, in a voice barely above a whisper, "as you walk through that barnyard she's asking you questions about those chickens. . . What is she saying?"

Grant opened his eyes and turned toward her. She was barely discernable in the dim light.

"It's not the chickens," he said slowly, thoughtfully. "I think I know what she was trying to tell me about that sick a lock business!"

"Go ahead," Sandra encouraged him. "Tell me."

Grant nodded.

"Two summers ago, Lee, Carol and I took a boat trip up the Trent Canal. We had a wonderful time, except. . . except, in the lift lock at Peterborough, Lee suddenly became very ill; probably the three hamburgers she had for lunch. Anyway, all the time they were hoisting us up into the sky, poor Lee was throwing up into the lock. It was actually kind of funny. The people in the houseboats and small cruisers in the lock with us were all very solicitous, offering help, but there was this forty-foot yacht just ahead of us with a big yuppie party underway on deck. At the first heave from Lee, everyone disappeared below, never to be seen again, at least not when we were around. It's become kind of a family joke. Every time we see a big boat somebody yells for Lee and we all get a chuckle."

He was pacing now, hands jammed into his pockets, agitated. "What is she trying to tell us? Do you suppose they have her in a boat someplace? Could there be a lock nearby? Could it be they have her in Peterborough for heaven's sake? Of course, we haven't solved the riddle of the silkie chickens either, maybe if we get that, we'll understand what she was trying to tell us about being sick in a lock."

Sandra was very pensive.

"They could have her in a boat," she said doubtfully. "That's possible, but let's talk a bit more about that trip up the Trent Canal and see if maybe there's something else."

Together they explored every avenue they could think of. Sandra took him literally screw turn by screw turn through the entire trip from Kingston to Trenton, then into the Trent Canal for four glorious days, ending at the municipal docks of Orillia.

They overnighted in Orillia, saw a play at the Opera House, then he and Lee headed home the next morning for an uneventful trip back down through the system to their cottage on the St. Lawrence. Carol had rented a car and driven home alone.

"For some reason," said Sandra, after he'd gone through it again, "I have this feeling that she's trying to tell you something about that trip, not the fact she's in a boat. Let's leave that part of it for a moment and get you back in that barnyard. Are you relaxed enough to let your mind just go free?"

Grant nodded assent.

"Okay, you're in that sun-filled barnyard. Chickens are scratching in the dust, white furry chickens. Silkies. Lee is with you. Tell me anything which comes to your mind."

"I'm holding one in my hands," said Grant in a soft, far-away voice. "Lee is laughing and patting it gently, telling me how funny it feels, 'like silk fur' she says." He paused momentarily, lost in thought, then continued slowly.

"Niki had a terrible time with them. We had trained her not to touch any of our other animals, but for some reason she just couldn't seem to get it into her head that these things were chickens. She wanted to play with them. I guess to her they were just fun little balls of fur, but when she played with them, unfortunately they didn't respond too well. She killed three or four of them. Lee was devastated. She couldn't believe her beloved Niki would do anything like that. I had to explain to her the dog just didn't understand, but then again, the dog wasn't the only thing which didn't understand about those chickens."

"Go on," urged Sandra, as his voice trailed off.

"The second year after we had the silkies," he began again, "Lee was determined to exhibit them in the poultry show at the Central Canada Exhibition in Ottawa. I decided we should have a little bit of fun, so we took a half dozen of them and spray painted them red and blue with some food colouring. They were the hit of the show, believe me. Lots of people who probably didn't know where eggs come from, let alone chickens, came tramping into the barn to see these strange-looking red, white and blue creatures. The Ottawa Sun even did a little feature on them.

"Unfortunately that year they imported some little prick of a British judge who saw no humour in it at all. Not only didn't he give Lee a prize, he berated her with a lecture about trying to make a fool out of him, and how in a real poultry show, like the ones in Britain, this kind of thing just would not be allowed. He walked off in a huff and for weeks after, almost every time she went out to feed them, Lee would affect a British accent, and tell the chickens to please not try to make a fool out of her."

"Grant, that's it!"

His eyes snapped open. "Whaa. . . ?"

"That's what she's trying to tell you. Whoever has her is British, or most certainly English speaking. She's trying to tell you that her captors aren't speaking French, they're speaking English and perhaps at least one of them is British!" Grant stopped his pacing, and whirled to face her. "I doubt it very much. Surely. . ."

Sandra leaned forward, staring intensely into his eyes.

"Don't you see? If they spoke English, it would be very significant to Lee. In fact, if they have her blindfolded, or are concealing themselves from her, just about the only thing she might know about them is the language they speak. Besides, growing up in Quebec, language would be significant to her. It would indicate a great deal more than just simply whether you say me or *moi*."

"But the voice on that first tape. . ."

"The French accent could have been faked," said Sandra, "or maybe one of them is French Canadian, but I'm convinced she's trying to tell you that not only are these bastards English, but that it's a very important factor."

Grant resumed his rapid pacing, talking more to himself than to Sandra.

"She tries to tell me something about the locks in Peterborough. She says they're speaking English. . . wait a minute, something doesn't ring quite true here. To begin with, what are Quebec separatists doing speaking English? And why would they be in a place like Peterborough?"

"Don't many French Canadians speak very good English?" asked Sandra. "Remember Trudeau!"

Grant nodded.

"Certainly, but when they are with each other, they speak in their mother tongue, just like everyone else in the world." Another thought struck him. "Of course, if they were in a place like Peterborough, they would speak English most of the time in an effort not to attract attention to themselves."

Sandra was shaking her head violently.

"Call it a woman's intuition if you want, but I still have the feeling Lee is trying to tell you they not only speak English, they are English. But you're right, I don't suppose there are too many English-speaking Quebec separatists. But if you were a separatist hiding out with a big secret, where better than in an English speaking province where nobody would think of looking, and no one knows you?"

She looked at him expectantly.

"True," he admitted. "Quebec is a pretty small and very insular place. Moving within separatist circles would shrink it even more. It would make sense if the whole country is looking for you and you speak very good English, to get yourself out of the province. Geeze, maybe they do have her at Peterborough." Then as an afterthought, "although you'd wonder how Lee would know that."

It wasn't until the early hours of the morning that, exhausted, they finally agreed the tape would reveal no more of its secrets to them that night.

"Sleep is what we both need right now," said Sandra. "Tomorrow, let's put Jake's mind to work on this as well and. . . what about Carol?"

Grant shook his head.

"I hate not involving her, I know she's hurting, but under stress you never know what she's going to say, or to whom, especially if she's had a drink. Booze has always had a very powerful effect on her. There's just too much bloody intrigue in all of this to take any chances. The RCMP and CICS should be called in, but for all I know, they've got somebody stashed away in high places who could blow the whistle to the wrong people. Hell, I'm beginning to wonder if the premier of Quebec might not be involved!"

Sandra regarded him thoughtfully. "You don't trust many people do you? You're thinking maybe you can do this alone aren't you? You and Jake?"

This caught Grant by surprise. "What makes you say that?"

"I've seen that look before. I know how you self-made men think."

"Tommy?"

"Yes, Tommy. You remind me of him. To hell with the consequences. Let's just get it done. Or as Tommy used to say, fuck the hurricane!"

Grant laughed softly. "Ya, I've met a few hurricanes in my life and I learned that when you're in one, no one is going to help you. You either save yourself or you're blown away."

Sandra was shaking her head. "Grant, you must understand that this time you need help. You need a lot of help, or to be more accurate, your daughter does."

"Maybe," said Grant. "Maybe you're right, but you know how deeply the separatists have imbedded themselves in the power structure of this country. Who do you suggest I trust? There's only you and I here right now and we haven't done too badly so far, and let's not forget coming here was your idea!" Chuckling lightly he added, "And I sure as hell prefer your company to that of our little friend Boisvert!"

He came over to where she was sitting on the bed and squatted so he could look her directly in the eye. "Sandra why are you here? You're going to a hell of a lot more trouble over this than you have to. Why?"

She stood up. "I've thought a lot about that. I think I know the answer. A few months after Tommy and I bought our place in Freeport, the whole place went a little nuts over an approaching hurricane. Everybody taped those big X's on windows, tied down lawn furniture, filled bathtubs with water and prepared for goodness knows what disaster their imaginations had concocted. Tommy, typically, refused to buy into any of it. 'Screw that,' is what he said, 'I plan to enjoy this.' He hauled an old lawn chair down to the beach and sat there as the sky got blacker and blacker, the wind whipping sand and salt spray into his face. I watched him from the kitchen window, fascinated and yes, afraid. Suddenly he jumped up, raced back to the cottage and shouted, 'Sandra, let's go for a ride!' I couldn't believe it; it was a bloody hurricane! He untied our little boat, which was pitching so badly he could hardly hang onto it, and jumped in. I'll never forget him standing their, water streaming down his face, his eyes blazing with excitement. 'Coming, me love?' Even though I was sure I was going to die, I couldn't stop myself. I ran out into the storm and threw my arms around him. As we headed out into those huge waves Tommy stayed on his feet, steering with one hand, almost blinded by the wind, spray and rain. He threw his fist into the air and screamed at the top of his lungs: 'Fuck the hurricane!' We didn't die, but Tommy did less than a year later. The very last thing he said was to remind me of how we handle hurricanes."

The room fell silent. "I'm not Tommy," said Grant at last.

"No you are not," said Sandra. "Maybe it's the hurricanes I can't resist."

"This isn't your problem, Sandra. God knows where it's all going to end. I can't ask you to become any more involved. I. . ."

"You could not possibly stop me," she said defiantly. "End of that conversation. Now, you were talking about sleep, so let's get some. We'll need fresh brains to tackle the rest of this riddle tomorrow."

"You're right," admitted Grant, "I'm half dead on my feet. I've got to get to that motel room, they'll be waiting for me."

"Grant," she said carefully, "I don't think you should be driving when you're this tired. You have everything you need here. Call Jake, or I will, and tell him you're staying here tonight."

For an instant, their eyes locked.

Grant felt a sudden surge of desire, his breath and heart quickening. 'My God,' he thought. 'What's happening here?' "Sandra, I . . ." he began.

She reached out and laid her hand lightly on his arm, shaking her head.

"No Grant, that's not what I mean. There are two beds here." But she too found her heart racing and was astonished by it.

DAY THREE

Ottawa 5:52 AM

The sudden ring of the phone on the night table between their beds startled them both. Grant glanced at his watch. It was a few minutes to six.

"Who the hell. . . ?"

The voice on the other end was familiar and venomous.

"Good morning Mr. Henry, I hope you slept well. Your companion as well."

"You son of a bitch," shouted Grant, "where is my daughter? if I. . ."

"Tut, tut Mr. Henry, this display of Daddy-concern is admirable, but time-consuming. Listen carefully. I will not repeat myself. Several days ago, you received a recording of some interesting thoughts by a certain gentleman, whose identity I'm sure you have by now discovered. This evening, for the entertainment of your listeners, you will play that tape, in the form it was presented to you, and then, because it is in French and most of your listeners are English speaking, you will identify the speaker, translate the words into English and read them to your audience yourself.

"In addition, you will find another cassette tape waiting for you in the lobby of your hotel. It is also to be played this evening, immediately following the first. Once again you will identify the voices for your audience, and provide the English translation. I am sure you and Mr. Thompson will have no difficulty in making proper identification.

85

"Copies of both recordings will be supplied to the Canadian Press Wire Service and to all three major Canadian television networks immediately following your broadcast at eight p.m. The most recent tape recording, the one now awaiting you in the hotel lobby, also contains a brief message from your daughter."

Click, then dial tone.

As Grant hurriedly dressed, he gave Sandra the gist of the conversation.

"Call Jake, would you please? Have him meet us here as soon as he can." He gave her the number and dashed down the hallway to the elevator.

The lobby was deserted except for the clerk who, disclaiming any knowledge of its origin, handed him a small brown envelope. "Found it here on the counter early this morning, addressed to you, Mr. Henry. I was waiting until a little later to give you the message. By the way, we're very honoured that you chose to stay at the Chateau Laurier. We all know who you are of course," she said, beaming what she no doubt felt was her most beguiling smile.

'Not only does everybody know me,' thought Grant grimly, 'but someone seems to know where I am and what I'm doing every minute!' Despite himself, he glanced around the lobby as he waited for the elevator.

Montreal 6:54 AM – Day Three

Notre Dame Cathedral, in the heart of Montreal's Old City, is one of the most famous buildings in Canada. It is one of the largest, most beautiful churches in North America. Since 1824 it has served as a symbol of the power of the Roman Catholic Church, which dictated most aspects of Quebec's daily life from the birth of the colony until the so called "quiet revolution" of the sixties and seventies. It still serves the religious needs of many Montrealers, but in recent years it has become best known as one of the province's main tourist attractions. From early morning until well past dusk every day during summer, tour buses and horse drawn calèches jostle each other for prime parking space within easy walking distance of the magnificent edifice.

As further illustration of the declining influence of the Quebec clergy, a grubby little store directly across from the cathedral delights in filling its windows with sex aids and T-shirts advocating every sexual perversion known to man – or the church! Far from being outraged at the juxtaposition of saints and sinners, most Montrealers are amused, even appreciative of the owner's defiance. One can only speculate as to the reactions of nuns and priests scurrying past the smutty windows every day, trying not to steal furtive glances at the vibrators, handcuffs and crotchless panties.

Notre Dame Street was not fully awake when an unusually well-dressed early morning worshipper strode purposefully past the sex store without giving it so much as a glance, climbed the stone steps and entered the cathedral; a wealthy businessman from the way he was dressed, or perhaps a lawyer from one of the nearby firms, in his late forties or early fifties, slightly stooped, greying at the temples, but still vigorous and powerful looking.

Moving quickly in the hush, he entered one of the confessionals lining the left side of the church, the third from the rear, pulled the curtain shut and glanced at his watch. In a moment he heard a slight scuffling sound, but could not see the bearded young man dressed in priest's robes who settled into the cubicle opposite.

There were no formalities as the younger man began to speak in slightly accented but cultured English.

"Our leader wishes to congratulate you. Everything has gone according to plan. You are to hold the girl captive, harming her no more than is necessary to obtain the proper, ah, sound effects, until you hear from us again. We will advise you of her fate at that time." There was a nervous cough from the priest's side of the curtain. The voice began again, less sure of itself now.

"We have one other duty for you to preform. Ahh, you will be paid extra of course." He paused for a moment, waiting for a response. There was none. He continued. "It has been decided that to hasten our objective, there must be another victim. Unfortunately, this has to be one of our own, killed in such a fashion as to indicate she died at the hands of. . . not English gutter slime, as was the case on Ontario Street last night, but the English ruling class.

"Your instructions are to proceed to the village of Ste. Anne de Bellevue on the western tip of Montreal Island, and choose a victim, female, under the age of twenty, and French speaking. She is to be killed as mercifully as possible this evening, and her body left on the campus of Macdonald College, less than a half kilometre to the east of the village. Are you wearing gloves?"

For the first time since entering the confessional, the older man spoke, in a strangely-accented English.

"Killing is an entirely different matter. We have never discussed it. How much are you prepared to pay?"

There was no hesitation. The voice was firm, matter of fact, as though it made this kind of statement almost every day.

"One hundred thousand dollars. Fifty thousand now, fifty thousand in our usual location after the job is completed. The payment will be there at six o'clock tomorrow morning, provided everything goes as planned tonight. You must not be there to pick up your money any earlier than six and no later. Right at six, that is very important."

Neither spoke for several seconds.

"All right," said the older man, "as long as we both understand that if there's to be any more of, of this kind of thing, the price goes up. Agreed?"

"Agreed," said the matter-of-fact voice. "Do you have gloves on?"

"Yes."

"Then here, take this. It's a sign which is to be attached to your victim's body. To spare your questions, it states that the death is in retaliation for the kidnapping of Lee Henry and other injustices endured by English Quebeckers under the regime of Jean Luc Menard."

The curtain between the two men parted slightly and a gloved hand appeared, holding a tightly wrapped piece of cloth and a larger parcel wrapped in brown paper.

"We will contact you when we wish to meet again," said the robed figure. A rustling of cloth and he was gone.

For several minutes the confessional's remaining occupant sat inside, immobile, scarcely breathing, listening intently, until slowly, without examining it, he shoved the piece of wrapped cloth into his pants pocket. Then, with a small knife produced from a sheath strapped to his inner left ankle, he carefully sliced open the parcel and counted the bills. Satisfied, he separated the package into two bundles, and reaching around to the lining at the back of his suit coat, dropped them into two specially designed pockets.

Carefully buttoning his jacket, he gave his tie a jerk of alignment and exited the confessional. The pews, deserted when he entered, were now dotted with early morning worshippers, none of whom showed the slightest interest in the well-dressed man who hurried out.

Ottawa 6:19 AM – Day Three

"To tell you the truth," Jake said to Carol, as they listened to the early morning news on the car radio, "I expected far worse. Two dead in Montreal, a few fights here and there, a handful of bomb threats, a couple beaten up in Toronto – piece a cake."

Traffic heading into Ottawa from the Quebec side was light at this hour of the morning. Jake figured they should be at the Chateau Laurier in no more than fifteen minutes, unless there was a tie-up on the MacDonald Cartier Bridge. He was driving as fast as possible. There had been urgency in Sandra's voice. "Come quickly," she said. "We've got another tape recording."

"Ya know," continued Jake, "it's really tough to get Canadians riled up. Geeze, if this was happening in the States, they'd start another civil war. They'd be picketing the White House. The KKK would be stealing white sheets from the clotheslines of the nation. They'd be lobbing grenades at each other on university campuses. But then, the Yanks really know how to do things up with a bang."

He was trying to cheer Carol up a bit, without much success. "Lousy humour, eh?" he asked, glancing sideways at her grim face.

Before agreeing to bring her with him to meet Grant at the Chateau, Jake had warned Carol that if she wanted to play any kind of role in the search for her daughter there could be no alcohol. "No booze at all, Carol," he said, "there's too much at stake. You know what happens if you even touch the stuff. There are things happening which, if the wrong people ever found out, could place Lee in even more jeopardy."

At first she had been indignant.

"Do you really think I would do anything to harm my own daughter?" she demanded angrily.

Jake snorted.

"Carol, let's cut the bullshit, okay? We both know all it takes for you is about two drinks and you don't care what the hell you say, or do, for that matter."

Her eyes telegraphed it. Jake easily warded off the blow she aimed at his head and grabbed her arm roughly.

"You bastard," she sobbed, "you bloody bastard. You don't understand. You just don't understand." She had great difficulty getting the words out between her sobs.

"There's something you should know," she was speaking barely above a whisper now. "I never wanted to leave Grant. I never wanted any of this to happen. And it's not all my fault either. Half the time he didn't seem to even notice I was around. Grant is the only one I ever loved, and I still love him. Why did this have to happen?" She was sobbing uncontrollably now.

Jake shook his head sceptically. "If you loved him so much, if you didn't want to break the marriage up, why the hell did you leave? Anyway, from what I understand you've met someone else."

The sobbing subsided somewhat as she slumped into a chair.

"I told you, you don't understand." Her voice was sad and tired and beaten down. "There's no one else who really means anything. I'm still not sure why I left. Maybe I was just lonely. Grant was always so bloody engrossed in his program. Maybe I resented being the one always tagging along behind the big radio star. Maybe I was just trying to get his attention. I don't know. It was all so stupid, so horribly stupid." She held her face in her hands, shoulders heaving, crying uncontrollably. Tears for her missing daughter, for lost love, for fading youth and beauty, for all the things which could have been but were not, and would never be.

Jake, subdued, reached down to touch her shoulder.

"I know, I know," he said, his voice soft and far away. "All those things just blowin' in the wind. Some of us just aren't meant for picking wild strawberries all our lives. I'm sorry. I was out of line. I didn't know. I don't think anyone knew."

She looked up at him, trying to smile, her eyes red and swollen. "That's the tragedy of it. I didn't know either. . ."

* * *

Grant was furious when Carol walked through the door into Sandra's hotel suite.

"What the hell. . ."

Before he could say anything more, Carol held up her hand. "Jake, can you and Mrs. Beale maybe grab a bit of breakfast or something, let me talk to Grant, just for a couple of moments. Please?"

"Excellent idea," said Sandra. "As a matter of fact, if I don't get out of this room for a few minutes, I'm going to go crazy. I'll tell Jake what we got this morning, then bring you back some toast and coffee."

"Please listen to me, give me a chance," Carol began speaking rapidly as the door closed. "I want to help with whatever it is you're doing to find Lee. Grant, she's my daughter too!"

He was shaking his head in adamant refusal.

"Carol, this is just too risky. There are some very strange things going on. We don't know who can be trusted. We're afraid to tell the RCMP what we know for God's sake. . . and there's something else. One minor slip of the tongue, by anyone, could mean serious harm. . . worse, for Lee. We just can't take the chance."

Carol was desperately pleading her case now. "Grant, I swear to you, I won't touch a drop of anything. Don't look at me like that. I mean it. Lock me in this hotel room if you like, and if something happens and you're afraid I'll say something wrong, just put me on a plane back to Vancouver, and I'll get out of your life forever. Please, you've got to give me a chance."

Grant had never been able to resist her pleas for long. It was no different this time. "All right," he finally agreed reluctantly, "but the conditions are these. We tell you everything we know. You help us if you can, but you stay in this hotel suite until we all agree it's safe for you to leave. Get someone to bring the clothes you need. You eat in the room, and the strongest we have to drink is root beer. Agreed?"

Carol didn't hesitate. "Agreed!"

Grant quickly brought her up to date on what they had been able to learn and their theories concerning the messages Lee was providing. "You were with us on that cruise up the Trent, so as soon as Jake and Sandra return, I want all of us to go back over that trip again and see if there's anything else we can think of that she might have been trying to tell us in. . ."

Carol interrupted him. "Grant, is there something going on between you and Sandra? You stayed here last night didn't you?"

"Carol, for Chrissakes, you're the last one to ask a question like that. Come on. What may or may not be happening between Sandra and me has nothing to do with finding Lee, and it sure as hell doesn't have anything to do with you."

She tried to make a joke of it. "Hey, hey, cool it man, just trying to get the lay of the land. . . oops, sorry, bad choice of words."

He shot her a malevolent glare but said nothing, as Jake and Sandra returned, loaded down with breakfast and inquiring looks. "In answer to your unasked questions," said Grant the moment they were through the door, "let's see if Carol can help us with the tapes, but first, let's grab a bite and have a look at what the rest of the world is doing."

They ate quickly, watching the latest TV coverage, which now focused primarily on the outbreaks of violence, the swelling public protest against Quebec and the ever-mounting political crisis.

Whitlaw's show featured a panel of three military experts, all with divergent views on the ramifications of the troop withdrawal which had already begun.

A flick of the channels and they were watching Premier Jean Luc Menard and his Secretary of State Marc (The "Hawk") Charbonneau flailing away at the federal government, which they claimed had caused the entire crisis.

Menard steepled his fingers under his chin and turned to Charbonneau who began to speak in measured tones.

"We invite the prime minister of Canada to re-think the entire matter of Quebec independence," he said. "We have no wish that this distrust, even hostility, which appears to be growing rapidly, escalate any further. The people of Canada should think long and hard about this and. . ."

Jake turned the set off. "Ya, ya. Sure thing Hawk. What a guy eh? Catches his wife in bed with a cabinet minister from English Canada and now he wants us all to pay through the nose for it. The more I see of this guy, the more I like his wife. Enough of this crap. Let's get to work. Sandra told me pretty well everything that's on the tape you got this morning. Let's have a listen and see what we can come up with."

Sandra, trying to buffer Grant from whatever trauma she could, took over. If she noticed the look Carol shot her across the room, she gave no indication of it.

"This is the recording we received at the hotel this morning," Sandra said. "As I've already explained to Jake, it contains two segments. The first is a slightly muffled recording of what appears to be some kind of private meeting between the premier of Quebec and our old friend Chief Inspector Boisvert. It's in French, but as you all speak it well, you should have no difficulty understanding.

"The second part of the tape is the man who identifies himself as the commander of the Quebec army of liberation. We know his voice only too well." She paused for a moment, looking directly at Carol. "It also contains a brief message from your daughter."

Carol nodded.

"Let me hear it," she whispered.

The premier's voice on the tape was unmistakable:

"Inspector, perhaps we should explain ourselves more clearly here. I am certain you know we all deplore what has occurred, but on the other hand, there are certain political considerations which must be taken into account. Could it be Inspector, that in your desire to protect your country. . . Quebec, from its enemies, you may have been overzealous? Did you, in this zealousness, attempt to create some doubt in the minds of some of our countrymen that this may not be the work of a separatist faction, but is instead another anglo plot to discredit our cause? To be blunt, I can find no fault with anyone whose devotion, or zealousness in defence of the cause of a sovereign state takes him over the bounds of what some would describe as lawful behaviour. We must remember we are involved in a revolution here and in a revolution there are always casualties, including, I hasten to point out, to the innocent and the truth."

There was a slight pause on the tape, then Inspector Boisvert's strangely quiet voice.

"To zealousness in defence of our cause, I must plead guilty." There was a loud snort and Jake muttered, "You little dick face."

There were two loud clicks on the tape, a moment of silence, then once again it was the voice of the man who claimed to command the army for the liberation of Quebec. Sardonic and mocking, he was obviously enjoying himself.

"Well, well, well. Interesting conversations aren't they? You just never know what you're going to get when you cast your ballot do you? I should think that after this evening, Premier Menard's chances of becoming the next secretary general of the United Nations, or Pope, I suppose, would be just about nil, although I am sure a good many of his fellow Quebecois, if they were totally honest with themselves, would support the premier's point of view."

His voice hardened.

"Our organization has no desire to be under the leadership of anyone as deceitful as Jean Luc Menard. We could insist upon Mr. Menard's immediate resignation, but in light of what you have just heard, I am sure no such insistence is required. His own party will take care of that very quickly. The matter of his replacement, however, is quite another issue. There are any number of pretenders to the throne, most of whom, I am sure, will begin preening themselves for the press the moment the contents of these tapes are made public.

"Our organization is fully aware of the qualifications of all of those likely to be considered to replace the unlamented Jean Luc Menard. As deputy premier, Mario Lefebvre would under most circumstances, assume the role until such time as a leadership convention is held. We are also aware that several members of the caucus will oppose such an appointment.

"It is our demand that not only must Mario Lefebvre be chosen to replace Jean Luc Menard, he must remain as premier until such time as Quebec, as an independent and sovereign nation, holds elections of her own for president.

"As you are aware, we continue to hold the twelve-year-old daughter of Mr. Grant Henry. Members of the government of Quebec should remember that they hold not only the fate of Miss Henry in their hands, but should our demands be ignored, there will be other civilian casualties before this war of independence is successfully concluded.

"I recognize that some members of the Quebec government will not be sympathetically inclined towards the plight of an anglophone, no matter what her tender years. So that no one can forget, what should I call it, the human side of this affair, here is a brief message, once again, from Lee Henry."

Her voice sounded weak and very tired. She spoke slowly, almost, thought Jake, as though she were drugged.

"Hello Daddy," she began. "I wish you would make them let me go home. Daddy, they say they will hurt me again if everybody doesn't do what they say. Please Daddy, make them do what they say. I don't want them to hurt me anymore. I wish this was at the end." She began to sob softly for a moment, before the first voice returned with its now familiar taunt:

"Same time, same place, tomorrow."

Grant, who had been listening to the tape all morning, still found himself trembling violently at the sound of his daughter's pitiful little voice. Carol was so badly shaken she had to be helped to the edge of the bed. Her face had turned chalky white, her eyes blinking open and shut rapidly. Grant, fearing she was about to faint, reached for her, but she mutely waved him away.

Jake broke the heavy silence.

"Kee-rist!" he whistled, "what a bucketful we've netted with this one!"

There was a crucial question however, which lay heavily in the air. It was finally Grant who voiced the unthinkable.

"No sense trying to kid ourselves," he said disconsolately, "there's just no way the Quebec government can go along with these demands. Mario Lefebvre is probably the strongest candidate to replace Menard, but under these conditions, I just don't see how it can happen. I don't believe any political party can allow terrorists to dictate what should be a free election, no matter what kind of club is being held over its head."

He slumped dejectedly into a small chair at the side of the bed, then in a bitter voice continued, "It's one thing to lower a bunch of flags or even remove troops, but forcing a premier onto a province just won't wash. This is one demand we can be very sure will not be met. We don't have much time left."

He fell silent, shrinking even further into the chair.

"Not only that," agreed Jake, "let's not forget that Menard is still there. He'll be in one big pack of shit after they hear this tape but. . ."

Sandra jumped in.

"Let's leave the politics to the politicians and see if we can learn anything more from Lee. Grant is right, we've got no time to waste, so are you guys going to sit around all day and mope, or are we going to get down to business here?"

They both looked at her a little sheepishly.

Again and again they played the tapes containing Lee's voice. Carol was in strong agreement with Sandra in her belief that Lee was trying to tell them her abductors were either English, or at the very least, English speaking.

"I remember her joking about that funny little Englishman judging her multi-coloured silkies," she said. "I'm sure he made a great impression on her and if there is someone around with a British accent, that's probably the first thing she would think of."

She listened carefully as the tape was played over and over again, paying special attention to her coughing, and talking about being sick a lock.

"I'm sure that's what she was trying to say," Carol nodded emphatically, "and I have an idea that the coughing or choking or whatever she was doing, is supposed to signify throwing up."

It was something they hadn't thought of before, and Carol was pleased she had been able to add to their knowledge. She gave Sandra a fleeting look of triumph.

It was almost noon when, weary, frustrated and disappointed, they decided to take a brief break. The recording they had received that morning appeared to be devoid of clues. They had explored hundreds of possibilities, none apparently plausible.

"She sounds so strange," mumbled Carol. "It's almost as though she was drugged or something." She was the first to say aloud what they had all been thinking.

"At least," said Grant, "they didn't hurt her this time." And, thought Jake, she's still alive!

Montreal 11:37 AM – Day Three

It was unusually warm for the time of year in Montreal, which meant that to get a good seat for lunch at the Algonquin Hotel's outdoor patio, you had to arrive early. The Algonquin, in addition to being one of the Old City's most famous landmarks, provided surprisingly good food, and an even better observatory from which to view one of the world's most interesting human panoramas. Sailors from just-berthed ships in the nearby harbour hurried by on their way to the famous brothels of St. Urbain and St. Laurent Streets a few blocks to the north, their eyes hungrily devouring the shop girls and office clerks in their mini skirts and flimsy blouses. Late season tourists from New York and Michigan strolled leisurely along the cobblestones, on the lookout for "quaint," unsure of what to expect from the mad separatists they had heard so much about, but titillated by the foreignness of it all, and the possibility of danger and intrigue. There were sudden bursts of barristers, some still in their robes, fresh from deal-making and plea bargaining in the nearby Superior Court. Nuns and priests from Notre Dame Cathedral, a brisk ten-minute walk away, joined the parade, mingling with the usual collection of bums and beggars, clowns and crazies.

As usual on warm days, a rag-tag group of musicians strummed guitars at the base of Nelson's Column, a peanut throw from the Algonquin's patio which, already, well before noon, was filling with Montrealers who were only too well aware that in a few weeks, sitting outside sipping beer or cognac would lose its appeal. Fall and winter weather in Montreal is usually measured in gradations of misery.

The tall, ascetic-looking young man sitting alone, full bearded face tilted towards the sun, eyes closed, right hand nursing a warming glass of beer, had the entire patio from which to choose, when he arrived shortly after eleven am. A careful observer would have noted he was not as relaxed as he tried to appear. While seating several American tourists at an adjoining table, a waiter accidentally tipped over the bearded man's shopping bag, causing some of the contents to spill out. With an angry cry, the bag's owner jerked it from the hands of the apologetic waiter and stuffed a black robe back in, glancing nervously about. No one paid the slightest attention. Even the just-seated tourists had missed the by-play, entranced by an organ grinder, complete with monkey, setting up shop a few meters away.

The young man chastised himself for his display of anxiety. He had been warned to avoid drawing attention to himself, and had begun to realize that coming here early was a mistake. A single man sitting alone for a long time might attract attention, but it was too late to move now. He glanced at his watch. Ten more minutes. He would be glad when this part of it was over.

To avoid drawing any further attention to himself, he quietly apologized to the waiter, blaming his bad humour on a date who, he claimed with a shrug of his shoulders, had stood him up. To avoid further conversation he ordered another beer and a bowl of chowder. It still had not arrived when, precisely at noon, he reached into the shopping bag, extracted a cellular phone and dialled a Quebec City number. He waited for a beep, then in an as authoritative and businesslike voice as he could muster said, "They've accepted our price and have promised delivery as scheduled. My appointment this afternoon has been confirmed for three. I'll check with you again at this time tomorrow. Goodbye."

When the soup arrived, he devoured it with the appetite of one, who, after a job well done, looks forward to a bit of relaxation.

Two very young men, hardly more than boys, strolled by, arm in arm. He checked his watch again. He had at least two hours. Quickly he dropped a twenty-dollar bill onto the table, picked up his shopping bag and followed the boys.

The West Island 1:20 PM – Day Three

Some forty kilometres west of the Algonquin Hotel, the streets of Ste Anne de Bellevue were awash with the ebb and flow of students and teachers from the nearby campuses of Macdonald Agricultural College and the Sir John Abbott CGEP, a junior college for much of the English speaking population of western Quebec. The fall term had just begun, and the cash registers of the little village were singing the song the merchants loved to hear, as the students, less impoverished every year, caught up with some last-minute shopping.

The mood on the streets was not as boisterous as usual. Despite the natural inclination of youth towards optimism, most could not help but feel anxiety over the events of the past two days. As members of a minority in what threatened to become an ever more hostile environment, the talk on the streets was of little else but the abduction of the Henry girl, and what lay ahead for them and other anglophones in the province. Many had long ago decided that upon graduation, their destiny lay someplace other than Quebec.

It was especially difficult for agriculture students, whose parents had expectantly packed them off to Macdonald Agricultural College in anticipation of their return a few years later, brimming with knowledge and enthusiasm, to manage farms, in particular dairy operations, which had been in the family for generations. How many of their children would ever return to a Quebec farm was a question which hovered over parts of rural Quebec like a dark and ominous cloud.

Fearing his finely tailored suit would make him too conspicuous amidst the college informality, the man who earlier that morning had visited Notre Dame Cathedral removed his coat and tie and left them carefully rolled beside him on the car seat and completed his reconnaissance in shirt sleeves. For more than an hour he drove slowly about the village, exploring side streets, parks, open areas, school yards and, in particular, student residences. Confident he knew the configuration of the streets well enough to navigate at night, he took a stop watch and small note book from the glove compartment and began a series of timing runs.

There were several downtown bars and hotels obviously catering to students. Meticulously, he recorded the time it took him to drive from each one of them to the stone gates guarding the entrance to Macdonald College. He conducted similar experiments from several other locations: a secluded park, a bus stop, and two large residence buildings. Finally, he clocked himself on a run from Macdonald's gates to highway 420, which, at the Ontario border some fifty kilometres away, became Highway 401, the Macdonald Cartier Freeway; four lanes to Toronto and beyond.

Preparations concluded, he drove several miles along Lakeshore Boulevard, pulled off onto a rutted sideroad and, finding a grassy embankment, sprawled on it, face to the afternoon sun, and fell asleep.

Mount Royal Park, Montreal 3:00 PM – Day Three

The winding gravel roadway which twists and hairpin-turns its way to the top of Mount Royal is a favourite of Montreal's hardier joggers and more romantic lovers. The climb, being arduous, induces some of the lovers to board one of the city's famous horse drawn calèches, thus sparing their legs, lungs and hearts for later tasks more pleasurable.

The sight of a single man in one of the gay little carriages during the middle of the day was sufficiently novel to draw the attention of several joggers who, recognizing the strange-looking passenger, waved a jaunty hello. Inspector Boisvert, deeply engrossed in other matters, did not acknowledge the salutations. He did not even notice them.

Not since the referee had taken his gloved hand and raised it in victory over the bloodied, prostrate form of the former Montreal Flyweight Boxing Champion had Boisvert been as exhilarated.

The driver, his bearded face partially concealed by a high-collared coat and broad-brimmed hat pulled low over his forehead, had begun speaking in very cultured French almost as soon as Boisvert climbed aboard.

"Please don't ask any questions Inspector. I have been authorized to provide you with certain information, but I am only a messenger so there are obviously many things I am not privy to."

Boisvert noted that from the nervous way he held the reins, his driver had very little experience with horses.

"Go on," urged the inspector gruffly. "This had better be worth my while. Whoever phoned said I would be provided information which would help solve the abduction of Lee Henry. Please proceed, and if I'm not satisfied, I will order you to immediately turn this animal and carriage about and return me to my car. Then I will handcuff you and take you to my office where I can question you thoroughly, in private."

"There is much more involved in this," replied the driver, unruffled, "than a simple kidnapping. My message comes from a source which, in a few days, will control most of the reins of power in this province. I am not at liberty to elaborate, other than to say that this new leadership has chosen you for an extremely important position."

Stunned, Boisvert began to speak, but the driver held up his hand.

"Please let me continue. A tape recording will be played during the Grant Henry show this evening which will cause considerable embarrassment to a well-known figure in this province. That same recording contains a segment which may cause you some minor discomfort. Unfortunately it cannot be avoided. I have been instructed to inform you that if there was any other method of achieving our goals, we would not involve you in this affair in this manner. It is our belief however, that in light of other information which will be revealed tonight, your very minor participation in the tape recording affair will be virtually ignored. To help insure that, and to enhance your reputation with the citizens of our new republic, we are providing you with information which will lead to the arrest of one of those involved in the Henry abduction."

Boisvert was about to say something again, but the driver continued uninterrupted. "Please make note of this."

Following instructions, Boisvert reached into his coat pocket and extracted a small computerized pad.

"At this moment," said the driver, "Inspector Marcel Charron, with whom you are familiar, is investigating a truck driver named Paul Larocque. He is a man suspected of robbing several convenience stores in recent months. Not only is Mr. Larocque guilty of those crimes, and many others, but an investigation of his garage at 1147 St. Cecile Street, Gatineau, will reveal an eighteen-foot outboard motorboat and trailer. Both of these items were stolen more than two years ago, but more importantly, this is the boat and trailer used in the abduction of Lee Henry. If Mr. Larocque is confronted with these facts and offered the opportunity of either admitting them or facing charges of the kidnap, rape and murder on April thirteenth of this year of an Ottawa prostitute named Andrea Snowdon, he will most certainly tell you everything he knows concerning the Henry case. It is our intent that you have your people arrest Larocque and lay charges in time for tonight's six o'clock television newscasts."

The driver reached into a shopping bag at his feet and extracted a phone.

"Obviously there is no time to waste." he said. "Inspector Charron is at his desk at this moment, expecting a call from you, although he has no idea what it concerns. Mr. Larocque is also at his home, expecting, not a phone call from a police officer, but a sizable amount of money. At this moment," the driver checked his watch, "the press is being alerted to expect a break in the Henry case and is standing by for your press conference, to be held at six pm in the Bourassa Salon of the Hotel Quebec. It would greatly enhance the impact of the story if the television cameras were able to switch from coverage of your statements here in Montreal to live coverage of the arrest of Mr. Larocque in Hull." He paused for a moment, pulling his hat down lower over his face, then continued in a somewhat apprehensive voice. "I regret very much having to say this, but please remember I am only a messenger. As you can appreciate, co-operating in this manner will provide you with a splendid opportunity to advance your career but if, for any reason you should feel obligated to reveal anything of what has been said here this afternoon, please be advised that there are, in safe keeping. . . ahh. . . several pieces of evidence which, if released to the press, could seriously damage, if not destroy, your usefulness to a newly constituted Quebec. Something about private interrogations, I believe."

Allowing the inspector no time to digest all of this, the driver handed Boisvert the phone. "I presume you know Inspector Charron's number?"

"I know his number," replied Boisvert, "but inform your superiors that I am accepting their offer, not because of potential rewards or threats, but because of my love for Quebec and my determination that we achieve our independence as quickly as possible." Increasingly, he was finding himself irritated, not so much by what the driver was saying, as by his mannerisms. Deeply homophobic, Inspector Boisvert suspected he was dealing with someone whose sexual orientation he'd like a shot at straightening out.

The driver sat for a moment on his small seat in front of the inspector, shoulders hunched, hands holding the reins lightly.

"Very admirable sentiments Inspector," he said finally, making no attempt to conceal his sarcasm. "Of course you don't know who it is that is bringing all this about, do you?"

Ottawa 4:12 PM – Day Three

It had been a frustrating afternoon for the four of them, crammed as they were into two small hotel rooms, the tapes refusing to reveal anything more to them. Sandra had tried her free association techniques on both Grant and Carol, but nothing worthwhile had come of it despite Grant's dogged insistence that, as with the previous tapes, Lee must be trying to tell them something on this one as well.

"She must know that by now we're aware she's up to something," he insisted. "It only makes sense she'd keep trying to get a message through to us, unless of course her captors have caught on and have put a stop to it."

"Or," added Jake, "she just wasn't feeling up to it. You know something," he said quietly, "not many adults, let alone twelve-year-old kids, would have the guts or the presence of mind to cook up signals as she's been doing, especially with a gang of thugs hanging onto every word. If what we suspect is true, if she really has been sending us signals, boy, she is something else!"

He checked his watch and got to his feet.

"I don't think we're going to accomplish anything more here with these tapes," he said, yawning in spite of himself. "The one thing we really can't do much with here is that buzzing sound we keep hearing in the background. I'd like to run it through the computer a few more times with Al Thompson back at the radio station, and see if we can't figure out what it is. Who knows, maybe it's some kind of clue. Give old Al a call, tell him I'm on my way there with two new tapes. We've already got the premier's knackers in a noose with that first recording of his complimentary remarks about his Indian and English friends. When the country hears that recording, along with this palsy-walsy, breaking-the-law-is-hunky-dory conversation with Boisvert, he'll be lucky if even his dog wants anything to do with him."

Chuckling at his own joke, Jake left. Sandra decided to go with him and make her calls to the network, advising them of what to expect at eight. They had already decided to follow the same routine as yesterday, with Vancouver and Toronto provided early feeds and told to be ready to initiate the broadcast if problems arose in Ottawa. They also agreed that, just like last night, police across the country would be alerted, although, as Jake pointed out, most of the protest tonight was likely to be confined to a few rooms in and around the legislative buildings in Quebec City.

4:44 PM – Day Three

Carol had fallen into a restless sleep in the other room, moaning softly from time to time as she tossed and turned. Rather than risk waking her, Grant donned a pair of earphones, plugged them into the tape recorder and settled back into a chair to listen to that final tape one more time. He knew the words by heart, but he was listening for something else. A tonal quality perhaps, an inflection, a hesitation, anything which Lee may have used to signal him. It began again:

"Hello Daddy. I wish you would make them let me go home. They say they will hurt me again if everybody doesn't do what they say. Please Daddy make them do what they say. I don't want them to hurt me again. I wish this was at the end."

There was no apparent signal, no hesitation, no change of inflection. Only a slight buzzing in the background, the same sound heard on all the tapes when she spoke.

Grant, as he often did when attempting to analyze a difficult problem, began to mutter aloud to himself. "Okay Henry, let's attack this from another point of view. We've listened for subtle signals, analyzed the hell out of every word she says, now let's zoom in on this from someplace entirely different. Let's think from the kidnappers' point of view. What do they wish to accomplish? Get everyone pissed off with them, right? Rile the country up until Quebec separation begins to sound like a honeymoon. Okay then, let's analyze the tape from that point of view."

He was unaware that he was talking loud enough to have awakened Carol, who lay on her bed listening, feigning sleep.

"Lee says 'I wish you would make them let me go home.' A natural thing for her to say. That's probably what she wishes more than anything else in the world. The kidnappers would like that, because going home is something everyone can relate to. It's bound to get everyone's back up; keeping this little girl away from her parents and her home. That's the phrase we'll probably see on most front pages tomorrow morning.

"All right, next sentence: 'They say they will hurt me again if everybody doesn't do what they say.' Again a natural sentiment. They've obviously already hurt her somehow (he couldn't bring himself to think how). Her biggest fear would be getting hurt again, especially if they have told her they will hurt her much worse next time. You can be sure they told her to say that, as a warning for us. I just don't see how she could have slipped us any kind of message there. It sounds too much like something they would tell her to say."

It was territory they had all gone over time and time again and come up with nothing. Grant was still certain there was something there. 'I know she wasn't feeling well when she made that recording,' he told himself. 'They may have her drugged or sedated or something, but there's just got to be a message for us there somewhere.' One thing which he knew would be in her favour was the fact that, in all probability, she would have very little to do other than think about her daily message and how she could slip something by her captors.

He began pacing the room, talking aloud to himself again. "Next sentence: 'Please Daddy make them do what they say.' Once again bound to be uppermost in Lee's mind. The idea that I can control any situation, can make governments and others to do my bidding, is not out of context for Lee. She's always been convinced that I pull most of the strings in the country, or if I don't, I could. Once again her abductors would instruct her to say something like that, as a further warning to toe their line. Doesn't seem to be anything out of context their either, damn. Okay, the last line: 'I wish it was at the end.' Once again a natural thought for her. Sure she wishes it would end and. . ." A sudden through struck him. "Wait a minute, wait a minute here." His pacing grew more rapid. "Would she think that? In her situation, given the grave danger she knows she is in, surely wishing it would end could very well mean. . ." his voice trailed off into a whisper. "Could mean she gets killed. There is a break in the pattern here. She's not telling me to make them end it. It's unlikely her abductors would make her say something like that. The thought is hers and hers alone, spontaneous, but out of context because she doesn't appear to be either following instructions, or imploring me to set things straight." He was growing very excited, almost running back and forth across the room.

Together they had listened, analyzed and speculated on those words hundreds of times during the day, but now, alone, energised, new ideas and theories came flooding into his brain. "Okay, okay, Henry, calm down, let's think about this. Let's analyze this. I wish this was at the end. At the end. . . at the end. . . What's she trying to tell us? Do they have her at the end of something? At the end. . . the end of what? She wishes she were at the end. . . so she's not at the end. Okay, let's think about this some more. The first tape – she's trying to tell us something about the locks or the Trent canal or a boat or something, now she says she wishes she was at the end. . ."

4:56 PM – Day Three

He had to choke back a scream; a thunderbolt, a million watts of light exploded in his head.

Carol leapt from her bed and stood in the doorway speechless with astonishment, as he began punching the air with his fist.

"Yes! Yes! Yes!" he shouted. He turned, saw Carol standing there and threw his arms around her. "Carol, I've got her message. I've got Lee's message. I know where she is!"

"Where? Where?"

"I'm sorry," he said emphatically, "I know all the promises you've made, but we just can't take a chance with this. You'll just have to trust me. I know where she is, or at least very close to where she is, but I'm not even going to risk telling the police, certainly not yet."

Carol was incredulous. "If you know where they have her, why don't you let the police know right away so they can rescue her?"

Grant shook his head vigorously. "First of all, I don't know which police can be trusted. Secondly, I only know the area where they have her. Lee didn't pinpoint her exact location. I don't think she could. She may not even know it. If the police start charging around at this stage of the game, goodness only knows what will happen. Even if we do find police we can trust, this thing is so big, the press is sniffing around so hard, it would only be a matter of time until the information got out and they'd either move her. . . or something worse."

There was another factor he didn't mention. In all probability, Lee's abductors felt very secure right now with the search centred in Quebec. He wanted them to keep thinking that way as long as possible.

"Are you going to tell her?" asked Carol.

"Who?"

"Sandra," she said.

Grant stared blankly at her for a moment.

"I'm not sure," he said. But in fact, he knew he was.

Hull 5:02 PM – Day Three

It wasn't exactly the kind of day Paul Larocque had anticipated. Expecting payment of ten thousand dollars for a truckload of smuggled booze stashed in a nearby warehouse, he instead found himself under arrest and charged with taking part in the abduction of Lee Henry. He was denying it vehemently and, having experienced Quebec police interrogation before, he was not surprised to find himself escorted by two of the Sûreté's biggest and surliest to a small room in the basement of Hull's Laval Street Police Station. As they shoved him onto a small metal chair in the middle of the room, his handcuffed hands instinctively darted to his crotch and he ducked his head down into his shoulders in anticipation of the blows which his past experience told him would soon begin.

"You fucking queers leave my nuts alone this time," he snarled in English, protecting them as best he could.

One of the policemen leapt forward and launched a thick-soled boot which caught Larocque on the outer thigh, knocking him to the concrete floor with a cry of pain and a rattle of the metal chair.

"Scum bag," the red-faced cop yelled at the injured man writhing on the floor.

There was a sudden knock on the door and a loudly whispered warning from the guard outside, "Charron's on his way."

Quickly, Larocque was yanked from the floor, plopped back on the chair and warned not to say a word about what had happened or. . . one of them gestured with his hand in a slashing motion across his throat. The prisoner, eyes watering from the pain, understood completely.

Charron, observing Larocque's attempts at concealing his discomfort, had a very good idea of what had occurred but chose to ignore it. Reprimand this pair and the moment they had the prisoner alone they'd work him over even worse. If the superintendent had had a better understanding of psychology, he might have concluded that a large part of his antipathy towards this piece of human flotsam sitting in front of him stemmed from a strong distaste for what he had been instructed to do.

"I'd like a private word with our friend here," said Charron. "Don't worry, Mr. Larocque understands what will happen to him if he's anything other than a nice little boy." Turning to the two guards he said, "Wait outside till I call you."

As the door closed behind them, Charron extracted a small sheaf of papers from his coat pocket and shoved them in the startled prisoner's face.

"Know what I have here?"

Larocque mumbled incomprehensibly.

"Well, let me tell you. Here we have signed documents from two of your friends stating that they watched while you raped a woman named Angela Snowdon on the night of April thirteen this past spring. One of your friends has even been so kind as to provide us with a photograph of you in the act. Lovely, just lovely."

Larocque, who until then had feigned complete indifference, jerked back in his chair as though he'd been kicked again and jumped to his feet. Charron took a step backwards and held up a warning hand.

"Don't even think about coming closer," he ordered. "Sit down, or I call my two friends in and let them loose on you for a couple hours."

Larocque, his face the colour of the whitewashed walls, dropped back into the chair. "I told those two other fucking queers I want my lawyer," he whined, "and I'm telling you right now here again, I ain't saying another friggin' word till my lawyer is here."

Charron eyed him coldly for several moments before replying. "All the lawyers in the world aren't going to get you off this one. You didn't stop at rape, as you very well know. When she threatened to go to the police after you had finished, you whacked her over the head a few times with a piece of pipe, killing her almost instantly. We have sufficient evidence to convict you of rape, forcible confinement and murder. I'd say even with good behaviour, you're going to be one very old and doddering man by the time you get to smell pussy again, with an asshole big enough to motor that boat of yours in and out. So what say you and I have a nice little chat about that motorboat! You know the one I mean. The one you used to give Lee Henry a midnight ride down the Gatineau River? How much did they pay you for that job? Five thousand? Ten? What's the going rate for kidnapping little kids these days?"

Larocque sat in the chair, handcuffed hands still guarding his crotch, and glowered at the superintendent. "I told you I ain't saying nothin' till my lawyer is here," he muttered, with a definite lack of enthusiasm.

Charron began slapping the papers against his thigh and walked pensively around behind the seated prisoner, who ducked. "Tut, tut Mr. Larocque," chuckled the wiry little policeman, "you don't need to be afraid of me whacking you. I don't need to pound a confession from you. I've got more than enough evidence right here," he waved the handful of papers inches from Larocque's nose, "to put you away till the Ottawa Senators win the Stanley Cup. But, supposing, just supposing, we could do some kind of deal?" He left the question smouldering in the atmosphere for a moment. "Interested?"

Larocque's interest was definitely piqued.

"What kind of a deal?"

"Well," drawled Charron, dragging the words out for maximum effect, "let's just say, for argument's sake, that you tell me everything you know about the Henry kidnapping, and in return, we drop the rape, and, yes, even the murder charges. The woman was a prostitute after all, she did a little performance for you and your good buddies, got into a dispute over her fee, one thing led to another, a scuffle broke out and she, accidentally, hit her head on something. What? The kitchen sink? That's only manslaughter. At the most, geeze, five years? Hell maybe only three if you're a really good boy. Plus of course, whatever the judge decides to lay on you for your role in the abduction of Lee Henry."

At this point, Charron took three quick strides towards the door and made as though to open it.

Alarmed, Larocque shouted, "Hey, wait a minute! Where are you going?"

"Out of this room right now," snarled Charron, in the most intimidating voice he could muster, "to lay rape and murder charges against you, you slimy bastard, unless you start talking, and talking fast, right now."

"Manslaughter you say. You drop everything else?"

"Yeah, yeah, against my better judgement. Except, like I say, whatever you get for your role in the Henry kidnapping." "All right," sighed Larocque, "but I don't know very much." "Tell us what you do know," urged Charron, opening the door to wave the two constables inside. "Get your notebooks out boys, our little bird here has a tune he'd like to sing."

As it turned out, Larocque didn't know much. He'd received a phone call only the day before the kidnapping and was told there was two thousand dollars in it for him if he'd take his boat to a small wharf just below Poisson Blanc and leave it there between eleven pm and midnight, motor in good working order, along with a set of oars. He was to retrieve the craft no later than 3:30 the next morning from the Des Flandres Street dock just above the dam at Pointe Gatineau. One thousand dollars was under a brick sitting on the Poisson Blanc wharf when he made the delivery, another thousand was on the floor of the boat when he reclaimed it later. He knew nothing else. He had no idea who contacted him, how they had learned about him, or how they knew he had a boat.

It was very little information, certainly not enough to justify dropping rape and murder charges, but Charron had his orders. Boisvert had been very explicit.

"The point now," the inspector had claimed, "is to show the public we're not sitting on our hands; that we're making some progress." His instructions were to keep Larocque in hiding until just before six pm, then bring him to Sûreté Headquarters in Hull in time for the TV networks to do a live insert on the early evening news.

"You are to make no comment to the press there," instructed Boisvert. "All information concerning the arrest and the charges will come from me during our press conference here in Montreal. The Hull coverage will be strictly your men bringing the prisoner into the police station for booking. Don't worry, I'll make sure you and your men receive the proper credit."

"I'll bet," muttered Charron into the dead phone after Boisvert had hung up.

Ottawa 5:46 PM – Day Three

"Orillia! They have her in Orillia?" Sandra and Jake were incredulous.

"I'm not sure where in Orillia, but there's absolutely no doubt in my mind that's where she is," said Grant. "Think about it. Somehow, Lee finds out they've taken her to Orillia. The only thing she really knows about the place is that two years ago we ended our trip up the Trent Canal there. So how does she manage to convey that information to us? First, she's got to let us know that the Trent Canal is involved. So she dredges up one of the most memorable events of that trip, her throwing up into the Peterborough lock, and figures out a way to get that message to us. We rack our brains to figure out what the connection with the Canal is and then in her next tape, as sick as she is, or as drugged or whatever, she puts it all together. Remember what she said? 'I wish it was at the end.' She's trying to tell us that she's at the end of that Trent Canal trip, which, now that I think of it, was also the last time the three of us were together as a family. Carol and I got into a fight after we came back to the boat from the Opera House that night and the next morning she rented a car and drove home alone. By the time we got back to the cottage, she'd moved out. It was the last straw for us.

"Orillia was the end of the trip up the canal as well as the end of our marriage," said Grant sadly, "something Lee was only too well aware of. Why it took me so long to put all the clues together I don't know. Now when I think about it, it was obvious, staring me in the face all along. The bit about feeding the silkies may have been only to alert us to what she was doing, or it could be that someone with an English accent is involved. Being in Orillia they must be speaking English."

Sandra and Jake had been very dubious until Grant mentioned the end of his relationship with Carol. It seemed to trigger something in Sandra.

"Wait a minute," she said, "I didn't realize that was your last trip together as a family. Maybe you've got something here. Would Lee remember Orillia as the end of a trip up the Trent Canal? Possible. Yes, it's possible. But remembering it as the last time you were all together as a family. The end of the marriage. The end of her nice, safe, secure life. Now that's something Lee might very well remember Orillia for!"

She grew more animated.

"Of course!" she exclaimed, "she would expect you to recognize that wishing it were at the end was her clue, because you would know it had to be totally untrue. She had to assume that by now you would understand she was referring to the Trent Canal trip. Did she ever talk about Orillia or any part of that trip as a happy time?" Sandra looked at Grant expectantly.

He shook his head slowly, trying to recall.

"Nooo." He stopped and looked at her. "Come to think of it, other than us poking fun at her once in a while about being a danger to big boats, we never discussed the cruise up the Trent very much."

"Because," declared Sandra emphatically, "that vacation wasn't something Lee recalled with pleasure at all. For her, it represented something very sad. The end of something very important. Orillia – the end of the trip – was not a place she wished to be and she believed you would understand that." She flushed. "Grant, I think you're right. She could be in Orillia!" The rosy glow began to extend down her throat. Her eyes flashing, she threw her arms about him and for a fleeting moment they gazed triumphantly into each other's eyes.

They were in David Parson's CBBY office. Jake, who had spent much of the afternoon with Al Thompson attempting to decipher more messages from the tapes, had remained uncharacteristically quiet throughout the discussion, listening carefully and watching them both with interest.

Sandra and Grant self-consciously drew apart and turned to the tall, spare figure who was by then staring pensively out the window.

"Well!" said Sandra.

Jake gave them a brief quizzical look decided not to comment on what he'd just seen.

"Okay, let me play cop here," he said. "Orillia. Famous as the home of Gordon Lightfoot, Stephen Leacock and the original Mariposa Folk Festival, right? A nice little tourist town, what, an hour's drive north of Toronto? Why Orillia? Any special reason? Anything symbolic about the place? I remember a few years ago, Sault Ste. Marie I think it was, creating a big stink when it declared itself unilingual or something, and in Brockville, remember that? They wiped their feet on a Quebec flag, which almost caused riots in Montreal and Quebec City. Anything ever happen in Orillia which would make someone pick that place as an up-yours gesture or something?"

Both Grant and Sandra shook their heads.

"I've been there a few times," said Grant. "Pretty little town; booms in summer with tourists. The only connection I can think of is that old Samuel Champlain visited there. Spent a winter in the area with the Huron Indians. There's a huge statue of him in Couchiching Park along the waterfront, which the seagulls love, but what possible connection could there be between Lee's abduction and an early French explorer?"

Their speculations were interrupted by a frantic pounding on the door. It was Dave Parsons, slightly breathless.

"Turn the TV on" he said, "there's some kind of break in the case."

They were just in time to hear Charles Whitlaw say, "We now switch you live to the Hotel Quebec in downtown Montreal where Inspector Paul Boisvert, who heads the investigation into the abduction of Lee Henry, is about to make a statement."

You had to hand it to Boisvert. He certainly made it look good. Staring intently into the camera lens, surrounded by a small forest of microphones, you hardly noticed his strange appearance.

The inspector's words were galvanizing. Speaking first in French, then English, he announced that there had been a dramatic breakthrough in the investigation of the disappearance of Lee Henry, the result, according to him, of around the clock investigations by more than 100 of Quebec's finest police officers.

"Right at this moment," he gravely announced, "a man is being arrested and charged with complicity in the abduction. We have reason to believe this man supplied the boat used to convey the kidnap victim downstream along the Gatineau River, avoiding the police roadblocks which had been very quickly and efficiently put into place the instant notification of trouble was received. This man we are now arresting will be thoroughly questioned and we have every confidence this unfortunate situation will quickly be resolved."

Boisvert's face was suddenly replaced by that of Charles Whitlaw who apologized for the interruption and announced that they were now going live to Sûreté headquarters in Hull where correspondent Margaret Tremaine was standing by. The suspect's arrival was expected at any moment.

Charron had done his job well. The timing was perfect. Just as the camera picked up the blond, attractive face of Margaret Tremaine, a convoy of police cruisers, sirens blaring, lights flashing, pulled up to a dusty halt in front of police headquarters behind her. There was a slight delay (to allow CTV to cut away for a commercial break), then Larocque was led out of one of the vehicles, hands cuffed behind him, surrounded by a small battalion of police officers, several armed with automatic weapons.

Their instructions were to make a display of getting everyone out of Larocque's path, but not provide any impediment to TV cameras which might want close-up pictures of the desperado. In particular, they were not to obstruct any attempts to show hard-working Quebec police officers risking their lives in the courageous pursuit of justice.

They did their job well. It was a first rate demonstration of how a desperate criminal, a danger to national security, should be handled. Only the most observant would have noticed that the desperate criminal looked more confused than dangerous.

Margaret Tremaine made a few comments, mostly about the crowd which had quickly gathered, and the extensive security precautions, then switched back to the press conference in Montreal where Boisvert made a show of examining papers which had been placed in front of him, then preened into the camera again and announced, "I have just been advised that the suspect, Paul Larocque of Gatineau, has already confessed to being an accomplice in the abduction. I wish to thank and congratulate all my men for a job extremely well done under very dangerous conditions. I assure all residents of Quebec we will not rest until the safety and security of everyone is assured, even. . ." he hesitated for a moment, staring intently into the cameras. . . "even if occasionally it requires some extraordinary measures."

He answered questions, mostly in French, for a few moments, then announced that additional suspects were being brought in for questioning and he was urgently required elsewhere.

6:12 PM – Day Three

The receptionist put Grant's call through to Charron immediately.

Charron apologized for not contacting him earlier. "I really didn't have the time," he claimed, "and to tell the truth, I didn't know if we had anything real here. In that regard Mr. Henry, I must tell you, I don't think this Larocque character is going to help us very much in our search for your daughter. I'm sorry to say that it doesn't appear he knows very much, although of course, we haven't finished our interrogation."

As he hung up the phone, Grant shook his head and laughed grimly. "The bastards! As far as they're concerned, this thing isn't about finding Lee at all. It's about politics. This big show with Larocque, or whatever his name is, is just for the folks back home. A little smoke and mirrors to convince Quebeckers that things are under control; that Quebec is capable of handling the problem. Carol thinks I should go to that bunch of cretins with the information we have, but who the hell knows what they'd do with it? Christ, from what we've seen so far, there'd be a stampede to see who could alert the kidnappers first!"

"But Grant," interjected Sandra, "if you're right, if Lee really is in Orillia, we're not talking about Quebec. I know how you feel about this, I understand your mistrust of anything to do with the Quebec police, but surely we can trust the Ontario Provincial Police, or the RCMP, or how about the Orillia Police for heaven's sake? We've got to tell someone where she is. We can't get her out of there on our own. We think we've located her, now I just don't see how we can avoid going to the police."

"Lady's got a point," said Jake. "I've never seen any kind of hanky panky between the Ottawa and Hull Police. Hell, they don't even like each other. The mounties though? That's a fart of a different odour.

Who can be sure about those birds? There's certainly been politics at or near the top plenty of times with them. One thing I do know. If we were to tell the red-coats anything, you can be as sure as half the Blue Jay's infield speaks Spanish that most of the federal cabinet will be in on it within hours, and God knows how many friggin' separatists there are in that bunch of piggies at the trough. But damn it all, surely we can trust somebody in this bloody country!"

Grant was not dissuaded.

"My biggest concern," he said, "isn't the police. It's the press. All that has to happen is just a whisper of a rumour that the investigation has been switched from Quebec to Ontario, and it will be on the front page of every newspaper in the country.

"All it would take is for one reporter to see me talking to the OPP, or even one cop's wife mentioning to a neighbour that her husband was looking for Lee, or her husband knew of someone who knew someone who was checking the situation out in Orillia, or anything like that and zap, the whistle blows, and not only is Lee moved, but any chance of her getting another message to us is gone."

Sandra was still wavering.

"Let's think very hard about this. We know the kidnappers are armed. We don't know how many there are. They appear to be very professional. Sure, Jake is a cop, but I don't think he's had any kind of anti-terrorist training or anything like that. Have you Jake?"

He shook his head slowly.

"Not really," he confessed, "but there are basic rules in situations like this. We certainly wouldn't have much firepower, but very often that's not what's needed. And I'll tell you something else," Jake added, warming to the subject. "I've seen some very highly trained cops screw things up royally. Remember Waco? Damn, they had the best brains in the United States and enough firepower to blow the State of Texas into the Gulf of Mexico and what good did it do them? You know something? It could very well be that two or maybe three people with a good plan might have a better chance than the entire U.S. Marine Corps, John Wayne, Rambo and Ross Perot." His enthusiasm was building. "Maybe you're right, Grant," he said, "maybe there are fewer risks in doing it ourselves than in bringing in the OPP or even the Mounties."

"You say two or three people," said Grant, "surely you're not counting Sandra in on this. I. . . ."

Jake waved a disclaiming hand. "No way, no way. But I do know one guy I trust completely; got all his marksman badges, been involved in some pretty tricky cases, including a hostage taking a couple years ago. Straight up kind of a guy. Balls as big as bulldozers. I can get him to book off a few days sick leave. There's a couple other guys I'd trust with my life too; problem is, if too many of my friends start booking off sick, somebody might start to ask a few semi-intelligent questions. . . We'll need at least three, though."

"Your friend makes three," said Grant quietly.

Jake had been expecting this. He didn't even look up when he replied, "Oh no we don't. This is no bloody job for amateurs. You, my friend, are going to be a long way from Orillia when this goes down. About 250 miles away, as a matter of fact, right here in Ottawa. What we sure as hell don't need is some over-the-hill radio man hobbling around, screwing things up!"

Grant snorted and stood his ground.

"Let's get something straight right now," he said in a voice which brooked no opposition. "If we go in for Lee, then I'm right there. And don't give me this crap about being an amateur. When it comes to this kind of thing we're all amateurs. As for my ability with a gun; Jake, we both know from the practice range I'm as good a shot as you, although I'll tell you right now, I have no intention of carrying any kind of weapon, unless it's absolutely necessary. The only problem I may have is that most of the country can recognize me, so we'll have to come up with some kind of disguise. But just get it out of your mind right now that I'm going to stay here in Ottawa while you and your buddy are taking all the risks in Orillia."

Grant was nervously pacing now, as was his habit when agitated, from one side of the small office to the other. "Our first problem," he muttered more to himself than anyone else, "is getting me out of this radio station tonight without anyone knowing it." Remembering the phone call he had received that morning, he added, more loudly this time, "Somebody is obviously keeping very close watch, they seem to know every move I make, every step I take."

Jake continued to protest but Grant was adamant. If lives were being risked he was going to be part of it. Reluctantly Jake finally agreed, but his mind had already begun to devise a plan which would reduce Grant's participation to a role well away from the scene of any hostile action. While he had no qualms about Grant's courage, he was very apprehensive that parental concern might override caution and common sense at a crucial point. Where Grant might be of use would be in determining Lee's exact location in Orillia, if in fact she was really there!

While Grant and Jake were by now both convinced that notifying police posed too many risks, Sandra was still doubtful. "As Grant knows, I don't scare easily. Hurricanes don't scare me in the least; what I'm concerned about is Lee. There may be a risk in involving the police, but it's nowhere nearly as dangerous as you two trying to do it alone. Right now, for heaven's sake, you don't even know where she is in Orillia. How do you propose to pinpoint her exact location? Sooner or later you're going to have to get help from the police. You don't have any choice."

Grant refused to budge. "Yes, we may have to involve the police at some point but right now, at least until we're away from this damn nest of separatist weasels, I'm not prepared to risk it."

They debated the issue until Dave Parsons knocked on the door, distressed and looking for advice.

"I'm being flooded with requests from the press again," he told them. "They've been tipped off that there's something even more spectacular than ever on the air tonight, and that Grant is going to be here to broadcast live. They want to know what's up, and want to photograph Grant while he's broadcasting. We're only forty-five minutes to air time, what shall I tell them? The publicity would be great if we let them in," he couldn't resist adding.

Grant recognized instantly that one of his problems was solved. "Absolutely no press inside during the broadcast," he told Parsons. "Tell them it would be too traumatic for me, but promise that immediately after the broadcast I'll give them an interview and pictures. Is Al Thompson still here?" Assured he was, Grant asked that he be summoned to their office immediately.

Jake flashed him two arched eyebrows as soon as Parsons was gone. "You've got something up your sleeve!"

Grant, preoccupied, nodded absently. Al knocked softly and entered. Grant grabbed his sleeve.

"Al, I need your help again. No one, and I mean no one outside this room, is to know what we're doing, okay?"

"Sure."

"What about the tapes we're playing tonight?" asked Grant.

"All ready to go," Al assured him. "The French has been translated into English and scripted for you to read." Al gave him an inquiring glance. "You are going to read it aren't you?"

"Yeah, I'm going to read it all right," replied Grant, "but not live. When those tapes go to air, I'm long gone out of here. Al, set up your recording studio. Make sure no one is around to know what's going on. We'll pre-record the whole broadcast right now. When we're finished, we give the tape to Sandra. At one minute to eight, she hands it to the producer and tells him to roll it from the top. By that time Al, you and I are half a city away."

Grant paused for a moment to collect his thoughts.

"When we've finished recording," he continued slowly, thinking hard, "bring the station van around to the loading ramp, back it up to the dock and open both van doors so no one can see me when I jump into it from the building. Grab something from inside the station, throw it into the van behind me as soon as I get into it, so anyone watching will think it's just a normal procedure, then close the doors and drive away. I'll tell you where to go once we're inside. And Al?"

"Yeah?"

"Sorry to impose on you like this, but this is really important. Understand?"

Al reached out quickly and grasped Grant's shoulder firmly.

"Hey, we old vets gotta stick together." And he was gone.

Sandra moved quickly. Picking up the phone she spoke briefly with Parsons. "David, I want everyone out of this building immediately, that includes all staff except for you and Al Thompson. You know how to produce a radio show don't you? You know how to operate the equipment? Good, because you're going to be rolling all the tapes this evening. This is too important to leave to anyone else. You're going to put the Grant Henry show on the air." As an afterthought she added, "And when it's all over, you can talk with the press along with Grant." Parsons didn't hear her dry chuckle as she hung up.

"The press is gonna love him after this," smiled Jake. "Geeze, maybe you two aren't such amateurs after all. Hell of a smart move Grant, you'll be nothin' but a blue streak, miles from here, while the whole country, hopefully including who's ever got the spy-eyes out there, thinks you're jes a sittin' here in front of the microphone chattin' away. One minor problem. As soon as Sandra hands that tape to

Parsons and makes sure it gets on the air all right, we've got to clear our butts outta here too, 'cause once whoever is watching you realizes he's been suckered, he's going to follow us, thinking we'll lead him to you. . . and he's gonna be some pissed off! Listen," he said thoughtfully, "there's a little park overlooking the Hog's Back Falls out near Carleton University. Meet us there. . . let's see. . . we'd better wait till it's good and dark. . . meet you there at ten. Al can hide Grant someplace until then, although you've obviously got to dump the station van."

"Good idea," replied Grant, "we'll switch to Al's car at his house, get lost for awhile, then meet you at Hog's Back, ten o'clock. See ya."

"There may be three of us," said Jake, "I'm going to try and track down my troubleshootin' friend." He peered intently at Sandra. "When I say three, that's if Mrs. Beale is coming with us."

Her eyes sought Grant's.

"Yes," she said quietly, a little exasperated, "I'll be coming with you."

Ste Anne de Bellevue, P.Q. 7:35 PM – Day Three

At the age of thirteen, Georgette Courville discovered that by crossing her legs while seated, then squeezing them lightly together, she could bring herself to orgasm. It was a practice she carried out so frequently that her classmates and her teachers considered her a kind of dreamy kid. With nine other children to raise, her parents scarcely noticed. Her school marks were always decent enough, she was never a discipline problem, just given to drifting off into a world of her own from time to time. No one ever suspected just what kind of world it was.

Some two years later, Georgette discovered that while self-administered orgasms were pleasant enough, they were nothing compared to the delights possible with the assistance of an experienced male.

She caught the eye of a professor of English at nearby Macdonald College, and for the better part of a year was almost monogamous, the professor's libido being every bit as robust as hers. As Georgette would be only too happy to admit, it wasn't that she needed a lot of men – just lots of sex.

"I'm built just like you men," she told her professor not long after meeting him. "Well, not exactly," she laughed, "but you guys go out, see a good looking woman and bingo bango, you want to toss her into bed. You don't give a damn about a relationship or even a conversation sometimes, you just want to get screwed. Well, why should it be different for women? It's like that for me, and I'll bet if most women had the guts to admit it, they'd tell you the same thing."

The professor, less than a month previously had married a teacher from nearby Sir John Abbot College, and while he indicated he was more than willing to continue the relationship with Georgette, she would have no part of it.

"Hey," she told him. "I'm no slut, and I'm not a home-wrecker. Why the hell should I wait around until you can sneak out once in a while? There's lots of good sex out there without you, mister!"

But so far tonight she hadn't been able to find anything that really interested her.

"Lots of boys," she mused. But it wasn't a boy she was looking for. Not tonight anyway. She waved to a couple friends as she walked into the Larry Moquin Hotel, but sat down at a table by herself and ordered a draft. The bar, which ordinarily would have been packed with college students by that hour, was almost half empty. Georgette, while not a particularly political person, was aware that tensions between French and English in the town had heightened dramatically since the kidnapping of some English broadcaster's kid, and that was probably what was keeping so many of them in their homes these days. She was vaguely aware there was supposed to be another radio broadcast from the kidnappers at eight that evening, in about half an hour's time, but unlike most of her friends, she had no great desire to listen. She'd hear all about it tomorrow. Tonight she had other things on her mind.

"Can I buy you a drink?" Before she had a chance to reply, a well dressed, middle aged man pulled out a chair at her table and sat down across from her. "You do speak French?" he asked.

"Doesn't everyone?" she replied.

"And you do drink?"

She arched her eyebrows. "Almost anything, but when someone with an expensive suit and tie buys, only the best scotch!" She watched him as he settled into the chair and ordered, his face impassive, dark eyes flicking from table to table. She had difficulty identifying his accent. Definitely not anglais. She was tempted to ask but something about him told her not to. Despite his age, he was powerfully built, and as she watched his muscles move beneath the fabric of his expensive jacket, she began to feel a familiar tingling crawling up the insides of her thighs.

"No little boy here," she told herself. "This could be a very interesting evening." There was something hard, almost menacing about him which she found tremendously exciting.

"I don't know your name," she inquired.

He looked steadily into her eyes. "I don't know yours either; why don't we just keep it that way."

Georgette burst into laughter. "Oh my God," she giggled, "you've been reading Erica Jong."

He clearly didn't understand.

"You know," she laughed again, delighted, "the zipless fuck; you don't know the other person, not even their name, you just fuck each other's brains out." She cocked her head to one side and giggled teasingly. "You're not getting too old to fuck somebody's brains out I hope?" He looked at her, unblinking, until she felt a welcome prickle of excitement race up her spine.

"You have a car here?" she asked.

He nodded.

"Well," she said, "why don't we go find out just how old you really are."

All his training and instincts told him that what he was about to do was wrong; too risky. Under most circumstances, he would have remained with her in the bar, fed her drinks until after nightfall, driven to a secluded spot, done what he had to do, then fled west as quickly as possible. The fact people in the bar would have seen him with her didn't concern him in the least. Canadian police had no knowledge of his existence. There was no record of his entry into the country, and by the time the investigation had begun in earnest, he would be several thousand kilometres away. It was her challenge to his masculinity which persuaded him to risk breaking the rules

"Okay," he said aloud and nodded, "I don't know this town very well, where do you suggest we go?"

She reached for his arm, dropped her shoulders and tilted her face up into his, smiling promises.

"You drive, I navigate," she said teasingly.

Halfway to her apartment she flicked on the radio. It was her favourite rock station, but instead of music she heard a muffled voice sounding like Premier Menard. She pushed the seek button several times but every station seemed to be broadcasting the same thing. Impatiently she turned the radio off and began to hum softly to herself as they drove the short distance to her apartment.

* * *

In bed she was voracious and demanding, not at all like the women he was used to, and despite himself, he could not hold back.

"You bastard," she said, "I told you to wait for me," and only half in jest, beat a light tattoo on his chest with her fists. "You'd better be a lot better at this," she told him, placing both her hands on his shoulders and pushing firmly down. "Dinner time, baby."

The blow to her temple flipped her over onto her side, almost knocking her off the bed. Carefully he rolled her back into the centre of the bed, onto her back. She was moaning softly, one leg twitching spasmodically. Still naked, he mounted her belly, sliding himself up until her flattened breasts pressed against his naked groin.

He reached forward and placed his large, powerful hands around her neck.

"Whore," he grunted in Spanish, "you deserve to die."

Ottawa 7:45 PM – Day Three

At fifteen minutes to eight, Al Thompson emerged from the CBBY building, walked briskly to the station van, threw both rear doors open, and slowly backed the vehicle up against the open door of the workshop loading dock. Only a very keen eye would have noticed the vehicle's slight settling as Grant quietly crawled from the building into the back of the van, where he lay on the floor as Al drove a large riding mower in behind him. Trying not to hurry, Al pulled the van ahead a few feet, got out, walked around behind, slammed the rear doors of the van shut and pulled the workshop door down.

So far so good! Al was certain no one was paying the slightest attention to him. As he wheeled out of the parking lot, several of the waiting reporters milling about the front entrance turned to glance absently in his direction, but none showed even a flicker of interest. It wasn't until the van was well out of sight of the station that Al spoke.

"Where to?"

Grant clambered slowly to his knees.

"Will this thing fit into your garage?"

Al assured him it would.

Grant was quiet for a moment, deep in thought.

"Okay, let's head directly to your house, keep an eye out behind to make sure we're not being followed. We'll make the switch to your car and be well away from your house before the broadcast is over and whoever has been tailing me gets wise to what's up. If they were at the station when we drove away, and they probably were, it won't take them long to put two and two together and figure out how I slipped out of there without them spotting me."

Precisely at eight, Al turned the radio on and they listened in silence as Grant's recorded voice introduced the tapes. He was identifying the premier of Quebec as the person making the racist statements when they pulled into Al's garage and the door closed behind them. Al's car, a tiny white Geo Metro, was parked beside the van. Grant sucked in his breath as he spotted it.

"Geeze Al, you didn't tell me you had a little matchbox. It's going to be tough for me to hide in that thing. If anyone spots me now it could blow the whole thing."

"Wait a sec," said Al, as he dashed into the house. He returned a moment later with an Ottawa Lynx baseball cap. "Slap this on your head, pull it down over your eyes, slump down in the seat and pretend you're asleep. It'll be dark in an hour or so, and you won't have the problem. Where to now?"

Grant glanced at his watch. 8:16.

"We've got an hour and three quarters to kill," he said, thinking aloud, "let's just get as far away from here as we can."

He reached down and snapped on the radio. Lee's quiet voice began as they turned from Al Thompson's driveway onto the street.

Within fifteen minutes they were on Highway 7 headed west. Less than ten minutes later, on instructions from Grant, Al turned right onto a narrow gravel road. It was territory Grant was familiar with. In what now seemed like another lifetime, he and Carol had belonged to the Valley Hunt Riding Club several kilometres further along this road, donning red jackets every Saturday afternoon one summer to pound off on horseback behind a pack of baying hounds. Grant remembered that one of the riding trails led back from the side-road and meandered up onto a ridge which provided a marvellous view of the area. The Geo had little difficulty navigating the trail and in a few minutes they were parked on the crest of the rise, completely shielded from the road, but with a clear view through the trees all the way back to the highway. If anyone was following them they would soon find out.

It was ten minutes before a car turned off the highway onto the side-road, but it sped past at a high rate of speed, throwing up a cloud of dust into the gathering dusk.

"I think we did it!" said Al.

Grant nodded grimly.

The two men sat wordlessly in the car listening as the radio talked of the rapidly mounting crisis in Quebec City.

The CBC had suspended regular broadcasting to provide continuous coverage and analysis of the situation. All commentators, including several editorial writers from La Presse and Le Devoir, agreed it was highly improbable that Premier Menard could survive the double scandal of being caught making racist statements and then appearing to condone illegal police action. Grant listened with growing apprehension as the commentators also agreed that no matter what the circumstances, the Quebec government could not acquiesce to the terrorist demands that Mario Lefebvre be named interim premier.

"The strange thing is," commented Jean Marc Soucey of Radio Canada, "there is no question that under most circumstances, Lefebvre would be the most logical choice to replace Menard, but in light of these demands, that is no longer possible. It is almost as though," he mused, "Lefebvre isn't really the man they want at all."

He was interrupted by an announcement that the leaders of both Quebec opposition parties were calling for an emergency session of the National Assembly, but that Premier Menard, still closeted in an emergency meeting of his caucus, was unavailable for comment. In Ottawa, the prime minister had advised members of his cabinet to make themselves available for an emergency meeting at any time.

By 9:30, when the little Geo began its descent from the ridge and the half-hour drive back into Ottawa, John Inglehart, Chief of the Association of Aboriginal Peoples, was demanding an apology from Premier Menard along with his resignation, but much more ominously, there were reports that armed Mohawk warriors from Kahanawake had begun stopping traffic on their reservation, including a large convoy of military vehicles evacuating troops and equipment from Quebec. Some of the trucks were stranded in the middle of the Mercier Bridge which spanned the St. Lawrence River between the Island of Montreal and the south shore. Warriors had blocked both ends of the bridge. The troops and equipment were trapped in between.

As Grant and Al Thompson pulled into the small parking lot overlooking the Hog's Back Falls, a bulletin announced that the prime minister had recalled parliament to deal with the growing crisis. He had made the statement only moments ago, while entering a special emergency session of the cabinet. The military vehicles were still captive on the Mercier Bridge and more than 100 members of the Sûreté du Quebec were rushing to the scene.

Quebec City 9:41 PM – Day Three

The premier of Quebec was beside himself with rage, ameliorated not at all by the fact that the entire caucus was jammed into an overcrowded office, which until recently had been used as a storeroom. The caucus room and two larger offices sometimes used for cabinet meetings were still being swept for listening devices. It had taken security only a few minutes to find the bug in his office. Not much larger than an aspirin, it was cleverly concealed in the gesso frame of a large painting of former Premier Maurice Duplessis which hung behind the premier's desk.

"Can you believe it?" shouted Premier Jean Luc Menard to no one in particular. "Security tells me they never thought of sweeping my office for bugs. They swear up and down they checked the caucus room a couple months ago and found nothing, but I don't believe the bastards for a moment." He slammed his fist down hard on the desk. "Stupid sons of bitches! They probably wouldn't recognize a listening device if it was jammed up their collective assholes. . . surrounded by fucking incompetents. . . Johnson, where in the hell did you find that dimwit who's supposed to be in charge of security around here?"

Undeterred as always in his profanity by the presence of female members, one of them in her seventies, he turned to confront Gerard Johnson whose ministerial responsibilities included security at the National Assembly. Johnson was one of those people found frequently in politics who had somehow managed to fashion a successful career while totally devoid of a single noteworthy talent save a well-practised obsequiousness. Under normal conditions, Johnson would have successfully shuffled the blame off onto other shoulders and performed a dance of placation, but this night, aside from a brief, almost bored glance in the direction of the premier, he didn't bother to respond. Had Menard been more in control of his emotions, had he been anywhere near as perceptive as usual, he would have recognized immediately that his fate was already sealed. When Gerard Johnson did not consider it necessary to kiss someone's ass, it meant only one thing. That ass was of absolutely no importance to him. And if Johnson didn't think Jean Luc Menard's ass was important, it was a dead certainty no one else in the room thought so either.

He could rant and rave all he wanted; deny, blame, alibi, justify till he was blue in the face, but Jean Luc Menard was finished as premier of the province of Quebec. For most of those now glancing uneasily about them in the stuffy little room, there were only two questions concerning his fate which held any interest for them. Who was going to win the battle to replace Menard? And how best could they ingratiate themselves with that winner?

Suddenly, as though someone had flashed a cue card up to his face, Menard, perhaps finally sensing futility, ended his harangue and dropped defiantly into his chair.

The uneasy silence which descended over the grim assembly was interrupted by the scraping of a chair on the tile floor as Secretary of State Marc Charbonneau rose slowly to his feet, his hawk-like face grim. He addressed the premier formally.

"Mr. First Minister, I am certain we all appreciate the anguish you are experiencing. Working as closely as we all have with you, and understanding fully the tremendous pressures you have been under during this extremely difficult and significant period in our history, I am sure I express the sentiments of all of us here when I say we have no little sympathy for the situation you find yourself in. However. . ."

He paused and looked slowly around the table, as though collecting not only his own thoughts, but those of everyone whose eyes he sought.

"However, we must face some very obvious facts and we must do it with some urgency. First Minister, I think we can all agree, yourself included, as painful as I am sure that must be, that under the circumstances which now unfortunately confront us, you can no longer continue to lead this party, can no longer serve as the leader of Quebec; not, at least, until a full investigation can be carried out to determine the exact circumstances of the recorded comments we have all heard. . . and of course have been heard by most residents of this province. Sir, being the fighter you are, I am sure your first inclination is to try and stick things out, battle back, explain that these statements were taken out of context or that the recordings have been altered somehow, and if this is the path you choose, I am sure we will all do our best to support you. But First Minister, I beg of you to think well what such a course would do to Quebec, and to our cause at this very delicate period. There are decisions which must be made, vital decisions within the next few hours, which I am afraid, if taken with you still heading this party, would cause many people, enemies as well as some friends, grave concern."

He paused for a moment and once again looked about him at the sober unturned faces. Seeing nothing there to deter him, he plunged on. "There is also another issue which must be addressed at this time. If you choose to remain as the leader of this province and anything were to happen to the Henry girl, the blow to this party and to the cause of Quebec independence could very well destroy us and our dream forever."

Throughout the entire dissertation, Menard's eyes had never left Charbonneau. He suddenly jerked forward in his chair.

"You fucking back-stabbing son of a bitch," he screamed. "I wouldn't be at all surprised if you aren't the slimy bastard who's behind all this. You'd love this job wouldn't you? Do anything for it, wouldn't you?"

There was a loud roar of protest from several of the ministers.

"Fuck you all, you bastards, there's not a one of you with the brains to see what's happening here with this son of a bitch." Menard was on his feet, face red, breathing increasingly laboured. "You've got your fucking resignation," he shouted, pitching his chair into the table. Several of those near him threw their arms up in front of their faces as though to ward off blows. The premier, the colour drained from his face, reached for the door. Yanking it open, he turned back to the shocked and silent table. "Rot in hell every one of you bastards." And then he was gone, the door crashing shut behind him.

The silence in the room continued until Menard's angry footsteps could no longer be heard pounding down the corridor. "Guess this means he's not paying for the coffee," muttered Johnson.

Someone giggled nervously, then stopped abruptly.

It was, they all realized, a momentous occasion in the history of the province. Never before had a premier resigned in such a fashion. Would they be dragged down into this horrible maelstrom? All were uncomfortably aware of the minefields in their path. Decisions reached around this table in the next few hours could blow their careers apart. Some understood that the very fabric of Quebec society was in grave danger and the dream of independence was teetering precariously on the edge of a precipice.

Finally, it was the venerable Mario Lefebvre who rose to speak, removing his glasses and rubbing the bridge of his nose as he assembled his thoughts. As was his style, he began slowly, some would say ponderously.

"I have no wish to comment on what has occurred here this evening," he said. "Let us leave that for the historians. . . and of course the press."

Someone snorted derisively and a low buzz arose from the table. Lefebvre erected an admonishing hand and waited for silence before continuing gravely.

"We have many decisions. . . vital decisions. . . crucial decisions to make here this evening. . . for our party. . . for our government and for our country." At this he glanced up, and catching several nods from those who understood that by the use of the word country he meant Quebec, he continued. "One of those decisions is choosing the person who, for the time being at least, will head this party." He paused for several heartbeats. "The kidnappers of the Henry child have insisted that I be that person, and as I am the Deputy Leader that would be the normal thing to do." Another murmur began to bubble up around the table, louder this time. Lefebvre continued without pause. "I suspect there are those who would support such an appointment." He looked up momentarily. The air was filled with expectant silence. "I am not one of those!"

Pandemonium! Cries of "Mario! Mario!"

Jean Claude Belanger, one of his oldest friends and staunchest supporters, leapt to his feet and shouted:

"If it's not you Mario, then it is no one."

Lefebvre stood motionless, his splotched and corded hands trembling slightly. When the uproar had subsided somewhat, he pressed on.

"It is surely no secret to any of you that it has long been my fondest dream to one day be leader of a sovereign Quebec. This party has been my life for more than twenty years. While this may sound vain to some of you, and perhaps it is, I also believe that I am well qualified for the job, I. . .”

"Better than any other, Mario," shouted Belanger.

"Ah dear friend, there are others quite capable of shouldering this responsibility, but. . ." Lefebvre's face became solemn and stern, his voice, which had begun to quaver, steadied.

"I will never be a member of any government which allows its leadership to be dictated by terrorists. The consequences of my refusal may endanger this young girl's life. I pray not, but, no matter what fate awaits us all, I can imagine nothing worse than an entire nation of proud people allowing itself to be tyrannized. When these. . . these thugs..these gutter criminals who believe they can subvert the will of a nation are apprehended, as surely they will be, I will fight with every fibre of my being to lead this great party. . . but. . . not under these circumstances. When Mario Lefebvre becomes leader of this party and leader of the sovereign Republic of Quebec, it will be because that is the will of the people. It will be through the democratic process. Until those wicked people who attempt to defile our way of life are brought to ground I will not accept a nomination for leadership of this party, nor will I take part in the selection of such a leader."

He reached down quickly to grasp his papers, jammed them into his briefcase and turned to leave. Almost as one, everyone present rose to their feet and applauded as Mario Lefebvre strode erect and proud from the room. Tears overflowed many eyes. But not all.

Ste Anne de Bellevue 9:56 PM – Day Three

"Holy Mother of God, there's something stuck in her vagina. . . looks like a rolled up piece of paper or something, it's not a tampon that's for sure. . . Jesus, Mary and Joseph, what kind of a freak. . ."

The police chief of the village of Ste Anne de Bellevue was shaken. In his fourteen years on the force, he had never investigated a murder, and there was no question that's what he had on his hands here. The naked body of a young woman had been spotted shortly before ten pm by two Macdonald College students returning to residence from the Larry Moquin Hotel. At first they thought she was drunk or that someone was playing a trick on them, but when they reached down to touch her, it was immediately obvious she was dead.

They were still being interrogated in a police cruiser parked nearby. The chief had no doubt they were telling the truth.

"Give me a rubber glove," he instructed the coroner, who had just concluded his examination of the body.

Wordlessly, the doctor reached into his bag and extracted one. "Are you sure you should do it here, now?" he asked.

The chief nodded. "Too risky to leave it there while the body is being transported. It could be a key piece of evidence, and I can't take the chance of it being lost."

Gingerly, trying to avert his eyes as best he could, he grasped the protrusion with his latex-encased fingers and pulled.

He carefully unrolled the scroll of paper, reading it in the bright headlights of the cruiser.

"Oh sweet Mary," he moaned. "Someone call Inspector Boisvert right away!"

Ottawa 10:00 PM – Day Three

A map or any official description calls it the Prince of Wales Falls. Everyone in the National Capital area knows it as the Hog's Back Falls. As rapids go they aren't much, a plunge of about fifteen metres between steep granite cliffs. During the spring run-off, the roar from the falls can be heard on the Carleton University Campus, a good half kilometre away, but by this time in October, the flow usually wasn't much more than a trickle between the rocks, the sound barely discernible a hundred feet away in the small park fringing the eastern cliffs which overlook the gorge.

Grant was surprised to see only two cars in the dimly lit parking lot as he and Al pulled in. He remembered Carol telling him that when she was growing up this was one of the favourite necking places for teenagers; the parking lot nearly filled every night with cars and pick-up trucks, windows heavily misted by the emissions of rampaging teenage hormones.

"Looks like the sexual revolution has pretty well emptied the groping spots of the nation into its motel rooms," said Grant, making a stab at levity as they stopped near the centre of the parking lot. Al had become extremely anxious and subdued as they drove back into Ottawa, listening to the gathering crisis on the car radio. During the last few kilometres he had hunched his shoulders over the steering wheel, his face taut with worry.

For all his concern, he couldn't help but nod and smile wryly at Grant's observation. "You got that right," he said. "When I was a teenager we used to call this place Blue Balls Falls. Young guys today don't know what the hell I'm talking about. You know it. . ."

The car at the far end of the parking lot flashed its brake lights twice. Grant inclined his head slightly.

"Must be them."

Al had seen it too.

"Geeze I hope so." Nervous again. "What if it's not Jake but. . ?"

"It's them all right," Grant assured him. "Pull up behind the car, but don't get out until we make absolutely sure. Don't turn the motor off."

Slowly, Al drove to within several feet of the car, a black Chrysler Imperial, and stopped, engine idling.

Grant didn't realize he was holding his breath until it rushed from his lungs when Jake emerged from the driver's side of the Imperial.

"Sorry about the James Bond stuff," Jake half whispered, affecting a grim kind of smile, drawling a bit, trying to make light of it all, "but we had to be sure it was you. No one told us old Al here would be driving a shitbox. By the way don't worry about our friends over there." He pointed his chin at a Ford Tempo nosed under a tree on the far side of the park. "Just a couple a kids panting it up, doin' a bit of exploring. We've been here better than fifteen minutes. Nothin' unusual. Looks like we both gave the bird dog the slip." He was talking in a rush.

Al's not the only one nervous tonight, Grant thought, surprised, since his own apprehension had been replaced by a vague serenity, born, he presumed, out of relief that at last the terrible inaction was ending.

Jake went on jangling.

"Shouldn't be hangin' about these parts too long," he said. "Jump aboard our old limo here Grant. . . and Al?" Jake reached out to grasp him firmly by the shoulder. "If anyone should ever ask, you don't know nothin' from nothin'. . . even if they put those shrivelled up old knackers of yours in a meat grinder."

Al grinned broadly. "Christ, Jake, at my age who needs em anyway?"

Grant, aware of the terrible burden he was imposing on this wonderful old man, found himself very moved. For all he knew, for all any of them knew, Al might very well be in some sort of danger. He turned to look directly into Al's worried eyes, and grasped his friend's hand firmly, fighting back tears of gratitude.

"How can I thank you?" he began. "You've been a great friend. I'll never forget what you've done for us. . . I . ."

Al threw both hands high into the air and shook his head vigorously. "You don't have to thank me. Look, this stuff has got to stop, Grant. This isn't the goddamn country me and my buddies fought for. I'm doing whatever I can, not just for you and Lee, but for me too. This is still my country, and damn it all to hell, I love this place and I hate what's happening. I'm not denying it, I'm a little scared, but don't you worry for one moment, I'm not so old I can't handle myself, and I'll tell you something else. I'm not finished with those tapes either. I'm going to keep listening to them until I come up with some kind of answer to that crazy buzzing sound. Whatever is causing it can't be too common, which means if we can figure out what it is, it just might help us find what we're looking for."

He found it difficult to mention Lee's name, unsure of Grant's reaction.

"I've got a couple more ideas I'd like to test out," he said. "If I turn anything up where do I contact you?"

Grant pursed his lips. "Not sure right now. Listen, we'll call you when we get this thing organized and check if you've come up with something new." Grant stopped as Jake signalled a vehement no. Then it dawned on him.

"No, we can't take that chance," he said, "the bastards probably already have a tap on your phone Al, and everyone else's they think we might try and contact."

He was interrupted by Sandra who had quietly slipped out of the Chrysler to hand Al a folded slip of paper.

"Here's a number they won't have a tap on. It's my telephone answering machine in the Bahamas. If you come up with anything you think might be important, go to a phone booth, call this number and leave a message. If you want to talk to us directly, here's what you do: Leave the number of the pay phone on my answering machine. As soon as I get your message, I'll call your home number and let the phone ring three times, then I'll hang up. Don't answer your phone; go directly to the pay phone. I'll call that phone in exactly, what, twenty minutes after ringing your home? Will that be enough time?"

"Sure," Al nodded. "There are plenty of pay phones around my house. I'll pick one not likely to be used much. If someone is using it twenty minutes after you call my home phone, I'll just wait till they're finished and you keep calling, okay? "

Sandra laughed softly and said, "Thank goodness for television, how else would we know how to do all this spy stuff? By the way Al, just make sure you've got enough change for the long distance charges."

They all stood silently, each lost in their own thoughts, watching wistfully as the tail lights of Al Thompson's little car bounced over the bridge and disappeared into the night. Jake finally broke the silence.

"Grant, meet someone who's going to help us. Charlie Dunn, Grant Henry. Grant, Charlie Dunn. And now let's get the hell out of here."

Orillia, Ontario 10:20 PM – Day Three

More than anything, it was the cold which frightened her. The terrible penetrating cold and dampness. Her thin blanket provided almost no protection from the frigid air flooding constantly into her tiny basement cubicle. She had spent most of the day huddled on the narrow mattress, coughing violently, chilled to the bone, teeth chattering, barely able to eat or stand up. What frightened her most now was the fact that during the past hour or so, the chills which convulsed her body periodically were now being interrupted by moments of warmth.

Groggy and increasingly disoriented, she at first believed her captors had turned off the cold air, or provided her with warmer cover, but in her more lucid moments she realized that the interludes of heat had nothing to do with kindness or concern. Lee had a fever, and it was growing worse. She understood the implications only too well, having experienced a frightening ambulance ride to the Ottawa Civic Hospital the year before when her temperature inexplicably climbed dangerously high.

It had been diagnosed then as a strange virus, probably picked up on a holiday trip to the tropics, but now, as she lay trembling on the sodden mattress, her mother's face began to float in and out of the mists swirling about her head. The lips didn't move, but from a great distance, a voice, unmistakably her mother's, kept repeating familiar words, which as a little girl used to make her and her friends giggle, but now drove an arrow of terror deep into her breast.

"Dress warmly now dear or you'll catch your death of pneumonia," repeated her mother's voice. "Your death of pneumonia, your death of pneumonia," reverberating off the encroaching walls, tumbling, twisting, spinning around and around her head like a giant whistling top.

The tiny chamber which served as her prison was cold and damp to begin with, constructed of flimsy plywood, years ago, directly on the basement's unfinished dirt floor.

Originally intended to accommodate students hired to help during the summer haying and harvest, it had more recently served as a storage room for the flotsam and jetsam households accumulate with the passage of time. Several dusty cardboard boxes, heavy with damp books, along with a large plastic Christmas tree, had been unceremoniously evicted to make room on the floor for Lee's mattress.

Uncomfortable as it was, the room would have been at least bearable were it not for the relentless air conditioning. One of the men upstairs, the same one she had overheard the first night in the car mention they were in Orillia, had some kind of skin disorder which he kept insisting only cold air would alleviate. From time to time she heard the other men complain about the cold, but the large air conditioning unit which stood just outside her room was very seldom idle.

Why her clothes had been taken from her, why she was provided only one tattered blanket she did not know. The morning after her arrival, not fully aware of the danger she was in, she had defiantly demanded a return of her clothes which had been removed sometime during the night as she lay in a drugged stupor on the back seat of the car.

She would make no such demands again.

The man with the accent she assumed was British shot a hand out, gripped the blanket at her shoulder and roughly ripped it from her body. In fear and humiliation she had dropped to the floor in a tight curl, attempting desperately to cover her nakedness, expecting – she dared not think what.

Standing over her, he straddled her body, one foot on either side of her chest, and jabbed viciously at her side with his pointed shoe until she was forced to roll onto her back, exposed and vulnerable. Slowly he squatted over her until the bulk of his weight rested on her stomach. Scarcely able to breathe from the pressure on her diaphragm, heart threatening to burst, she was certain she was about to die.

He bent his head forward until his face was within inches of hers, his eyes screaming a rage which wanted to rip and tear at her. Spittle sprayed her face.

"Get used to it. . . like I did," he snarled.

He clambered to his feet, livid with menace.

"Bring down the tape recorder," he shouted up the stairs, "the little princess here is ready to talk to her daddy."

DAY FOUR

Montreal 1:17 AM

The most dangerous of the crises the new premier of Quebec had to deal with was the Mercier Bridge standoff between Canadian troops being evacuated from Quebec and the Mohawk warriors. It was also the crisis with the most potential for political gain. The bridge remained blockaded at both ends by the warriors who had erected makeshift barriers of large trucks. Trapped in the middle of the kilometre-long span was a column of more than forty army vehicles, mostly troop carriers, carrying close to 200 soldiers, men and women. All civilian vehicles caught in the trap had been allowed to break out of line and escape the bridge shortly after the barricades went up.

Thus far, the situation remained tense but calm. The troops were under orders to remain where they were, all night if necessary, and make no move which could in any way be construed as hostile. Many of them had left their vehicles and were stretched out on the roadway and sidewalks, heads propped on kit bags and knapsacks. Despite the abductors instructions that all small arms were to be left in Quebec, many of the soldiers still had rifles and were keeping them close at hand.

The Indians guarding the bridge had lit a number of large fires at either end. Several hundred yards away, police had cordoned off the areas with wooden barricades and ropes, establishing wide buffer zones between the Indian encampments and the throngs of the curious, the thugs, louts, and the idly stupid, who were oozing into the area by the hundreds from the back alleys, the strip joints, the tattered street

135

corners and bars of Montreal, drawn like vultures to carrion. They stood, bloated beer bellies pressed to the police barricades, hurling curses, stink and despair into the night.

Earlier in the day, National Home Security Inc. had purchased every minute of advertising time still available that evening on three Canadian networks. It was the deal of a lifetime. Tomorrow, the overnight ratings would indicate that almost three quarters of all Canadians over the age of eighteen watched the unfolding drama well into the night – more than fifteen million viewers. Within a week, National's sales would increase more than 35%, its market share would be up an incredible 10%, and the bright young marketing assistant who had persuaded National to make the investment accepted a job a month later with a major competitor at more than double his previous salary. The Nielsen overnight ratings showed that only a rerun of the final episode of *Seinfeld* and the *Million Dollar Wheel of Fortune Play-Off* had attracted more viewers in the United States.

Quebec's new premier was by no means oblivious to the potential. Well aware that others, in particular Mario Lefebvre, were much more popular and trusted figures in the province than he, and that a leadership convention would have to be held soon, Marc Charbonneau acted swiftly. Shortly after one am, not much more than an hour after being selected to replace Jean Luc Menard, Charbonneau, accompanied by the TV cameras of the nation, strode confidently through the police barricades, disdainful of the hoots and jeers of the restless mob, across the bridge approach to an Indian campfire.

It was a noble sight: this tall, spare man, alone against the night-mob, a hawk marching resolutely into hostile Indian territory. What the TV viewers didn't see was the horde of reporters and cameramen jostling and scurrying in his wake, like so many Hamelin children.

Four warriors, the lower parts of their faces covered with bandannas, armed with semi-automatic rifles, stepped from the dark into the stark glare of the arc lights. Several cameramen darted forward for better angles. Anxious commentators providing live coverage found their hearts pounding, their breath quickening, as the four, dark and menacing, approached the premier. Charbonneau's face revealed no discomfiture.

"I would like to discuss a peaceful settlement to this impasse." He addressed them formally in English, then French, loudly enough for the microphones to pick him up clearly. "With whom should I speak?"

The four conferred briefly with each other in Mohawk.

"Come with us," and they motioned the premier to a large van parked on the outer fringes of the barricade. One of the camera crews made as though to follow, but was blocked by three of the warriors who wheeled about, rifles at arms length, horizontal at chest level.

Inside, it was obvious the van had been rigged as a kind of headquarters. A large television set teetered precariously on the tiny sink, empty beer and liquor bottles were scattered about, several cellular phones were in evidence. The lone warrior who had accompanied Charbonneau inside, his face still partially obscured by a bright red bandanna, brushed a partially emptied chip bag from one of the upholstered seats, and motioned him to sit.

The premier glanced briefly about, then in a very determined fashion shook his head.

"No way, not here. You're going to have to do better than this my friend."

The warrior, silent until now, laughed loudly, the sound muffled strangely behind the cloth. "Afraid of bugs in the night are you Mr. Premier?" He spoke in English. "Okay, you pick the spot then." He turned abruptly and dismounted the vehicle, barking orders in Mohawk to the three warriors still holding the pack of camera crews and reporters at bay.

Charbonneau selected the cab of an ancient logging truck which formed part of the barricade. The passenger side window had obviously long since either been broken or refused to be cranked into position. A large sheet of graffiti-covered plywood plugged the hole, effectively blocking the interior of the cab from prying camera eyes. Red Bandanna nodded agreement, and with his three compatriots continuing to mount guard, they climbed aboard.

Charbonneau twisted himself about to face André Johnathon, better known to most as Crowbar, in recognition of feats accomplished two years ago during a blockade on the Kahanawake Reserve. Johnathon, with the assistance of a four-foot-long crowbar, had pretty well demolished a line-up of more than thirty cars caught in a hastily erected blockade on the provincial highway which slices through the heart of the reservation. A rookie Sûreté cop had made the mistake of stopping a car for speeding on Indian land, despite warnings from the band council that they would police their own territory.

Johnathon had served several months behind bars for his escapade, but his position as one of the most influential of the leaders of the Warrior Society was firmly entrenched.

Charbonneau used his proper name to address him. "André, I hope you will not be offended if I ask you to open your shirt and turn out all your pockets for me."

The laughter was raucous this time. "Now Mr. Premier, you're afraid of bugs on Indians!" He ripped open his shirt, exposing a broad expanse of chest, then with a great flourish began turning his pockets inside out, scattering coins, keys, a wallet and several bullets onto the ragged seat and floorboards.

"Maybe you think I've got something hidden behind this," he said, pulling down the bandanna. "See Mr. Premier, nothing here but store bought teeth." He grinned broadly to display a perfect set of uppers, obviously the product of a chemical rather than genetic formula. "Guy knocked 'em out with a crowbar," he said, shaking the old truck with an explosion of laughter. In reality he lost them playing lacrosse. The laughter suddenly stopped, his face slipping into narrow-eyed menace.

"We got a few guys handy with crowbars, and plenty other things when people don't come through on promises." He sat stock still, staring intently at the premier.

Charbonneau closed his eyes and jerked his head quickly left, then right. "André, André, no need for threats. The Quebec government will approve your application for a casino on the reserve just as soon as this thing is all over with. That was the deal I made with you. Now, how about your end of it? Barricades down, big toothy smiles for the cameras, the statement we agreed upon to the media and then let's all go home and get some sleep. On second thought, we'd better sit here for a while, let the good folks back home think their new premier had a real tough time persuading you savages to let my people go. Got a peace pipe or anything like that we can smoke? How 'bout maybe just a smuggled cigarette?"

This time both of them laughed uproariously.

Ste Anne de Bellevue 1:46 AM – Day Four

Ordinarily, dealing with the grieving friends and relatives of the victims of violent death was not something which gave Inspector Paul Boisvert a great deal of difficulty. He had, after all, acquired considerable experience at it. Besides which, it was his observation that more often than not, the victims had only got what they deserved anyway. Tonight, though, was different and he wasn't quite sure why.

It had taken Ste Anne de Bellevue police less than an hour to make a positive identification of the body found propped against the stone entrance of Macdonald College. Georgette Courville was well known in the town. Finding people to identify her wasn't difficult. She was well liked too, as far as the inspector could determine, a fact which, he suspected, may have played a role in her selection as the target for murder.

Perhaps it was the note, more specifically the manner in which it had been attached to the body, which was giving him so much discomfort. The girl's parents and brother, summoned in the middle of the night from their home in Huntington, about an hour's drive away, sat in white-faced disbelief as Boisvert struggled painfully to describe the circumstances of her death.

His original inclination was to avoid mention of the scrawled message, but whatever else he was, Inspector Boisvert was too good a cop not to quickly realize that it could not be avoided, besides which, they would soon learn all the details from the media. Opening a drawer in his desk, the inspector extracted the note now completely enclosed in clear plastic.

"We found this on your daughter," he said, tactfully avoiding any reference to the method of attachment. "Would you please examine it very carefully and tell me if you recognize the handwriting, or if any of the words mean anything to any of you."

The room became still as the three carefully examined the note then slowly shook their heads. The inspector, who had been observing their reactions intently, was satisfied.

"I really am sorry to have to do this," he apologized. "I hope you understand we have to follow up every possibility. Can you think of anyone, anyone at all, who would have any reason to dislike your daughter? Does. . . did she have a jealous boyfriend? Had she ever been in a relationship with a violent man? Can you think of any reason, other than that stated in the note you have just examined, for Georgette's death?"

Her mother, small and worn, began to weep quietly, mashing her fists into her eyes. "Everyone loved Georgette, she sobbed, "she had no enemies."

There was something about the woman, a faint whisper perhaps of his own mother, half a life-time ago, which made him exceedingly sad.

"Yes," he sighed, "you are probably right. There is an excellent chance your daughter was killed precisely because she was so well-known and so well-liked."

The woman, hunched over on her chair, hands still twisting in her face, began to sob more loudly, her shoulders shaking with the effort and the pain. Her husband and teenaged son made no attempt to comfort her, ignoring her anguish while continuing to stare unblinkingly at the inspector.

"As you can see, the note says your daughter's life was taken in retribution for the kidnapping and torture of Lee Henry and supposed injustices perpetrated on the English speaking population of Quebec. It does not say why Georgette was chosen specifically, but it would seem to make perfect sense to choose someone whose death would cause maximum consternation, and your daughter, well known and well-liked was a prime target."

The boy, who appeared to be about sixteen, tall, whipcord thin and already displaying the fine features and jet-black hair which, as a man, would render him exceedingly handsome, shook his head violently and protested, "Georgette had no politics. Her friends were both anglophone and francophone. For her there was no difference. I. . ."

"Yes," interjected the inspector, "you are right. For her there was no difference but. . ." here he paused briefly in an unsuccessful attempt to conceal the anger and bitterness in his voice, "for those who killed her. . . she had one fatal flaw. . . she was French!" The last three words reverberated loudly off the walls of the small office.

Alphonse Courville, thirty-one years the manager of the George H. Cavan and Sons dairy farm, one of Quebec's largest, began to rock back and forth on his chair, moaning softly.

"Those bastards, those English bastards."

His son eyed him coldly.

"Yes, and you helped make those English bastards rich, and you did it speaking their goddamn language the whole time!"

It was said with such force, such loathing, that even the inspector was stunned. He was about to respond when an aide entered the room.

"There's a telephone call for you, Inspector Boisvert. Someone says he knows who killed Georgette Courville."

The inspector looked up tiredly.

"Aah not already. Before this is over, we'll have them crawling out of the woodwork claiming they know who did it. We'll probably have a dozen or two claiming they're the ones responsible. I'm sorry but. . ."

The aide held up a hand.

"Inspector, I'm aware of all that, but this man says he knows you. Says he's taken a ride with you. In a calèche. On Mount Royal."

Without excusing himself, the inspector bolted from the room.

Lindsay, Ontario 2:06 AM – Day Four

It was Jake's idea to avoid the obvious, and take the slower drive along Highway 7 to Orillia rather than the faster four-lane route. "These guys aren't exactly fifteen minutes short of a full morning you know," he said. "If they have any idea we're on to them, or, maybe just as a general precaution, they could have someone watching along the 401 or 400 highways. I know, I know, the chances of that are about as good as me winning a lottery, but let's play it safe and take the back roads instead."

There were no objections, so with Jake behind the wheel they drove west along the tortuous two-lane route, through the rusty red and grey granite outcroppings of the Canadian shield until, just outside Lindsay, listening to breathless radio analysis of Marc Charbonneau's triumphant march through Indian territory, they pulled into a Comfort Inn and booked two adjoining rooms. Orillia was less than an hour's drive away.

For most of the trip, the four sat silently listening to radio reports of the incredible events unfolding: the resignation of Jean Luc Menard, the refusal by Deputy Premier Mario Lefebvre to assume the post, the selection by the caucus of Marc Charbonneau as interim premier and his seemingly miraculous mediation of the Mercier Bridge crisis.

An announcement from the prime minister's office in Ottawa stated tersely that the emergency meeting of the federal cabinet had been suspended in light of the peaceful resolution at the Mercier Bridge, but that parliament was already assembling to deal with the situation and in particular, the demands of the kidnappers.

Incidents of scattered violence were reported across the country. There were several injuries following a brawl between Indians from the Six Nations Reserve and a group of locals in a Brantford, Ont. tavern; police had to be summoned when fights broke out among the spectators at an interprovincial hockey tournament in Brandon,

Manitoba. Officials admitted that under the circumstances they should never have allowed the two Quebec midget teams onto the ice. In Montreal, roving bands of punks returning from the Mercier Bridge barricades broke a few windows. But everywhere else it was a far different story. Streets were almost vacant. Clubs and restaurants reported only a fraction of their usual business. Airlines were flooded with cancellations. Commerce and most normal social intercourse was grinding to a halt. Many churches were holding special services, but for the most part, frightened and worried Canadians remained at home, bolted their doors and hoped for the best. Some prayed.

By the time Grant and his companions had settled into their rooms, television coverage was confined to wrap-ups of the day's events, and in the case of the CBC, a detailed analysis of the situation by a panel of journalists and university professors.

Sandra reached for Grant's hand as the panel began to discuss what reaction might be expected from the kidnappers in light of the refusal by Mario Lefebvre to assume the premiership of Quebec.

The panellists agreed that any predictions of that sort were impossible. The real question, according to Charles Whitlaw, was what reaction parliament would have to the decisions already made by the government in its attempts to comply with the terrorists' demands.

"It's obvious," said Whitlaw, "that lowering flags and removing troops from Quebec was a mistake which has led the country to the brink of separation. . . perhaps even civil war."

There was sharp disagreement with this last statement from the other panellists, but all conceded national unity had been dealt a desperate blow, and it was highly unlikely parliament would consent to any more demands from the terrorists, no matter what the consequences. There was some speculation that the first action parliament would take would be to send the troops back into Quebec. This was followed by several minutes of heated debate over the wisdom of such a move.

The discussion then moved to safer ground – Charbonneau's performance at the barricades, which all agreed had been nothing short of spectacular, almost guaranteed to solidify him in his new position.

Whitlaw pointed out that despite the fact Charbonneau's late father had been a much-loved political figure in Quebec, one of the architects of the quiet revolution, his son had never elicited anything more than grudging respect.

Whitlaw turned to the panel. "The widely held belief is that Charbonneau has spent most of his life trying to live up to his father's reputation, but is far too cold a fish for most Quebeckers. Is that accurate?"

"Very much so," nodded Marie Chaput, political correspondent for Montreal's *La Presse*. "If Premier Charbonneau had not been so successful at the Mercier Bridge, there is no way Quebec would ever have accepted him as premier. They loved his father, but have, at least until now, distrusted his son. I suspect Premier Charbonneau has achieved his lifetime ambition in just one night. There is no question," she continued, "that had Premier Charbonneau not defused the situation at the Mercier Bridge, the province, perhaps even the country, could have been plunged into the worst violence it had seen since the FLQ crisis. We had an incredibly volatile combination with armed troops trapped and exposed on the bridge, heavily armed Mohawks, the Sûreté, which has been feuding with the warriors for years, and a growing crowd of angry Montrealers threatening to storm the barricades. I was there," she told the panel. "I can tell you the mood was very ugly."

"And," retorted Whitlaw glumly, "I can tell you the mood of the country is very ugly as well." His statement was greeted with the silence of assent.

Jake reached down suddenly and snapped the set off. Grant made a sound of protest, which was brushed aside by Jake.

"The day a talking head like Whitlaw, or even worse, some pie-in-the-sky professor, can enlighten me about anything," muttered Jake, "is the day I head out for some place sane, like maybe Haiti or Bosnia or something. Besides, we've got some planning to do and old Charlie here is as dry as a bone." Grant and Sandra turned to face the big, powerfully-built man overflowing a leather chair in the corner, feet propped on one of the beds.

* * *

Charles Bertram Dunn was one of those men who never seemed content unless embroiled in some sort of crisis, and over the years, had acquired an uncanny ability to create his own if necessary. A hockey player of sufficient skill to have attracted the notice of several NHL clubs, he had somehow managed to alienate them all with a series of escapades which included: breaking a leg while trying out for the

Canadian Olympic bobsled team, despite being under contract to the Ottawa Senators at the time; barroom brawling with one of the scouts for the Boston Bruins who had been quoted (incorrectly, he maintained) in a Toronto newspaper as saying Dunn skated like a duck; and breaking the nose of one of the Buffalo Sabre's brightest young Russian players during a training camp scuffle.

By then the word was out that Charlie Dunn was a hell of a hockey player, but as one of the Sabre's coaches is reported to have said, trouble stuck to him like beautiful women to Corvettes.

And not just in the arenas of the nation either. At the tender age of twenty-eight, Charles Dunn was into his third marriage and would admit privately he was about ready to cash that one in too. He confessed ruefully to Jake one day that he just couldn't seem to help himself.

"I go through women like shit through a goose," he laughed. "Must be something I eat!"

But he was a hell of a cop. Extremely bright, honest, hard working, street wise, tough and afraid of absolutely nothing, Charlie Dunn was the man you wanted to shoulder up to when the going got rough. Someone once compared him to Gordie Howe heading into the corner after the puck during the deciding game of the Stanley Cup final: straight ahead, elbows up!

And what did Charles Dunn think about this most recent crisis? Well, he was about as happy as he could recall himself ever being. "Plunk down in the centre of the biggest action in the country. Man, this is really livin'!"

"Grab us a beer would ya," said Charles, pointing to the mini bar. Then, feet landing loudly on the floor, he waded right into the heart of the matter.

"Been doin' some thinkin'" he said. "What's the population of Orillia? Twenty, twenty-five thousand maybe. Lots more in summer with all the tourists and such, but right now not that big a place. Most likely small enough so's lots of people know lots of people, know what I mean?

"These guys, these bastards who took your daughter, Mr. Henry, it's not likely they live in Orillia, or if they do, chances are they're weird enough so's some people may have noticed, know what I mean? But most likely they've moved into town in the past few weeks, probably rented a place or something, maybe they have a cousin or something like that around here, maybe even one of them's got a cottage or camp or the like. But in a town as small as Orillia?" He arched his eyebrows. "Pretty hard to hide. Pretty hard. Maybe you think you're hidden, but in most small towns, half the population knows every time you take a leak. Excuse me Mrs. Beale, but you know what I mean, eh?"

Grant couldn't disagree. Raised in a small town in northern Ontario, he was only too familiar with the curiosity and suspicion strangers could generate. But as for Lee being held captive in a cottage or camp, Grant thought it highly unlikely. That buzzing noise on the tape sounded almost as though they were near some kind of factory or plant.

"I agree with you Charles," nodded Grant, "in. . ."

"Hey, call me Charlie, eh?"

"Yeah sure, sorry. . . Charlie. Anyway, in all probability, the kidnappers presence has aroused some interest in town. Just being strangers, and yeah, I agree they probably are, would create some kind of curiosity. Being from Quebec, it's likely that they act, and for all we know, sound a little different as well. Let me tell you, if any of them has a French Canadian accent and has spoken five words in Orillia, a lot of people will know it by now! A French Canadian accent, any kind of accent, is something Orillians sure as hell would take note of, and talk about. Having said that, how is any of this going to help us find Lee?"

Jake and Charles glanced briefly at each other. It was Jake who replied. "Charlie and I have done a lot of scheming on this, and we've come up with a plan which just might work. Let me run it past you two and see what you think." Grant and Sandra nodded.

"Okay, we can assume that somewhere in this little burg, somebody has seen something or someone that looks maybe just a bit funny, okay? Maybe not funny for New York, or Ottawa, or Montreal, but funny for Orillia, different. So how do we track down this information without looking kinda flutterplate ourselves? Most importantly, how do we set out to track down these funny people without tipping them off we're looking for them?"

He glanced around briefly. They were staring expectantly at him, including Charlie Dunn, who presumably knew what he was going to say. "We figure. . ." he darted a sideways look at Sandra. "No offence Mrs. Beale. We figure the ones in a small town who do the most looking and the most talking and the most nosing about are the women. Anyone disagree?" He looked directly at Sandra, who with an impatient upward flick of her wrist and a slight frown told him to get on with it.

"All right, so we agree women are the ones most likely to have spotted anything a bit different. They're the ones most likely to talk about it with neighbours and friends. So how do we reach these women? Once again keeping in mind we can't tip off the kidnappers what we're in town for. Well, Charlie and I figure if there's one thing women hate more than anything else, it's a guy who's skipped out on his wife without paying the bills, especially if there's a couple a kids at home. Women, and most men, okay, okay, I grant you, will do almost anything to catch these bad dad guys and pin their pointy little arses to the wall. So here's what we've gone and done.

"Old Charlie here has got himself and me deputised as special agents of the family court of Winnipeg, Manitoba. By sheer chance you understand," Jake chuckled, "by sheer chance, Charlie here just happened to have a few of these special deputy documents just hanging round his locker, begging to be filled out. So the first thing that happens after we check into Orillia later this morning is special agents Dunn and Barr, alias Kibble and Berton, the good guys, go looking for one, maybe two skippers who've moved into town in the past few weeks, trying to crap out on their duty as husbands and fathers. We start out in the grocery stores, the market area, maybe some coffee shops, anywhere women get together, all the time flashing our documents and asking questions about a couple escaped husbands. We figure once the word gets around that special agents Dunn and Barr, alias Kibble and Berton, need the co-operation and assistance of observant Orillians to track down skunks of this odour, the phone lines should be burning up, no time flat. Special agent Sandra Beale, alias what? Bahama Mama? you pick a name – can take calls from our hotel room headquarters, assisted by special agent Grant Henry, alias Night Talk Man, who because of his distinctive voice and famed brain, will have to be confined to checking addresses and any other duties which don't require him to talk to anyone other than us."

Jake paused for a moment, looking cautiously around the room. "Well whataya think?"

Sandra was shaking her head sadly.

"It's just that we have so little time," she said without thinking.

Grant who had been pacing back and forth across the tiny room, stopped abruptly and slumped onto one of the beds as though struck.

A canyon had opened up somewhere inside of him. Sandra gasped and turned to him, throwing her arms about his shoulders.

"Oh Grant, I'm so sorry. I spoke without thinking. Grant, we're going to find Lee. She's going to be all right. Oh, I'm sorry, I'm sorry!" She wanted to hold him, to comfort him, but he turned away. Lee was the one who needed comforting. She was out there, perhaps not far away, alone and in danger. Choking back his despair, moved by Sandra's concern and tenderness, he reached out tentatively to lightly touch her arm. Feeling the warmth and smoothness of her, it was all he could do not to gather her into his arms and lose himself.

"It's all right Sandra. It's just I can't bear the thought of anyone harming her. . . or. . . or not ever seeing her again. You're right though. We don't have much time, but we've got to go with their plan. It's all we've got."

His sleep, when it finally came, tenuous and troubled, was filled with nightmares of spiderwebs, and a particularly horrible dream from his childhood in which he was falling from a haymow onto the upraised tines of a pitchfork.

But just before dawn, he found himself running hand in hand with Lee through a lush green meadow, the sweet song of crickets ascending from the tall autumn grass.

4:56 AM – Day Four

The prime minister was a heavy sleeper, a trait acquired, or so he claimed, during his university days, when in order to pay for his studies, he worked most of the night grinding bearings in a local plant.

"When you only get to sleep four or five hours a day you soon learn to use every second of it," he had explained to his wife, who was now having great difficulty shaking him awake.

"Wake up, wake up," she shouted directly into his ear. "For heaven's sake wake up, the premier of Quebec needs to talk to you. It's urgent."

The prime minister slowly rose to consciousness. Eyes still sealed, he groaned loudly enough for an aide, jigging anxiously just outside the bedroom door, to hear.

Suddenly wide awake, his wife's words penetrating the fog, he threw both legs over the side of the bed and took the phone from her outstretched hand. He was surprised to find his heart pounding.

There was no congratulatory salutation. His questions spilled out in a flurry. "Marc, what's the problem? What's happening? What the hell time is it anyway?"

The voice at the other end was calm, measured, speaking English.

"Mr. Prime Minister, are we on a secure line here?"

The remaining vestiges of woolliness had by now been swept clear of his head. The prime minister replied in French.

"Of course! Marc, what's wrong?" The hour and the long-standing antipathy each man had for the other was making him more testy than usual.

Charbonneau wasted no time in coming to the point. "Prime Minister we have another terrible tragedy on our hands and I am afraid the consequences may thrust us into a situation from which there will be no returning without much harm and. . . even bloodshed."

The prime minister caught his breath. "For God's sake what is it?"

The Quebec premier pulled no punches. "A young lady, Quebecoise, has been brutalized and murdered and thrown onto the lawns of Macdonald College in Ste Anne de Bellevue. Do you know the place?"

"Yes, yes of course. Go on."

"Rolled up and placed in this young woman's vagina was a piece of paper upon which is written. . . in English. . . here, just a moment, they wrote it down for me, word for word." There was a brief rustling of paper as Marc Charbonneau sorted through his notes. "Here, I'll read you the exact wording. . .'

"This francophone life has been taken in retaliation for the kidnapping, rape and torture of a twelve-year-old anglophone child and for the injustices perpetrated upon the English speaking population of Quebec by the racist policies of the Quebec Government.

"We represent a group of English speaking Quebeckers who have decided to fight back in a war which has already been launched against us. This is a war we did not start, but from which we will not run. Our policy from now on is, an eye for an eye, a tooth for a tooth. A French life for every English life." Another rustling of paper. "There is," said Charbonneau, "no signature. Quite a piece of literature isn't it?"

The phone fell silent. The only sound was that of the Prime Minister of Canada distractedly rubbing the dark stubble on his chin. Both men had been in politics long enough to know that in situations like this the first one to speak was the loser. It was the prime minister who caved in first.

"I don't suppose there's any chance this can be kept from the press? At least the note?"

Charbonneau's reply was terse. "Too late. They've already got the whole story, including a copy of the note." Relishing the discomfort he was creating, he couldn't resist volunteering additional information. "They know where it was found too!"

The prime minister groaned aloud and began a tentative entry into the carefully laid trap.

"What do you think will happen?" he asked.

At the other end of the line, the premier silently shot a triumphant fist into the air. "Got ya," he shouted exuberantly to himself.

Aloud, exerting considerable self-control, he answered the question calmly and quietly, managing even to affect a grim note of sadness. "Prime Minister, if something isn't done immediately to defuse this situation, we're going to have a lot more trouble on our hands than either of us wants to tackle. I wouldn't be at all surprised if we didn't see some blood spilled, maybe even more deaths, in my country, and yours." Once again he let the phone fall silent.

Aware he was floundering badly, ambushed, but unable to extricate himself, the prime minister waded in further. "What are you suggesting can be done to prevent further. . . ahh difficulties?"

Charbonneau snapped the trap shut in English. "Prime Minister, the only thing which can prevent a total breakdown in law and order, from all hell breaking loose, as you English would say, in both Quebec and Canada, is to immediately begin negotiations with us to create a totally independent, a sovereign Quebec."

His voice assumed a new note of authority, the rhythm of his speech changing perceptibly, as though he were addressing a political rally. He continued to speak in English. "This is the only course which will deflect us from the highway to destruction we seem inexorably headed down at this moment. Among many other things, an announcement that we are entering into amicable negotiations on separation might very well result in the freeing of Lee Henry. That, after all, has been the kidnappers' demand from the start. The national outpouring of joy and relief at such an event would go a long way towards relieving the immediate tensions, and overshadow much of the resentment bound to occur in some quarters with the separation of Quebec."

He continued in a more placating fashion. "Naturally any announcement concerning the start of independence negotiations would be accompanied by assurances from the government in Ottawa that Quebec would not be impoverished by federal policies, and that our borders will remain intact. The federal government will make it very clear that it will not support any efforts to partition off any part of Quebec. This will remove much of the fear here. We, on the other hand, will assure English speaking and native Quebeckers that their concerns will be thoughtfully addressed. I should tell you I have already talked with several Indian band councils and all are prepared to negotiate. It's really only a matter of money."

This time it was the Quebec premier who was compelled to break the silence.

"Prime Minister, are you still there?"

"You know I am Marc. . . So it has to come to this has it? Must we. . . this includes you too don't forget. . . must we allow terrorists to map our paths? What will history say about us Marc? Hells bells, what will our people say about us today? Damn it all anyway, I've fought against a divided country all my political life. I believe it to be wrong. Wrong for all of us. From the deepest part of me, I believe it to be wrong, foolish, dangerous even and totally unnecessary. . . I. . ."
Charbonneau interrupted coldly.

"Prime Minister, you asked me what would prevent disaster and I told you. When the people of Quebec learn of the young woman's murder and that despicable note, the howls of protest and demands for retribution will spill over well beyond our borders. Any chance at an amicable parting of the ways may be irretrievably lost unless that information is tempered by news that the process of allowing our two cultures to complete their journeys along separate paths has begun. Prime Minister, you know it as well as I. The time has come. We cannot continue to live together as one family. Too much water has now flowed under the bridge. Let's make sure we don't stain that water with any more red. And you know something?" There was a prolonged pause before he continued. "The rest of this country wants it now, just as much as we do in Quebec!"

The prime minister, stung by what he feared might very well be the truth, responded carefully, his voice rising barely above a whisper.

"You may announce that I have agreed to a debate on the question of entering into negotiations with Quebec on the matter of separation. It will begin during this afternoon's emergency session of parliament."

Replacing the receiver carefully on its cradle without saying goodbye, the prime minister sat motionless on the edge of the bed, his shoulders sagging in defeat. His wife, without a word, rose from the bed, knelt in front of him and placed his head on her nightgowned shoulder. Neither one could hold back tears.

Toronto 6:00 AM – Day Four

On an ordinary work day, tens of thousands of people pass through Toronto's Union Station, which serves as railway station, subway stop and central hub of the GO commuter rail system. When the Blue Jays are in town, thousands more pour over its tiled floors to the enclosed walkway leading directly to the nearby Sky Dome.

Although not yet fully charged with the energy of morning rush hour, even at six am, Union Station is a very busy place; the subways already beginning to discharge their briefcase-clutching cargoes.

This morning, Via Rail from Vancouver had arrived at 5:35, four hours late, as was the frequent custom, and a few of its bleary-eyed, rumpled passengers, shaking kinks from their bodies, were still making their desultory way to cabs parked outside along Front Street. A few sought directions to nearby hotels.

The middle-aged couple slumped over hard plastic seats in one of the departure area's waiting rooms found it difficult to resist the temptation presented by the pervasive odour of freshly made coffee and muffins emanating from the tiny coffee shop directly across from them.

To the casual observer, the couple looked like any other. A little down-at-heels perhaps; why else would they be taking the train? Waiting for. . . who knew what? The eight am Via Rail to Windsor perhaps? But a trained eye, if suspicious, might have detected something just slightly out of place. Something hard to put your finger on. Were they just a little too alert for this early in the morning? Their movements too brisk?

The same could be said of the floor washer vigorously attacking the nearby tiles with his bucket and mop.

The original Union Station was built in a giant T. The huge lobby at the top of the T, called the Grand Hall runs parallel to Front Street at ground level. It is reputed to be the largest room in Canada, and one of the most spectacular, accommodating ticket outlets, waiting areas and restaurants.

The longer part of the T had recently been redesigned to serve as both the arrival and departure concourse for VIA Rail and is, in fact, a long narrow underground tunnel constructed so that the railway tracks actually pass over it. The rumble overhead as trains rolled in and out sounded like distant thunder.

One of the few concessions to the demise of the age of steam were two small gates at the very rear of the passenger concourse through which, every work day, passed thousands of commuters from the outer reaches of Metro Toronto and beyond. They were now being used as both arrival and departure gates for the GO commuter rail system.

At exactly six am, Andres Rodique Saurez strode purposefully down the sloped floor from the Grand Hall into the hurly burly of the arrivals and departure concourse. Nine years surviving the brutal streets of Bogota, Columbia as a homeless urchin had taught him well. He was as cunning and predatory as a jungle cat stalking its prey.

His path down the concourse was slightly diagonal, a course which, if continued, would bring him directly to a row of luggage lockers lining one of the walls, a few feet from where the couple was seated.

Barely three strides from colliding with the lockers, he glanced up as though in surprise, turned slightly to his right and continued on down the concourse at the same brisk pace. His dark wrap-around glasses masked eyes which darted intently about, alert to the slightest flicker of interest from anyone as he approached the lockers. He was watching for any sudden movement, the tensing of a body, a hand unconsciously creeping inside a coat to check a hidden weapon.

He had spotted the couple and the floor washer immediately upon entering the concourse, but even when he was close enough to the lockers to reach out and touch them, he had been unable to detect the slightest indication the couple was even aware of his presence. Nor had there been a minimal flicker of interest from the long-haired young man just now opening the small news stand in front of the lockers. The floor washer had not stayed his mop for an instant.

Perhaps it was because he was weary and cramped from the six-hour drive from Ste Anne de Bellevue, or it may have been contempt for Canadian authorities for their laxness and naivety. Whatever the reason, for the second time in the past twenty-four hours he was about to make a mistake, this one much more serious than having sex with a young woman in her apartment before killing her.

Satisfied there was no danger, Andres wheeled slowly about and casually strolled back to the lockers, cold cat's eyes sweeping back and forth behind their camouflage, muscles bunching, prepared to spring.

There was no need for him to seek out the proper locker. Having retrieved parcels here several times in the past few days, he knew exactly in which one his payment would be. Reaching into his pants pocket, eyes still prowling behind glasses, he extracted the large key, inserted it into the lock and began to open the door.

The departure lounge erupted in pandemonium. Before the locker door was fully open the couple was dead; two shots, fired so quickly from the gun which had appeared as though by magic in Andres' hand that many eye witnesses later claimed they were positive only one shot had been fired.

The man, Metro Toronto Police Sergeant Brian Hanlan, died first, a bullet through the centre of his chest. His hand had just reached the butt of his service revolver which still rested, cold and useless, in its shoulder holster. The woman, Constable Miriam Jessop, also Metro Police, had either reached for her weapon earlier than her partner, or was faster. Her gun was out of its holster, on the grimy plastic bench where it had fallen when the bullet caught her.

The instant he fired, Andres dove to the dusty floor, plunging head first into the legs of an elderly woman, one of the last stragglers from the Vancouver train. She crashed to the floor, purse and luggage scattering. Her screams of pain and fright could scarcely be heard amidst the cacophony of sound erupting in the station.

It was impossible to determine how many people were in the concourse of Union Station when the shooting started. Some newscasts estimated 200. Toronto newspapers claimed their must have been close to 300, counting the staffs of the shops, almost every one in a panic stricken frenzy to escape.

Exacerbating the chaos were some 100 arriving commuters from the Oshawa Go train who were beginning to enter the two narrow rear gates, just as the panicked horde came charging out. Dozens went sprawling to the floor in screaming tangles.

Thus far, Andres had been able to spot four policemen with guns trained on him. The floor washer had dropped behind a small magazine kiosk no more than fifteen metres away, a sawed-off shotgun poked around the corner. There was another cop partially hidden behind a large granite column directly behind him, near the top of the sloping floor at the entrance to the Grand Hall, and two others were crouched behind a row of waiting room seats near the entrance to one of the two GO train exits, a good twenty metres to his right.

For a moment he was puzzled by their actions.

Why weren't they shooting at him? Then came understanding. 'They're afraid to fire because of all these people around,' he told himself, 'Andres you're not dead yet!' He knew only too well that in his country, bullets would be flying everywhere by now, with little concern for the innocent.

Grasping the front of the old woman's dress, he sprang to his feet, dragging her upright with him, his gun pressed to her temple. Her screams had subsided to loud moans, her face ashen, spittle dribbling from the side of her mouth.

Although less than a minute had transpired since the shots, most of the occupants of the departure area between Andres and the Grand Hall entrance had managed to flee up the sloped floor and steps to safety. Those trapped between him and the rear of the departure lounge were confronted with a much more difficult and dangerous situation.

Standing between them and escape to the Grand Hall was a madman who had already shot two people and was holding another captive in the very centre of the corridor. Adding to their dilemma was the fact that fleeing to the inviting safety of the Grand Hall meant having to cross the direct line of fire between him and the three armed policemen who were alternatingly shouting at Andres to drop his gun and at everyone else to drop to the floor, something no one appeared inclined to do. None of them could see the fourth policeman completely hidden behind the pillar at the entrance to the Grand Hall directly behind Andres.

The only safe means of escape for those thus trapped appeared to be through the two narrow GO train exits completely blocked by a confused jumble of panic stricken humanity.

Some passengers, still unaware of the chaos inside the station, continued to make their way towards the gates. All other exits leading to the various train platforms, were firmly locked at this hour. Scores of people were jammed into the rear of the corridor, shouting, crying, screaming, pushing, several still flailing about on the floor, all trying desperately to claw their way out, certain that death was only a heartbeat away.

Panicked even more by the gunman's sudden movement and his loudly moaning hostage, several people broke away from the scrambling throng at the rear exits and charged towards Andres. For an instant he thought they meant to attack, but as he raised his gun to face them, they veered away, like a herd of stampeding cattle, and tore past him. A much larger group immediately gave chase.

The streets of Bogota had taught him well. In a flash he realized he wasn't what they were after. What they sought was the safety of the Grand Hall about the length of a soccer field behind him; safety which, with swiftness, luck and nerve, could be his as well.

With a grunt, he hurled the woman aside, and jamming his gun into its holster under his coat and throwing his dark glasses to the floor, he sprinted after the fleeing mob, overtaking the slowest of them in a few bounds. He passed the laggards quickly so he was running in the middle of the pack. They paid him no attention, unaware of his presence, their only concern the Grand Hall, the street and safety.

The three policemen behind them, the floor washer and the pair crouched behind the seats, lost a precious second or two in frozen indecision. By then it was too late. Dozens more of those attempting to escape through the Go train exits, spotting the general exodus in the other direction, turned and stormed after the fleeing throng.

The officer with the shotgun sprang to his feet and was immediately bowled over by the rearguard of the stampede. Down he went, with a dozen or more sprawled about him like so many ten pins.

The two policemen who had ducked behind the seats for cover lost sight of Andres in the middle of the throng, then found they could barely move amidst the humanity swirling about, let alone give chase.

For Andres, there remained but one obstacle: the lone officer he had spotted behind the pillar at the top of the sloping platform. He would have to run right past him, within a few metres. Where was he?

The madly charging herd was now half way up the ramp, the leaders almost into the Grand Hall, when the missing policeman suddenly appeared, whirling around from behind the large pillar, gun in both hands, crouched in the classic stance. He was young, his fright obvious, his shout barely audible above the din: "Halt or I'll shoot."

The sight of the gun inspired the mob, not to obey the order, but to run faster, Andres in their midst. The secret, Andres knew, was to avoid making eye contact with his adversary but in the one brief glance he allowed himself, he knew he was going to make it. The young policeman was confused, unable to determine with certainty which of the running men was the gunman. The lighting was dim in the departure area. It had all happened so quickly, at least 100 metres away from his position behind the pillar, and without the gun and dark glasses, in his finely tailored suit and stylish haircut, Andres Saurez looked like most of the other middle-aged businessmen running with him. In an instant, Andres was past the crouching officer and then, amazingly, past two more policemen charging from the Grand Hall down into the concourse, guns drawn. They didn't even glance at him.

* * *

Now, out onto the street! Several of those who had unwittingly shielded him during their mad dash dropped to the sidewalk in breathless exhaustion.

Andres didn't pause. Barging roughly through the large crowd which had begun to assemble on the street, he threw open the door of a parked cab and leapt in. As it peeled quickly away from the curb, police began pouring out of the station onto the sidewalk. A cruiser, lights flashing, siren blaring, came tearing down Bay St. and made a careening left turn onto Front, coming to a fishtailing stop just past the station, blocking eastbound traffic.

It was about ten seconds too late. The cab was already turning north onto Yonge.

"Jesus," said the driver, "what the hell was going on in there?"

"Ahh," said Andres, "just some stupid kid freaking out, pumped on drugs. You know the cops, always trying to make a big deal out of nothing." The cabby was shaking his head.

"Yeah, but all those people running around and all that yelling. . . geeze yuh know, this used to be a nice place to live but not anymore. They've gone and ruined it. Christ, yuh know we invite the druggies into the country. . . we invite them I tell ya. We put ads in all the fuckin' foreign papers telling all the crooks of the world to come to Canada. You're welcome here we tell 'em. Come on in. . . and if you can't make enough robbing banks or beatin' up little old ladies, then just take a little trip down to sunny Florida and we'll send you your welfare cheque air fuckin' mail so's you don't have to line up in the snow or nothin'. Shit man, worse here now than New York! Where yuh headed?"

Andres, rage already beginning to supplant the exhilaration of escape, managed only a grunt in reply to the cabbies's musings, then, "Yonge and St. Clair."

'I was set up! Those bastards set me up like some kind of bloody amateur!' Furious he hadn't smelled the trap the moment he entered Union Station, he berated himself. 'I should have known they'd try to weasel out of my fifty thousand.' In the brief instant before he had seen the two cops reach for their guns, he had caught a glimpse of the locker's interior. It was empty.

Andres had only a vague idea who "those bastards" were. His only contact with his employers had been by telephone, and most recently, through the confessional in Notre Dame Cathedral. He directed most of his anger at himself for being so careless, for not having realized this was more than a bunch of crazy Frenchmen fomenting revolution. It wasn't the double-cross which was bothering him so much though. Betrayal, after all, was something he had come to expect. It came with the territory. If anyone had asked, he would probably have admitted he'd have done the same thing, but for him to fall so easily into the trap was inexcusable.

He was distracted momentarily as two police cruisers tore past, heading south, followed by an ambulance, then as he had taught himself to do so well over the years as a drug courier, he forced his mind away from his anger and self recrimination. There was no time for it. No profit in it. As the cab wove its way through the ever-thickening traffic, he began carefully to review his options.

The safest course was to keep right on going to Pearson International Airport and catch the first flight out of the country (they might be watching the flights directly to Columbia, so stay away from any of those), and from there, back to home and safety. Take the portion of the money they had paid him and run.

He was strongly tempted except for one thing – the girl. She could be worth a fortune. Not only to those who had just set him up, but to the beleaguered Canadian government, which by now would surely be willing to pay any amount for her safe return. Snatch her from her hiding place and someone would have to pay him a lot of money. He didn't care who. Whoever offered the most money was welcome to her.

He would have to be very careful though. Much more careful than he had been until now. Canadian authorities might be something less than competent, but whoever had paid him to kill the girl in Ste Anne de Bellevue and then tried to have him blown away in Union Station was smart enough.

'Not bad for amateurs,' he told himself, 'but if they want to play for keeps, they're no match for me. Not even close!' They simply didn't have his experience.

One thing was certain. They'd likely be ready for him if he went back for the girl. They'd be half expecting him to make a grab for her. He couldn't just tear up there, barge into the place and walk away with her. It wouldn't be that easy. On the other hand, he told himself, it wouldn't be all that difficult either. A plan was already beginning to form in his mind.

As the cab passed a doughnut shop he remembered he hadn't eaten anything since noon the day before.

"Hey," he instructed the cab driver, "drop me off here. Think I'll have some breakfast."

Montreal 6:38 AM – Day Four

Inspector Paul Boisvert, awakened from a deep sleep with news that Andres Saurez had escaped after killing two police officers in Toronto's Union Station, had less than a minute to be furious. That was the length of time it took to reach Premier Marc Charbonneau by phone at his Quebec City residence.

"My, my, Paul, why do you think this is bad news?" To Boisvert's amazement, the premier began to laugh delightedly. "This is wonderful Paul! Can you imagine? You provide all the information necessary to capture the man who murdered the Courville girl, and Toronto police are so incompetent, not only do they let him escape, but two of them get shot in the great fuck-up. Half the city of Toronto gets terrorized for good measure. Paul this is marvellous! Better even than had they caught this man! You must call a news conference immediately."

The premier grew more excited. "Yes that's it. Call in the news clip boys. Express extreme indignation that Toronto police have bungled things so badly. Tell them the magnificent job you and your people have done in tracking down the killer is now out the window. . . all for nothing. You must of course, express sympathy over the fact two people died in this unfortunate affair, but remind everyone that the brutal murderer of an innocent Quebecois child is now free. You might even suggest that the whole thing was handled poorly in Toronto because it involved the murder of a francophone.

The premier was about to hang up, still chuckling drily, but couldn't resist sharing good news. "Paul, there is something else you should know."

Boisvert, still trying to wrap his mind around the astounding developments and his new instructions, didn't hear him, and began asking a question concerning the news conference.

The premier interrupted impatiently. "Listen to me. I spoke with the prime minister earlier this morning." His voice grew husky and excited. "Paul, parliament is going to debate Quebec separation this afternoon. . . We've won!"

Morning – Day Four

The nation, which had gone to bed in the early hours of the morning breathing a sigh of relief at the successful conclusion of the Mercier Bridge crisis, hoping for a brighter dawn, awoke instead to angry disbelief and shock.

The brutal murder in Ste Anne de Bellevue, the fiasco in Union Station, and the spreading violence and vitriolic rhetoric dropped a curtain of black despair over the country.

The melancholy did not last the full morning.

In most nations, news that the federal government was about to negotiate the terms of dividing up their country would be catastrophic, but the premier of Quebec was correct. The announcement, shortly after seven am, that parliament would begin debating that afternoon whether to enter into negotiations with Quebec on the terms of separation, was greeted by most Canadians with a tremendous sense of relief. Many welcomed it openly. The agony, they believed, was to be prolonged no longer.

Orillia 7:26 AM – Day Four

"Do you think we'll really do it? Do you think we'll break up the country? My God, Grant, we've come through so much together. Do you really think this is the end?" Sandra tried to sound hopeful, but she doubted hope was warranted. "And what do you think this means for Lee? If separation is what they're after, do you think they might let her go now?" She was gazing out the window of their suite in Orillia's Leacock Hotel, admiring the tidy little harbour fanning out below.

Jake Barr and Charles Dunn had been on "backyard patrol," as they dubbed it, since daybreak, circulating their carefully constructed story of a Winnipeg husband who had skipped town, leaving his wife and two kids destitute.

As planned, they checked in by phone every hour, but so far had to confess rather glumly that they hadn't been able to turn up a thing.

"Everybody's friendly enough," admitted Jake, "but nobody seems to know nothin'."

Both Sandra and Grant were fretting at the inactivity. Sitting by the phone anxiously waiting for a call was almost unbearable, but Jake had been insistent.

"We're leaving your phone number with everyone we talk to," he explained. "I know you'd like to do some poking around yourselves, but we've got to leave the line open as much as possible. You never know when somebody might remember something, and try to contact us." He didn't have to reiterate that Grant's voice would be immediately recognizable. Nor did he think it wise to mention that he wanted Grant as far away from any trouble as possible.

Grant, understanding the politics involved better than most, was not surprised at the announcement concerning separation negotiations. Nor was he hopeful the announcement would, in any way, alleviate the danger Lee was in.

"It's impossible to know what they'll do with Lee," he said. "I suppose there's a chance they'll simply let her go, having won a victory, but. . ." his voice became bitter, "it's very unlikely they'd do it until all the terms of independence were agreed upon. They've used her up until now to get what they want and you can be pretty sure they'll keep her at least a bit longer, if for no other reason than to see if they can continue to win concessions. Another possibility. . ." his voice trailed off into in a faint whisper. "Another possibility is that, if they are satisfied she has served her purpose, they might think it would be too dangerous for them to simply let her go." He did not elaborate, nor did Sandra ask. What he meant was clear enough.

Turning his face from her, ashamed of the tears gathering in his eyes, he managed to continue. "What it means is that it's more important than ever to find Lee as quickly as possible. She could be in even more danger."

An emotion-charged silence settled over the room. Sandra desperately wanted to take him in her arms, but held back. Something told her that Grant would not accept any form of solace right now.

The best she could hope for was to get him thinking about something other than Lee for a few moments. She asked her question again. "What about Canada? Do you really think this is the end for us?"

"Probably," replied Grant sadly. "Yeah, we'll do it all right. What a stupid tragedy isn't it? In the end we turned out to be no different than some bloody eastern European banana republic whose citizens revel in dredging up every damn grievance, real and imagined, from the past couple of hundred centuries." He shook his head disgustedly. "Our great and noble experiment. . . two languages, two cultures. . . existing as one nation, just too goddamn magnanimous for those who are supposed to be leading us. And let's not forget all the narrow minded peewee-brained bigots on both sides, who are right now gleefully tapdancing on the country's grave."

His anger exhausted, he sat, spent and subdued, for several minutes, staring bleakly out into the harbour. Sandra didn't prod him.

"You know," he began again, "there are going to be some who will claim it's all because of the kidnapping of one little girl." He shook his head vigorously. "That's not what's happening here. We're destroying our own country, not because of this crisis, but because we didn't have the imagination, the courage, the determination, maybe even not enough love to save it. What it all boils down to in the end is that we just didn't care enough. If we Canadians really wanted to keep the country together, really believed in it. . . really loved it, nothing on earth could divide us. The seeds of destruction weren't sown by the cruel bastards who abducted a twelve-year old girl, or who murdered that poor woman in Ste Anne de Bellevue. The ones killing Canada are those of us who didn't care enough, who just couldn't be bothered to explore the country, to learn about our people, our history, who didn't care enough to try and find out who we are, and how we got that way. You know," he said, "Hugh MacLennan once described Canada as a land of two solitudes, but we could have changed that if we had really wanted to. We're losing our country because damn it all, we didn't work hard enough to keep it."

Grant turned from the window to stare at her, passion spent, his face drawn and grim. "So help me God, Sandra, if anything happens to Lee, I swear I don't think I could ever broadcast another word in this country. I would never forgive myself or anyone who lives here, for allowing a situation to develop where innocent children can be used as political pawns. We all stood by and let this happen. . . to Lee and to Canada."

"Wait just a minute," she interjected, "I understand how you're feeling right now, but just remember this. Everyone in this country is appalled, horrified at what has happened to Lee. And I'll tell you something else," she said thoughtfully. "We've been hearing a few people expressing relief because they think that an end to all our squabbling will soon be here, but if we do separate, a lot of Canadians, I suspect the majority of us, are going to be a whole lot sadder. If ever we needed reminding how much most Canadians love this country, let's not forget that big rally in Montreal just before the last referendum. Grant," she said, leaning forward with her face only inches from his, "it just might be that if we do take separate paths we'll come to like and respect each other more. It just might be that there was no other way, that Quebec separation was inevitable and this just hastened the process."

"Yeah," replied Grant bitterly, "we might respect each other more the morning after, the only problem is, it won't be Canada anymore."

Sandra made no reply. Grant, despondent and increasingly restless over their lack of progress, rose from his chair, slid the large glass door aside and stepped out onto the small concrete balcony, the familiar tangy fish and seaweed smell of the lake assailing his nostrils.

The municipal harbour, spread out beneath his feet, with its sprinkle of small boats bobbing gently in Lake Couchiching's swell, dredged up a flood of memories for him. This was the harbour into which, not that long ago, he had so happily sailed with Carol and Lee.

That trip up the Trent Canal, despite its unhappy ending, had been a great adventure. He remembered Lee's sparkling eyes as she took the controls through Rice Lake; how proud she was picking out the compass points and helping navigate through the dense fog of Lake Simcoe.

"Now," he realized sadly, "she's out there somewhere, maybe not far from here, alone, frightened. . ." He couldn't bear to think the rest.

His mind drifted to Carol. With a pang of guilt, he thought how frightened she must be right now, back in her Ottawa hotel room, not knowing what was happening, where they were, alone with her devils. He knew she would be beside herself with anxiety and fear, and was surprised to find himself drawn to her. They had lived together too long, he supposed, shared far too much, for him not to want to shield her from the pain he knew she would be in. There was something still there between them, a tiny, unpredictable flicker of the flame which had once burned brightly.

Inside the hotel room, lying on the bed, watching the breeze ruffle his long blond hair, feeling his anguish, Sandra ached for him, and was astonished. For months after Tommy died she was certain she would be forever after incapable of caring for another man. She had found the thought of sex repugnant. But now, as she watched Grant leaning over the balcony railing, taut and brooding, she felt the blood racing to her female organs, a magnificent electrical kind of shock racing down her legs and spine. She had experienced nothing like it since those first few dizzying months with Tommy, when a single moment alone meant falling on each other in a frenzy. But, as with Tommy, there was more than sex. It took every ounce of her willpower not to rush out onto that balcony, throw her arms about him and hold him, have him hold her, comfort him as she knew he needed.

She understood he was attracted to her but sensed that he was suspicious of his feelings, and would not allow himself to succumb to them until he was sure it was something more than succour, a shelter from the storm. He was a man who, self-made and fiercely independent, would be unwilling, perhaps unable to admit need or vulnerability, at least until assured it would not be perceived as weakness. But Sandra also knew that despite her fragile, almost waiflike appearance, she was every bit as tough as Tommy had ever been. No, make that tougher if the need arose, and far more determined. She wanted the big blond man out there on the balcony and that moment resolved to have him.

Stepping through the sliding door into the slight chill of the morning, she reached out to take his hand gently in hers and sought out his troubled eyes.

"Talk to me Grant. What are you thinking?" And then, as though reading his mind she whispered softly. "This is where it ended for you and Carol isn't it?" Tilting her head in the direction of the harbour she said: "Out there."

There was a long silence, and Sandra grew afraid she had gone too far.

"No," he replied finally, "it ended long before we arrived here, I just couldn't accept it. Accept it? Hell, I didn't have the guts to face the truth. In the end she had more courage than I. She's the one who called it quits, who packed up and left. I sometimes wonder if I would have ever pulled the plug."

She didn't believe it had anything to do with courage though, he had plenty of that. 'No,' she told herself, 'he's a lot like Tommy was. Too damn stubborn to admit defeat. If Carol hadn't walked out, he'd probably still be in there slugging away, still trying to salvage the relationship.'

Sandra was four or five years older than Grant, but in many ways his was the philosophy of a generation which predated hers. 'A real old-fashioned, stubborn son of a bitch,' she thought wryly. 'Till death do us part and all that, and probably not the least bit afraid of hurricanes either!'

The phone startled them both. Sandra, nearest the door, took the call. It was Jake again. They'd talked with a woman who was certain her next door neighbour was the man they were looking for. He'd moved in only a few weeks ago and she'd been shocked to see him drinking beer on his front porch, in full view of people passing on the street. But when they checked, turns out the guy was just visiting his girlfriend who'd lived there for more than ten years.

"Other than that, not much," reported Jake, "but we're sure getting the word around. Something will turn up soon. Try and reassure Grant for us will you? We'll find her."

As she hung up, Sandra's hand flew to her cheek.

"Oh my God, Grant," she said, "we forgot all about checking in with my voice mail in Freeport. Maybe Al Thompson has come up with something."

Grant, pacing now with anxiety and frustration, responded only with a sceptical look.

He should not have dismissed his old friend so readily. Because Al Thompson, working through the night and well into the morning, had discovered the secret of the tapes. He knew the source of the strange buzzing sound in the background when Lee was talking.

Orillia 7:42 AM – Day Four

During the night, one of the men upstairs must have brought Lee another blanket. Perhaps prompted by a spark of human kindness or pity, perhaps simply because her dreadful coughing was keeping him awake.

Although she was by now too delirious to notice it, the air conditioning had been turned down as well. It made little difference. Her fever had worsened during the night. She was burning up with it. Her breathing had grown laboured, her coughing weaker.

Shortly after dawn someone brought her breakfast but she was too weak to eat, or even sit up. Nor did she notice the anxious and perplexed look on the young man's face as he watched her feeble attempts at feeding herself. For a moment, he seemed about to assist her but after casting several furtive glances in the direction of the stairway leading to the main floor, he apparently thought better of it and left, leaving the food on the floor beside her mattress.

Terribly thirsty, she did manage, from time to time, to rouse herself sufficiently to turn on her side and draw on a straw protruding from the water filled coke bottle they had left her earlier. She made several unsuccessful attempts to crawl to the nearby bathroom, then found herself much too weak to move from the warm wetness spreading beneath her hips.

She was fighting it with all the strength her robust young body could muster, but she was losing. The fluids filling her lungs were slowly drowning her.

In her delirium she began to make little sounds, like the mewing of a tiny kitten. "Mummy, Mummy, Mummy."

Hull 9:14 AM – Day Four

Chief Superintendent Marcel Charron was deeply troubled. Since an obviously tipsy Carol Henry had phoned earlier that morning, he had locked himself in his office and instructed his secretary to hold all calls. He needed time to think.

Carol had launched her call with a rambling invective about how unfair it was that she had been left behind in Ottawa to rot in some bloody hotel room while everyone else was out looking for Lee. In particular, she was very disconcerted by the fact Sandra Beale had accompanied them on their search, while she, the mother, had been left behind.

At first, Charron had only half listened, feigning politeness, having no desire to become embroiled in a domestic dispute. He was about to plead an important incoming call in order to get rid of her, when she said something which galvanized him. He shot forward in his chair and switched on the tape recorder at the side of the phone.

"They've been getting messages from Lee," Carol was saying. "Grant says he knows where she is. . . I'm pretty sure I know too."

Astonished, but not quite sure if he believed her, Charron let her continue uninterrupted.

"They're on their way to find her right now," she said, confusing the days, then corrected herself. "They should be there now. . . they didn't trust me enough to take me with them." Then she added bitterly, "They took Sandra Beale though!"

She was silent for several seconds although Charron could hear her breathing. He still hadn't responded.

Her voice had lost most of its belligerence when she began again.

"I haven't heard a word from them. . . Grant, Jake, Mrs. Beale, and I think another man. . . I'm really worried. I wanted them to go to the police, to get some help anywhere, but they said they couldn't trust anyone. . . not even the Mounties. . . especially not you."

"Mrs. Henry, why are you telling me this?" asked Charron.

"I don't know. . . I just. . . something just tells me I can trust you. I had to talk to someone. I. . ." She began to cry softly. "I'm really scared." Her voice dropped to a tiny whisper. "Do you think you can help? If I told you where they are, do you think you could help me?"

The superintendent seemed to take forever to answer.

"I don't know, Mrs. Henry," he said finally. "Honestly, I really don't know."

If Carol heard his response, she ignored it.

"They're somewhere on the Trent Canal system. I overheard Grant talking to himself when he thought I was asleep. . . I'm almost positive it's Orillia where they've gone."

"Orillia! Why Orillia?"

"Well, we knew from one of her first tapes she was somewhere along the Trent Canal, and in her last tape she talked about being at the end, or wishing she was at the end, and that's where we ended our trip up the Trent. . . at Orillia."

Charron didn't sound convinced.

"And you say. . . how many people have gone there to try and find her? Three? Four?"

"Four I think. Grant, and of course Jake and I think some other guy, a friend of Jake's, and the ubit. . . ubiquitous Mrs. Beale."

"And they didn't tell anyone else? Didn't notify any police? They're doing this all on their own? My God, Mrs. Henry, if you're right, if your daughter really is in Orillia, we could have a disaster on our hands. It's obvious whoever took Lee is not afraid of violence. Did Grant or anyone say if they knew exactly where in Orillia your daughter is?"

It took Carol a moment or two to respond. She seemed to be having trouble concentrating.

"Noo," she replied finally. Then as though the realization of what she was doing was just now dawning on her, she asked a question which would take Inspector Charron the better part of the morning to answer.

"Listen" she said, "you're not going to tell any of this to that little chicken-faced guy are you? I don't trust him as far as I could throw him."

Charron's hand slowly reached out to rest on a small metal toggle switch atop the tape recording device attached to his phone. He hesitated for a moment, then slowly flicked it to the "off" position.

"I don't know Mrs. Henry. I certainly should report it to Inspector Boisvert. As you know, he's in charge of the investigation. . . and I. . ."

Alarmed, Carol screamed, "If he does anything to hurt Lee, I'll kill both of you. . . you. . . you bastards!" and slammed down the phone.

Ottawa 10:32 AM – Day Four

Carol knew that if Grant hadn't left her alone, if he had taken her with them, if at least someone had remained with her in the hotel room and most of all, if being kept in the dark about everything wasn't so frustrating, she would never have taken a drink. She just knew it!

Mind you, she hadn't had very much. She had to give herself credit for that. Just a couple small ones. She hadn't gone crazy or anything. Besides which, there was only so much stress a person could take. . . any person, without cracking up.

That damn phone call though! Why in hell had she called Charron anyway? What could he do? Stupid thing to do.

Well. . . maybe not. He was right when he said it was a police matter. And when you really get right down to it, what the hell do a couple bumbling idiots like Grant and Jake know about finding a missing girl. . . but that Boisvert guy, what a package he was. You couldn't trust that wormy bastard with a nun!

She glanced around the lobby of the Chateau Laurier, from where she had made her call, almost expecting to see the little chicken-face charging through the revolving door. No! No question about it. She had done the right thing. Lee was her daughter, damn it, not Sandra Beale's. Phoning the police was the responsible thing to do. The only thing she could do. The police would find Lee. Everything would be fine. As a matter of fact, everyone would be so happy that she had called the police, who knows, maybe Grant and she could. . .

"Hi." He was just standing there. Tall, slim, immaculately dressed. With a wide friendly grin and teeth as white as a child's.

"Hi," said Carol, with a little smile.

"I'm new in town," he said, glancing at his watch, "I realize it's a little early for lunch, but they tell me Wilfrid's makes wonderful pre-lunch martinis. Would you care to join me for one?"

It was a game Carol understood very well.

"No."

"No?"

"But I might join you for two!"

They both laughed delightedly at her wit, and Carol clambered rather shakily to her feet.

"Mr. Just Blew Into Town, show us the way to Wilfrid's."

He really was delightful. Witty and extremely attentive, interested, fascinated by her and everything she said and did. She knew she was drinking a bit too much, but what the hell! It wasn't every day a woman had the chance to spend time with a man like this. Besides which, he didn't seem to mind if she rambled on a bit too long. If Grant didn't want her back, well, there were other fish in the sea.

Well before lunch was over, he knew the entire story. He gazed with intense sympathy into her eyes as she explained how the four of them had gone off to Orillia looking for her daughter, leaving her behind.

"My God," he said. "How terrible for you. Have you heard anything from them? Have they found your daughter yet? Do they know anything about the people who abducted her? Did your daughter manage to give you any information about the people who kidnapped her or anything like that?"

A little warning bell began to sound in her head, but its tiny tinkling was quickly drowned out by the alcoholic buzz. She poured out her heart to him, but hardly touched her lunch.

He escorted her back to her room. As best she could, through the haze, she invited him in for another drink. He politely declined.

It was just as well. Within minutes she had dropped into her first sound sleep in two days.

Hull 1:23 PM – Day Four

Superintendent Charron finally gave up trying to reach Carol by phone. He could only assume she had left the hotel unnoticed, despite the desk clerk's insistence she must still be somewhere in the building.

"I saw her take the elevator upstairs less than half an hour ago Superintendent," said the clerk. "I would certainly have noticed her if she came back down. She's really. . . uh. . . she's very attractive. I assure you, I wouldn't have missed seeing her if she came into the lobby. She may have fallen asleep in her room, she. . . aah. . . she did seem to have had perhaps a bit too much to drink."

Charron didn't doubt that, but found it difficult to believe anyone could sleep, sober or drunk, through the prolonged ringing of the phone from his repeated calls to her room. Having agonized most of the morning over his course of action, he was anxious to make her aware of his decision. His failure to locate her made him faintly uneasy.

Marcel Charron was not a man to take risks. Intelligent and honest, he had worked his way up through the ranks slowly, methodically, one step at a time, each step well planned and thought out. Which was the way he had set out to unlock the puzzle of Inspector Paul Boisvert. A puzzle which was disturbing him deeply.

Minutes after Carol's call, he had extracted a blank sheet of paper from his desk drawer and began to write down, point by point, some of the events involving Boisvert for which there appeared to be no reasonable explanation. He used his own form of shorthand developed during years of compiling accident reports, and began to write:

– Verbal attack on Henry (lied about having a daughter). Why?
– Tried to prevent the playing of the first tape on the radio Unlikely the order had come from the Solicitor General as Boisvert claimed. Why?
– Changed his mind the next day and allowed tapes to be played. Why?
– Instructions re: playing of tapes. Who from?
– Told me he'd been talking with both the premier and the prime minister – couldn't tell me why! Why?
– Met privately with the premier (former) – taped admission re: overzealous.

– Info – re: Paul Larocque – very detailed – where from?
– Info – re: Ste Anne de Bellevue killer!!! – Where from?
– Meeting in Boisvert's office – told me "there was a great deal more involved in all of this than you may suspect!"

When he had written it all down, Charron sat at his desk staring at the sheet for several minutes, his mind churning. He grew more and more disturbed as he contemplated what lay in front of him. Taking his pencil once again, he began to heavily underline his last sentence. "There is a great deal more involved in all of this than you may suspect!"

Flipping the pencil onto his desk, he pushed his chair back, swivelled it round and stared out the window into the parking lot below.

"Just what the hell is going on here anyway?" he asked himself. "Could Boisvert be involved?" He found the idea extremely difficult to believe and began to search his memory for every word the little Montrealer had spoken, every nuance, every inference, turning it over and over again in his mind.

There was no question that Boisvert hated anglos. He made no bones about that. There was also no doubt of his sentiments concerning Quebec independence. The tape recording during which he admitted to being overzealous was proof enough of that, and Charron recalled the incident (it seemed a lifetime ago) when Boisvert had justified his attacks on Grant Henry as necessary to lessen the damage to the separatist cause. But despite that, Charron, who considered himself an excellent judge of character, was convinced the little detective was in no way involved in the kidnapping. Or if he was, he was one hell of an actor, his performance at the Henry house worthy of an Oscar!

'No,' he told himself. 'Boisvert could not have been involved in the kidnapping, but something, something happened after that. He seemed to know far too much, far too soon. Part of it may have been puffery but somewhere along the line someone must have begun providing Boisvert with inside information.'

He lifted himself out of his chair and stood by the window, continuing to stare out but seeing nothing.

There was something else about little Chicken Face. Try as he might, he couldn't quite put his finger on it. Not only did Charron have too much information too soon, something basic about him had changed between their first meeting in Grant Henry's garage "command post" until that time he had been compelled to cool his heels in Boisvert's Montreal office.

What was it? A new dimension to his arrogance? Yes, there was certainly that. Some new ingredient had been added to the soup of his personality. During that meeting in Montreal it was almost as though Boisvert was seeing himself in a new role.

He'd seen that almost overnight assumption of a new identity once before, and remembered it well. It had been years ago, when, as a probationary constable, he had struck up a friendship with another rookie, who, until the day he became engaged to a Quebec cabinet minister's daughter, was just one of the boys.

But the moment she said "yes" he became, in the opinion of everyone on the force, a "bona fide asshole." In his friend's mind, his impending marriage meant he had metamorphosed from rookie cop to privileged member of one of Quebec's most powerful families and was free, obligated even, to exert that power.

"Boisvert was always an asshole," thought Charron wryly, "but from one day to the next, he became a different kind of asshole. It's almost as though someone said yes to him!"

It all kept coming around and around again to that one portentous statement Boisvert had made to him in Montreal. He read the underlined words again.

"There is a great deal more involved in all of this than you might suspect!"

At the time Charron had dismissed the words as mere bravado; the crowing of a banty barnyard monarch. Now he began to see it in a clearer light. It was a boast yes, but much more than that. Much more!

What it really meant was that not only was there a great deal more going on than simply a police search for a missing girl, but that whatever it was, Paul Boisvert was privy to it. Whatever was going on behind the scenes, Paul Boisvert was part of it!

The implications were enormous. If it were true it meant, among other things, that someone Boisvert was involved with knew who killed that poor girl in Ste Anne de Bellevue, and – this thought so startled Inspector Charron he unconsciously reached for his desk to support himself – and whoever knew the girl's killer, also knew he would show up in Union Station to retrieve his blood money and must have tipped off the Toronto police.

He shook his head, as though to clear it, or at least re-assemble the thoughts.

'Wait a minute here,' he admonished himself, 'let's not get carried away. Just because Boisvert may know some of the inner workings of the investigation doesn't mean he, or anyone he's involved with, had anything to do with the Ste Anne de Bellevue murder. That information,' he tried to convince himself, 'probably came from one of his regular informers, or perhaps even anonymously.'

He fell back into his chair, feeling relieved but unable to erase the flickers of doubt crawling across his consciousness like storm warnings on a TV screen.

He began to examine the backs of his hands resting in front of him on the desk, noting the thickly corded veins, the ever-expanding brown splotches. Not yet the hands of an old man but soon to be. He felt old and sad and very lonely. So much was changing. So many things were happening which he could not understand, nor, as he realized, did he care to.

Something was certainly up. As his wife would have said with that pseudo-British accent she affected at times, something is mighty rotten-smelling in the state of Denmark. Boisvert could hardly have been involved in the Henry girl's abduction, but there didn't appear much doubt he was now caught up in some kind of conspiracy. A political chess game was being played, with a young girl one of the pawns, and Inspector Paul Boisvert one of the players. Charron understood little of it. For him, it was a world gone mad.

Was Grant Henry correct in his assumption the police could not be trusted in the search for his daughter?

Had the political whirlwind sweeping the country overtaken all else, including concern for the girl's safety?

The superintendent had to conclude it had. Henry was probably right! The stakes were so high, no one knew who could be trusted. As slim as their chances were of finding and rescuing her, Lee Henry's fate was probably best left in her father's hands. He was staggered by the knowledge. Fully aware the decision might cost him his job, Charron pushed a button on his telephone tape recorder, carefully extracted the cassette and pocketed it. He would burn it later in his fireplace.

Charron would tell no one of his conversation with Carol Henry and the conclusions he had arrived at, except perhaps his wife, and maybe not even her. All he could do was hope that his decision to remain silent was correct, that somehow fate would allow the rescue of that poor little girl.

Montreal 1:34 PM – Day Four

The instructions Inspector Paul Boisvert had received had been very explicit.

"You take no action, no action of any kind. You do not even think of doing anything about the Henry case until you check with me," had been Premier Charbonneau's exact words. In view of the political implications of the investigation, Boisvert did not find those orders in any way strange or out of the ordinary. He did find the premier's reaction to the news of the Orillia search a little surprising though.

"Well done, Paul," said the premier. "So they worked that fast did they? Rather amazing really. The girl, you say, was sending them messages on the tape. . . huh. . . can you imagine!" Then anxiously. "But you're sure she didn't send them any information about her captors?"

"Carol Henry certainly didn't know anything about it if she did," Boisvert assured the premier.

"And this guy who talked with her. . . I gather that's all he did. . . talk?"

"Talk, yeah, that's all. Just talk. How the hell was she to know the guy's gay, eh?"

The Premier apparently did not find this as amusing as did Boisvert, whose giggle was pinched off by Charbonneau's next terse question.

"He didn't get her so drunk she didn't get a chance to tell him everything did he?"

"Absolutely not, First Minister. I can assure you, Phillipe Castonguay is the best at this kind of thing I have ever seen. His technique is about as good as you can get. The information can be fully relied on. I guarantee it."

"You guarantee it, do you?"

"Absolutely."

There was a long silence.

"Inspector Boisvert, what do you recommend we do?"

Boisvert was taken aback. Until now the premier had been calling all the shots.

"Well First Minister, I. . . ahh. . ."

Charbonneau seemed amused.

"Yes, Inspector!"

"Well, if you really think there's anything to all this Orillia business, I suppose I should go there as soon as possible." He sounded anything but enthused at the prospect.

"You think you should go to Orillia? Really? And what happens if while you're in Orillia, the girl turns up in Sherbrooke, or St. Louis de Ha Ha for Christ's sake?"

"Well. . . aah. . ."

"And what happens if the girl does turn up in Orillia? How are you going to explain to the world's press how you found her so quickly? No Paul, you know what I think you should do? Nothing! Absolutely nothing, and I'll tell you why. If, by some incredible stroke of luck, her father should find her safe and sound, then the whole country can have a big blow-out party. Except of course, here in Quebec where the murderer of Georgette Courville runs around loose, thanks to the incredible bumbling of Toronto police.

"That's it Paul," said the premier, becoming more animated. "That's the answer. We just sit tight. If there's any kind of trouble in Orillia and someone gets hurt, the father is in the soup for taking matters into his own hands. If nothing is found, who knows, the press might just find out about the little expedition, and decide there's something mighty queer about four grown up people who think they've heard taped messages and go dashing off into the English countryside to tilt at windmills. And as I said, if they do find the girl, it isn't going to make the average Quebecois feel all that much better. Besides which, it's too late to turn back from our destiny now Paul, far too late."

He warned Boisvert once again not to take action of any kind on the case without first consulting him and then hung up, obviously in excellent spirits.

Inspector Boisvert was relieved he didn't have to go to Orillia. The thought of setting out for the heart of English Canada was not something he had any great enthusiasm for. Besides which, it sounded like a wild goose chase.

Or did it?

Inspector Boisvert was a man who relied heavily on his instincts. It was the way he had fought in the ring – uncanny in his ability to slip under a left jab, to bob just in time to avoid a bomb to the chin. A story had been floated once that he was so fast, his instincts so honed, he could anticipate when his opponent was going to blink, and thus launch blows they never saw. Right now those instincts were signalling frantically. Something the premier had said was jangling away inside him, semaphoring wildly, demanding his attention. What was it?

He closed his eyes and began to roll the conversation with Charbonneau back in his mind. There it was! Right at the start. When he first told the premier of Castonguay's conversation with Carol Henry. What was it he'd said? Yeah, that was it. Something about how fast they had worked. The implication, when you thought about it, was pretty clear. Charbonneau didn't snort with derision at the thought of the girl being held captive in some little jerkwater place like Orillia. "So they worked that fast did they?" was what he had said, as though. . . as though. . . he knew the girl was there! And then there was all that concern over whether there was any information concerning the abductors.

"Yeah!"

A smile began to crease Boisvert's strange face, getting broader and broader until finally he broke into loud laughter, behaviour so unusual, workers in the outer office shot each other worried looks. The buzzer on his secretary's desk made them all jump.

"Find Detective Phillipe Castonguay and have him come to my office immediately," said the inspector, the glee still evident in his voice.

Less than an hour later Detective Castonguay, somewhat apprehensive (in this office most visitors were) sat across the desk from Boisvert expecting the worst. It was well known that Castonguay's soap-star looks and his sexual preferences infuriated the inspector.

But not this day.

"Early yesterday morning," said Boisvert cheerfully, "I met a man driving a calèche on Mount Royal. It was probably the first time he'd ever been that close to a horse. He was a tall man, six foot one or two I'd say, very thin, mid to late twenties, black curly hair and a very long black well-trimmed beard. He spoke excellent French, no patois. Come to think of it, he sounded as though he had been educated in France, or had at least lived there for some time. Whoever rented him that calèche would certainly remember him.

"I want you to find our friend as quickly as possible, and I want you to bring him here to me. No one else is to know anything of this. Do I make myself perfectly clear?"

"Yes, I understand Inspector, but finding a guy like that will be a real bastard of a job. There must be dozens, hundreds of men who fit that description in Montreal. Do you know anything else about him? Where he hangs out. Any of his friends? Do we even know in what area of the city he lives?" The task, as presented, appeared overwhelming.

Boisvert shook his head.

"I can't help you with any of that, but there are two things I am almost certain of. . ." A strange, almost embarrassed look flitted across his face. "Number one, this man is most probably involved in separatist politics, perhaps radically so, and. . . my observations have led me to suspect he may be gay!"

"Ahh," said Castonguay slowly, nodding the upper part of his body in understanding. "I see. If you're right Inspector, this shouldn't take all that long."

Boisvert dipped his head over his desk and began to scribble on a piece of paper.

Castonguay reached the door then paused for a moment and turned to face him again.

"Excuse me inspector. Will this man be dangerous? Will he be armed? Ahh. . . how careful should I be?"

Without even glancing up, Boisvert replied so softly Castonguay barely heard him.

"Very! Be very careful!"

Orillia 1:42 PM – Day Four

It was Al Thompson's perseverance which led to his discovery of the source of the strange buzzing sound on the tapes. After spending the entire night in a vain attempt to get the computer to unlock the secrets, shortly after dawn he began to randomly telephone friends and acquaintances, often rousing them from sleep, playing the tape into the telephone, hoping against hope one of them might recognize the sound. None did.

Although increasingly discouraged and exhausted, he refused to give up. Running out of friends to call locally, he began phoning long distance to the town of Renfrew about fifty kilometres west of Ottawa where he had grown up, and still had relatives. He had made about a dozen such calls when he finally struck pay dirt.

Hughie Patterson was an old friend of the family who owned a small used car dealership on the western fringe of Renfrew. Al had bought a Dodge from him several years ago, so Hughie, sniffing another sale, greeted him in a jovial fashion which quickly changed when the purpose of the call was explained.

Hughie's reaction was immediate when he heard the tape.

"Hell Al, ya shoulda come here first. That there sound is one of them heat pumps from the earth."

Al was taken aback.

"Geeze, Hughie, this is no joke, this is serious stuff we're talking here. I don't app. . ."

"It ain't no joke, Al. That there sound is one of them heat pumps they're installing in some of the new houses roun' now. Thermal something-or-other they call it. They lay a few hundred feet of plastic pipe a couple feet deep in your back yard, the pipe sucks up all the heat out of the ground and condenses it down like. Sometimes instead of takin' the heat from the ground they pump well water through the pipes and get heat from that. Couple a guys just up the line here put their pipes out into the Ottawa River. I was down to see one of em, Ben Willard, only last week, sold him a 93 Colt, still in pretty good shape, and he shows me his new heatin' system. Says it costs him pig feed to operate and. . ."

"Hughie, why the hell would anyone be running a heat pump when the weather's as warm as it's been this past few days. It can't be a heat pump."

"Kee-rist," said Hughie. "Don't you fellas in the big city know nothin'? Them same heat pumps is used for air conditioning as well. Some folks they tell me, is usin' em to heat their swimmin' pools."

Al's heart began to pound.

"Hughie, are you sure? How can you be so positive?"

"I'm tellin ya, that's what that there sound is. I mind listenin' real close to it up at Benny's place and rememberin' how strange it sounded. Never heard nothin' like it before. Yep, no question about it, that there sound is what they call a ground source heat pump. Not too many about, but they sure's hell sound like one great idea."

"Hughie," said Al, thinking fast. "If I wanted to get one of those heat pumps installed in my house, who would I call?"

"Well, so far's I know, no one's installin' 'em around here, but there's a couple a guys I understan' up in Ottawa handlin' 'em now. I guess you'd best just let the ole fingers do the walkin' in the yella pages eh!"

"Hughie, I can't thank you enough," said Al.

"Sure you can," said Hughie, "just call on me when you're lookin' for a real car."

Al Thompson, so excited he could barely dial, immediately called the Freeport number Sandra had given him, left a brief message, then spent the next several hours in a near frenzy waiting for his phone to ring three times.

"What the hell is the matter with you people anyway," he shouted into his empty kitchen after about two hours of staring at the silent phone. "For heaven's sakes, call!"

When Grant finally signalled him with the three rings, Al tore off down the street so quickly he arrived at the designated phone booth well before the twenty minutes had elapsed and had to pace nervously for several minutes. By then, he was so agitated, he screamed into the mouthpiece.

"Kee-rist Grant, why the hell haven't you called before this? Our deal was you were supposed to call Sandra's Freeport number first thing this morning I. . ."

"Al, Al, calm down. I'm sorry I didn't call sooner. Your message said you thought you knew what the buzzing sound was and it should help us. What do you mean?"

Calmly now, and carefully, Al Thompson explained.

Afternoon – Day Four

By the time Jake and Charlie Dunn checked back in by phone, Grant and Sandra had not only tracked down the sole installer of ground source heat pumps in the area, but had winnowed the hunt to nine prime targets.

It wasn't all that difficult since, as Bert Tricky of Tricky Plumbing and Heating explained to Sandra, he'd only been installing "them kinda heat pumps" for a "couple a years" and so far only had about fifty "on the go". Sure he'd be glad to talk with Sandra about installing a unit in her home and no, he didn't have a problem providing her the names and addresses of his customers, all of whom he was certain would give him an excellent reference.

Sandra was in a cab and on her way to Tricky Plumbing and Heating in less than ten minutes.

Bert Tricky, presented with a willing audience, was quite prepared to let commerce (and just about everything else) grind to a halt while he shared his knowledge, points of view and current gossip. Bert Tricky, in fact, was an old windbag, who, prompted by Sandra, provided a lengthy discourse ranging from marital status to morning disposition of everyone for whom he had installed a ground source heat pump.

Using the information so gaseously provided, Sandra and Grant, through the process of elimination, reduced his list of forty-seven installations to nine "most likely" suspect locations. Some of the exclusions were reasonably obvious – two schools, a garage, the local library, a large poultry barn and the homes of several older residents of the central part of the city were immediately eliminated. Several more were discounted because they were occupied by well-known business people, and in one case a United Church minister.

The nine were left with were all single family homes, occupied by people about whom even Bert Tricky knew very little.

One of the houses, just west of Orillia, was, according to Bert, owned by "some big shot mafia guy from Toronto," although he confessed he'd never actually seen the man. Another house had been sold to a couple from Barrie only about a month ago and two others, one a farmhouse, had been recently rented out and Bert hadn't met the new occupants. The remaining five on their list were chosen simply because there was no reason to eliminate them. It was conceivable they would have to check all forty-seven buildings, but these nine, they agreed, were the most likely.

By the time Jake and Charlie Dunn barged into the room, full of questions, Grant and Sandra had a plan of attack almost completed. Grant checked his watch – almost three pm. For one brief instant his mind flicked to Parliament Hill where he knew MPs would at that moment be settling into their seats in preparation for one of the most momentous debates in the country's history. It was a momentary distraction. Something far more important to him was much closer at hand.

"Okay," said Grant, "here's what we're going to do."

Orillia 5:14 PM – Day Four

Andres Saurez was puzzled. There was no sign of life in the small white house sitting in the middle of a clump of lilac bushes about 100 meters away. The young guy, the nervous one, should have appeared outside the kitchen door three, maybe four times by now.

In the three days Andres had spent with them in that house,

Twitch, as they had begun to call him, had been unable to resist the urge to step outside and dart anxious looks up and down the road and into the fields at least once an hour and sometimes more often than that.

Andres, dressed in khaki pants and a Blue Jays jacket, had been lying and sometimes sitting on the dusty barn floor peering through a crack in the boards for almost four hours but had seen no movement from the house. He had parked his rented car at the bottom of the hill, about half a kilometre away, then, careful to stay out of sight of the house, he made his way on foot to the old ramshackle barn. There was only one farm within sight and if anyone had spotted him from there they would have just assumed he was out for a late afternoon stroll. He had kept his rifle as inconspicuous as possible, but he knew it was not uncommon for strangers from town to spend a few hours wandering these fields shooting groundhogs.

The plan he had worked out in the Yonge Street doughnut shop was very simple and, he was certain, would be very effective. He would wait until nightfall, set fire to the old barn, which would go up like a torch, run to the house before the flames were visible, then lie in wait in the lilac bushes just outside the kitchen door and shoot anyone who stepped outside to investigate. He would then have plenty of time before neighbours arrived to snatch the girl from her basement room and escape with her in the car he knew was parked in the small shed snugged up to the side of the house. His only concern was that in his absence, reinforcements might have joined the two men he had left behind to guard her. The intent of his surveillance was to determine if in fact that had occurred.

At some point during his vigil, Andres was visited by the suspicion that, aware of his escape from the Union Station trap, and fearing he might come looking for them with vengeance on his mind, they might have taken the girl and fled. He rolled this thought around in his head a few times, then discounted it as highly improbable.

'Too risky,' he told himself. 'Moving that girl in daylight would be just too dangerous.' But what the hell was going on down there anyway? Not a sign of life! Where was that stupid Twitch guy anyway? Afraid to step outside? Did they suspect that he might be lying in wait for them? Had someone warned them to be on the lookout for one very angry Andres Saurez? Yes, that was possible. Probable even. That would explain the quiet. They were probably waiting until nightfall to take the girl and run.

He relaxed a little, then rolled to his knees and grabbed a handful of loose hay, stuffing it beneath him.

'A couple hours yet till dark.' He chuckled grimly. 'If our timid friends down there don't come popping out on their own to see a barn fire, we may have to see how fast they move when their happy home starts to go up in flames as well!' His only regret was that the drug cartel for which he worked would have to find another safe house for couriers like himself. This one, isolated but only an hour's drive from Pearson International Airport, had served them well. He had no fear the cartel would ever find out he had taken on some freelance work. Those guarding the girl had no idea who he was. Besides which, they were unlikely to survive much past dusk!

Drowsy, fighting sleep, he was jolted into full alertness when a car came bouncing up the lane, stopping in the driveway of the house which was now deeply etched in early evening shadows.

Squinting in the freckled light of the barn's interior, Andres watched a big man in grey pants and a brown windbreaker approach the house and knock on the screen door. A second person, who, as best Andres could tell through the reflected glare of the windshield, was also male, remained at the wheel of the car.

Carefully Andres reached behind him for the rifle and thumbed off the safety. Earlier in the day he had worked one of the rotting barn boards free from the nails fastening it to the beam at his feet. Lying prone on his belly, he eased the board aside several inches to provide a clear line of fire, snugged the rifle's stock to his shoulder and watched and waited.

Afternoon – Day Four

Grant's strategy was simple enough. Form two teams, visit the nine suspect dwellings, pretend to be interested in buying an earth source heat pump and ask for any suggestions or recommendations and a chance to see it in operation. Throw Bert Tricky's name into the equation and see what happened. If they were invited in and nothing seemed suspicious, stroke it off their list. If something didn't smell just right, the situation was to be sized up as best as possible on the spot, but nothing was to be done until all four of them had agreed on a course of action, which at Sandra's insistence, might very well include the police.

Not everyone who refused them entry was necessarily a suspect of course. Even in towns the size of Orillia, many people were more than a little reluctant to allow strangers into their homes, but there was something Bert Tricky had said which they planned to use to their advantage.

"One thing about most everyone who has one of these little babies," said Bert, "is that they just love to talk about them. Most of the folks who go in for this kind of doodad fancy themselves as being pretty concerned about the environment and all, and are usually as anxious as all get out to let everyone know how concerned and smart and up to date in Kansas City they are."

So the plan was, even if they couldn't get invited in for a look, keep whoever answered the door talking as long as possible and see if anything out of the ordinary cropped up. And above all else listen for that strange buzzing sound they were all familiar with.

"One thing is for sure," said Jake, "kidnappers and terrorists aren't likely to give a good hoot in hell about heat pumps and they for sure won't be at all anxious to talk to anyone about anything with half the world looking for a little girl they've got stowed away."

By mutual consent, the first house selected was the one reputed to house the mafia don.

"On this little peeky boo," said Jake, "all four of us are there." There was no disagreement. He and Sandra would play the careful shopper role, while Charlie and Grant waited anxiously nearby in their parked car.

To their surprise, Sandra and Jake were immediately invited in by a lovely little old gnome of a man, who puttered cheerfully about on a gimpy leg, which he admitted ruefully was the result of a recent attack of gout. He insisted not only that they examine his heating system to their heart's content, but stay for a glass of sherry, and be damned with the gout, while he dug up some recent hydro bills to prove just how efficient his heat pump was. Sandra was shaking her head, and despite herself, grinning, when they finally emerged.

"Some mafia don!"

"We have to get two things," announced Jake thoughtfully, as they pulled away from the curb, "another cellular phone and another car. Grant's right, we've got to break up into two teams, otherwise, at the rate we're going it's going to take us the rest of the week to check on those final eight houses." "Better yet," said Charlie, "let's rent a car with a phone already in it. Economy has them I know, and we passed one of their agencies on the way out here. Let's divy up the houses right now, drop Grant and me off at the rental place, we'll pick up a car and phone while Jake and Sandra are checking out. . ." he ran his finger down the list. . . this place." He selected the house which had recently been sold to the couple from Barrie. "But we gotta be very careful here, okay? No chances. No hero stuff. We plan this thing so each team stays as close to the other as possible. We let the other team know every time we leave the car to check a house and we immediately report back after the call is over. If we suspect anything. . ." He turned sideways to look directly at Grant. "If we suspect anything, atall atall, we get out as fast as we can. We move away so they can't see us, but we can see them, and immediately call the other team. Together we plan what we're going to do. If we think we need the police, then we call the police. And Grant, I don't have to tell you, keep that Lynx cap pulled down and those sunglasses on all the time. Everybody agree?"

There were murmurs of assent.

Orillia 5:14 PM – Day Four

"Okay, we're here. It's a two-story white frame house on top of a small knoll. Left side of the road. It's a gravel road all the way, exactly. . . let's see. . . ahh. . . yeah, one point three kilometres east off the highway. It's the 9th concession all right, just like tricky Bertie said, but there isn't much of a sign to indicate it on the highway. You could miss it easily. You turn off number eleven highway onto the 9th concession at a big junk yard called, believe it or not, Margaret and Pierre's Antiques. You can't miss it. The yard has enough junk to fill the Titanic.

"The name on the mail box here is Werner. That's spelled W-E-R-N-E-R. From what we've been able to learn he's a widower. Lost his wife a couple years ago and rented this place out more than a year ago to a man supposed to be from Sarnia. We checked with neighbours up the road, but no one seems to know anything about the people who've moved in here. In fact no one we talked to seems to have ever seen anyone here. The nearest neighbour is a good kilometre away so they wouldn't see much anyway.

"Charlie is walking up to the door right now. Doesn't look like there's anyone around. We'll get back to you as soon as we check things out."

Having reported in to Sandra and Jake as agreed, Grant disconnected the cellular phone and watched while Charlie knocked loudly on the screen door.

It was their second house-check since the "mafia don." The first place turned out to be the home of a local high school teacher and his wife, who, exactly as Bert Tricky had predicted, would have been only too pleased to spend an hour or two with Charlie extolling the virtues of their environmentally friendly heating and cooling system.

Jake and Sandra, meantime, had driven half way to Barrie, only to find that the couple who'd bought the place weren't even aware it came complete with air conditioning and had never even bothered to turn the unit on. They were now on their way to their second location, which according to their information, was near Washago, about halfway between Huntsville and Orillia and about twenty kilometres from where Charlie Dunn was right now pounding on a screen door.

5:17 PM – Day Four

There was something bothering Charlie, something unsettling about this prim and tidy little white house. The place certainly looked innocent enough, nestled in the centre of a large, well-trimmed stand of lilac bushes, but he found himself unconsciously tensing his body and had instinctively tucked his left elbow into his side several times, seeking the reassuring feel of hard steel.

Grant, alone in the car, could sense it too. The sagging old barn at the end of the lane, its rusty, torn metal roof flopping and rattling in the suddenly-chill evening breeze; the uncut hay fields throwing their heads violently from side to side and the silence of the house, wrapped in rippling shadow, sent an involuntary shiver down his spine. He closed the car window and reached for his jacket in the back seat.

By cupping both hands to the side of his face against the door's window, Charlie could see inside. His heart quickened. The kitchen was a shambles. Open boxes of food, bags of garbage, cans, dirty dishes and beer bottles were strewn everywhere; on counters, on chairs, on top of the refrigerator and the kitchen table.

It was that table which interested him the most. Small clearings in the debris had been created at both ends. In the centre of the clearings were plates half filled with what looked like spaghetti. At one end of the table, cutlery was scattered on the floor and a chair lay tipped on its back. The evidence was obvious. Two people had sat down for a meal at that table, then bolted in one hell of a hurry. Who? When? Where were they? Still in the house?

Charlie knocked once more, pounding vigorously, then cautiously reached for the door knob and turned it. It wasn't locked. Gently, he pushed the door ajar, ready to drop to the ground, his right hand just inside his jacket, millimetres from his gun.

"Hello! Hello? Anybody home? Bert Tricky told me to call on you and check out your heat pump. Hello!"

Alarmed, Grant watched as Charlie pushed the door completely open and stepped inside the darkened interior. Grant was tempted to shout at him; this wasn't in the plan, they should wait for Jake and Sandra, but he held his tongue. Charlie Dunn was, after all, an experienced cop. He was armed and so far hadn't pulled his gun. He must know what he's doing.

Charlie blinked several times, trying to adjust his eyes to the murky interior, then looked around, standing perfectly still and listening. Nothing. But damn the place was cold!

It hit him then. He felt the blood rush from his body, and ice flood in. With a vicious kick, he sent the table crashing to the floor, spewing food, garbage, bottles and dishes wildly about. He crouched behind this barricade, slithering in the spaghetti and the garbage, safety off his gun, ready to fire at any sound or movement.

Cold! Of course! The air conditioning! It had to be running almost all the time in order to be heard on every one of Lee Henry's tapes! This was the place! She's here! Who else? Where? Jesus, what was that?

From behind a narrow wooden door set into the far right hand corner of the kitchen, had come the faint sound of. . . what? There it was again. Louder this time, but still faint. A gasping, sucking, whine, then something else. . . a rasping kind of sound, like a hungry dog licking an empty tray across a concrete floor. And then he remembered. It was in a grubby arena in a dingy little northern town years ago, a defenceman down on the ice, gasping for life, his throat gashed by an errant skate, blood squirting between desperate, faltering fingers, that same horrible sucking sound. . . the rasping. . . the terrified, pleading eyes!

With a cry, Charlie tossed the heavy table aside as though it were made of cardboard, and lunged for the door. Although almost certain the diners were gone, and desperate to reach the source of that terrible sound, his training insisted he take as few chances as possible. Standing with his back jammed to the wall, he reached out with his left hand, grasped the metal latch and threw the door open, keeping his body well away from the entrance. There was no movement from below, no sound save the sucking and rasping, muffled now by a loud buzzing drone which had just clicked on.

Charlie recognized it immediately – the mysterious background accompaniment to Lee Henry's agonized recorded pleas.

If Charlie Dunn had been a more cautious man, if he had followed regulations, he would never have plunged down into that dark and dingy basement. At the very least he would have yelled to Grant to call for Jake and police backup. But Charlie Dunn had already used up his caution quota for the day.

In one swift, powerful motion, he whirled from his position beside the door, grasped the top of the handrail leading down the basement stairs and using it as a fulcrum, vaulted to the dirt floor below without touching a single step.

Crouched low in the dim light, almost on his knees, he pivoted 360 degrees, gun outstretched in both hands, alert to the slightest movement. The basement was empty, save for a few cardboard boxes and what appeared at first glance to be a very large white refrigerator with pipes protruding from its side and top.

'Son of a bitch,' said Charlie to himself, 'the famous ground source heat pump. Now little girl where are you?'

And then he knew. As his eyes grew more accustomed to the dim light, he could see that the sounds were emanating from a corner of the basement which had been partitioned off into a small room, raised slightly from the dirt floor. Certain the guards had fled, he completely abandoned caution and was inside the room in a bound.

For a moment he was immobilized. She lay there, head and shoulders on the floor, the lower part of her body on a dirty mattress, her nakedness covered only partially by a filthy blanket. At some point, food and water must have been placed beside the mattress because it was now pasted into her hair as her head lolled from side to side on the floor, reacting, it seemed, to each gasp of air she forced into her drowning lungs. The sound which had drawn Charlie down into the basement was Lee Henry's desperate fight for life. Every breath another agonizing victory, punctuated by frequent rasping, hacking coughs, which shook her pale, fragile body.

A low guttural moan escaped her lips as Charlie scooped her into his arms and bounded up the basement steps and through the shambles of the kitchen.

He was outside on the grassy lawn, less than five metres from the car, sprinting, when the bullet struck him. It tore through his left shoulder, deflected downward, exiting at his elbow, missing Lee by less than a millimetre.

It wasn't the bullet which killed him though. It was a piece of bone, not much larger than a matchstick and as sharp as a scalpel which splintered off his humerus, sliced through the flesh of his inner arm, through the rib cage and plunged deep into his chest cavity.

Charles William Dunn crumpled into a heap on the grass, his precious cargo spilling from his grasp like a fragile vessel, to lie exposed and white as chalk against the green.

The second shot, fired into the echo of the first, crashed through the car's windshield and caught Grant on the left side of his head just as he was throwing open the car door to rush to his daughter. The force of the blow spun him partially around and knocked him sprawling back onto the front seat, his legs protruding through the open door.

Blood sprayed wildly as he bounced off the seat, crashed into the steering wheel snapping off the bottom half, then rolled down between the seat and the dash, partially onto the floor. Two more shots thudded into the back of the seat, only centimetres above him. A shower of broken glass pattered gently down over his head and shoulders.

A part of Grant was paralysed by disbelief, shock and terror, certain he was dying. He fought it desperately. To succumb to panic meant certain death for him and for Lee. He must not allow that.

He was amazed to find that at that moment, his own life meant nothing to him. He was not in the least concerned about dying, or pain. Only Lee mattered. The discovery seemed to pump strength back into his muscles. His breathing slowed to almost normal. He could feel his mind detaching from his body and the horrific events of the past few moments. He viewed it all as though from a distance. Reaching out with his will, he shut down the engine of panic which threatened to overpower him and replaced it with a dispassionate calm. Time slowed. He felt no pain. The profuse bleeding from his head and face concerned him in a distant, hazy kind of way, but he sensed the wound was not mortal. Most of the blood was pouring from his left ear, which a quick probe with his hand revealed was missing most of its lobe.

There was also a deep gash high on his cheek and he suspected a bone had been broken.

For just an instant, he was confused by the loud roaring which seemed to tear at his head. Dazed, he believed it was the result of his wound, but when he shifted his body slightly, trying to stop the blood from running into his eyes, the roaring changed for a moment, and he understood it wasn't his head at all. It was the car's engine. He had started it the moment Charlie Dunn burst from the house with Lee in his arms. The motor was racing wildly now, only inches from his head, the accelerator wedged against the floor by the weight of his body.

Grant was almost certain he had not lost consciousness when the bullet struck, but the shock had confused his mental clock. How long had he been lying here, jammed like this between the front seat and the underside of the dash? The instant or two he could recall? Longer? Long enough for whoever had fired the shots to have fled? Or, what he really feared, had sufficient time lapsed for the sniper to be even now approaching the car, ready to finish the job?

A moan from the lawn a few metres away, loud enough to be heard over the engine's roar, snapped him into action. It was Lee.

Quickly, he folded his legs into the car, involuntarily wincing from the imagined impact of another bullet. With every movement he knew he must not adjust the pressure on the accelerator. Any change in the engine's sound would be an instant tip-off to whoever was out there that he was still alive. Groping around behind him with his left hand, he managed to grasp the lever he sought, slippery with blood, and wrenched it sideways. By pushing against the seat with his body, he managed to move it back enough to give him the room to scramble to his knees on the car floor, right hand still firmly jamming the accelerator down.

Slowly he raised his head to peer over the dashboard, steeling himself against another bullet. The shattered, blood speckled windshield, while screening him from the view of anyone in front, made it virtually impossible for him to see out. To compound the problem, his left eye had swollen almost shut. Finally, he found that by twisting his head sharply to the left and ignoring the pain now washing over him in waves, he could get his right eye close enough to one of the bullet holes to squint out, although his line of vision was severely restricted. If the sniper was near the car Grant knew he might not be able to see him, but the barn was clearly visible directly in front.

There was a long narrow dark gash in the weather-beaten greyness of the barn's wall. A board had been removed. He could see nothing behind the gash nor anywhere within the restricted scope of his vision.

He caught his breath. In the long shadow of the barn's east side there was movement. And again. Out of the shadow and into full view in the sun's setting rays, a man was moving, bent almost double, running hard, a long-barrelled gun in his right hand. He was coming directly towards the house and car, fast.

Charlie Dunn and Lee lay no more than five metres from Grant's precarious refuge. The idea of making a dash for them, and in particular Charlie's gun, flitted for the briefest of moments into his mind. 'No,' Grant warned himself. 'The instant I let up on this gas pedal, he knows I'm alive. I'd be a dead man before I got out of the car.' It was obvious that whoever was out there knew how to use a gun very well.

Taking great care not to alter pressure on the accelerator, Grant shifted his body on the slippery floor of the car, managing to jam his right knee onto the pedal, freeing his right hand. He readied himself for battle.

One of those strange fleeting thoughts which sometimes jump into the mind at times of crisis came to him as he calmly kneeled on the car's blood-soaked floor. He recognized it as an Old Testament passage from his grandfather's bedtime reading of the Bible: "And they girded their loins for battle." He found himself abstractedly rolling the phrase over and over in his head. . . only a few seconds more.

* * *

Andres Saurez had no doubt that both men were dead. He had great confidence in his marksmanship, even with one of his targets moving. Besides which, the big man lying on the lawn hadn't moved since going down, and as he drew closer he could see no sign of life. Andres had seen sudden and violent death often enough to recognize it, even from a distance.

The girl was still alive. He could see her moving, but she appeared to be either very ill or badly injured.

"Damn!" He didn't need another complication. As for the one in the car, from the amount of blood he could see and the bullet holes dead centre on the driver's side of the windshield, it was obvious his aim had been perfect. The body must have fallen onto the accelerator.

Andres couldn't help gloating. But he was puzzled. Who were these men? If they had been sent to help guard the girl against him, why had one of them knocked so long on the door while the other waited in the car? And most importantly, where were the two men he'd left here only two nights ago? And what about that one lying dead there on the lawn? He had come charging out of the house with the girl in his arms, which meant either the guards he had left behind had fled earlier, leaving the girl alone or, the man now lying sprawled on the grass had killed them. But Andres hadn't heard any shots inside the house. Which left a third, worrisome possibility. Could there be someone still in the building waiting for him? Was this another trap? He didn't think so. If it was, it was incredibly stupid, with two men already dead, but as he drew closer to the carnage he had created, he grew more cautious; careful always to stay out of the line of fire from any of the windows in the house; ready to dive into the chest high hayfield which bordered the laneway between house and barn. After his experience that morning in Union Station he was taking no more chances.

* * *

About halfway between the barn and the house, the man, who Grant could now see was dressed in army fatigues and a blue jacket, stopped abruptly, dropped his left hand onto the gun's steel barrel and stared intently first in the direction of the house and the two prone figures on the grass, then with narrowed eyes at the car.

Grant held his breath, remaining motionless, still hidden, he hoped, by the cracked, blood-splattered glass and the deepening shadows.

Apparently reassured, the man resumed his progress, walking briskly now, no longer running, still slightly in a crouch, both hands on the hip level rifle. He was watching the car intently but Grant could see, for some reason, he was becoming more and more apprehensive about the house. Once he almost turned his back on the car to stare at the building, gun half raised to his shoulder, when a small flock of sparrows fluttered up from the lilac bushes.

"Turn your back on me again like that you murderous son of a bitch and you're a dead man," muttered Grant. "Come on you bastard . . . come on. . . just a few steps closer. . . that's it..closer. . . closer. . . keep coming. . . keep coming. Shit! Now what?"

Less than five car lengths away, the man stopped abruptly and dropped into a deep crouch, eyes fixed on the house. Another three or four strides closer and Grant would have risked it, but from this distance; too far.

5:21 PM – Day Four

It was the lack of cover the rest of the way to the house which was bothering Andres. Thus far, he had been able to keep out of the line of fire from any of the doors or windows. If someone had leapt from the house in an ambush, he would have dropped into the dense hayfield. Until this point, he had been able to stay close enough to the field to feel the tall stalks of timothy brush against him. At the first sign of danger, he would instantly duck into their concealing shelter. Another couple of strides however, and the hay ended.

From here to the house, about twenty metres directly in front of him, he would be fully exposed. Too risky! He stared hard at the car, its engine still roaring loudly. It was sitting, he estimated, no more than ten meters to the left of the building, directly in front of the kitchen door.

'That's the answer!' he told himself. 'Get the car between me and the house. Use it as cover.'

It meant he'd have to make a dash across open ground, fully exposed for several seconds, until he could get behind protective cover, but there would be far less risk doing that than in continuing to approach the house directly. He suspected that anyone watching would be expecting him to continue straight ahead, directly towards the house and the two sprawled figures on the grass and would, at least momentarily, be caught off guard by a sudden change of direction. More importantly, he knew that a target moving laterally was more difficult to hit than one approaching directly head on.

Not wishing to signal his intentions, he continued staring straight ahead at the house, then without warning wheeled abruptly left and began to sprint, crouched low.

5:22 PM – Day Four

It took Grant a fraction of a second to understand what was happening. He didn't have more time than that to act. Still kneeling sideways on the floor, his knee jammed against the accelerator, he reached up with his right hand, grasped the gear shift and held his breath.

Andres was less than ten metres away, running awkwardly, bent almost double. He was twisting his body in an effort to keep his eyes fastened on the house over his right shoulder, when Grant ripped the gearshift down.

For what seemed an eternity the car stood still, the spinning wheels frantically clawing at gravel, stones and dirt.

That millisecond of delay, while the car's spinning wheels sought purchase, might have been enough to save Andres, but he made a fatal mistake. Instead of leaping to one side, or making a dash for the lawn and Lee, Andres chose to trust his marksmanship. Straightening to full erect, he slapped the rifle's butt into his shoulder and fired two quick shots through the windshield, where the driver's head should have been, before the wheels struck solid ground and the car launched itself at him like a stone from a catapult.

Refusing to believe what was happening, he got a third round through the windshield before the car was upon him.

The impact tossed him like a sheaf of wheat more than two metres to the left as the car tore past, wheels spitting stones and dirt.

A blinding pain rushed up from the lower part of his body. He knew he was seriously injured, but was not yet ready to die. Even as he felt his bones breaking and his body being hurled through the air, he refused to relinquish his grip on the gun. Lying on his back in the dust and the dirt, left shoulder, ribs, pelvis and legs shattered, he managed to raise the weapon with his right hand and begin firing it like a revolver in the direction of the car, which had stopped only a few metres from the barn.

He continued firing though a fiery red haze of pain and shock until, out of bullets and the lower part of his body unable to respond to his brain, he could only watch in helpless horrified fascination as the car with no driver began to move again.

His screams were not of fear, but of impotent rage as the vehicle began to back up directly towards him, slowly at first, then faster and faster. With his last ounce of strength, Andres raised the rifle over his head – a defiant club against the onrushing enemy.

* * *

For one brief horrible moment Grant was certain the car was going to miss the man planted there in his path, feet braced, pumping bullets into the windshield only centimetres above his head. The spinning wheels were slewing the car wildly from side to side, and steering with the broken wheel from his kneeling position was virtually impossible. At the last second his eye lost the bullet peep hole and he was driving blind.

He heard the thud of contact and felt the car hesitate for an instant, but it seemed so inconsequential amidst the bedlam, he suspected it was only a glancing blow or perhaps only a wheel catching a rock and death remained standing astride the laneway.

It was not until the shadow of the barn dropped a curtain of darkness over the car's interior that Grant jerked his knee off the accelerator and stabbed the brake pedal with his hand. A few metres short of crashing into the stone foundation of the old barn, the car shuddered to a halt and stalled.

Stunned by the sudden silence, Grant was momentarily frozen to the floor, heart pounding, breath coming in long gasps, blood dripping from his face.

The crack of the rifle shocked him out of his daze. It sounded far away. Then again, this time from the direction of the barn, but when he scrambled from the floor to peer cautiously through the shattered rear window, he realized what he had heard was the shot's echo off the barn wall.

The gunman was lying on his back in the middle of the laneway behind him, his legs twisting away from his body at strange angles. The gun in one hand was pointed at the car but the bullets ploughed up dirt several metres short of their target. Andres did not have the strength to raise the rifle high enough for the bullets to reach the car. As he grew weaker, the bullets fell shorter and shorter.

What galvanised Grant was the sight of Lee lying on the lawn only a few meters away from the injured killer. If he turned the gun on her. . . !

Grant turned in the driver's seat, twisted the ignition key and as the engine roared to life, jammed the gearshift into reverse. Twisting about on the seat to peer out the rear window, he could see enough to line the car's rear wheels up with the malignant lump of blue and brown in the dust of the laneway and tramped the accelerator to the floor.

At the last instant, Andres jerked away from the onrushing wheels as they brushed past his head. The sound Grant heard was the rear fender striking the rifle sending it spinning onto the lawn near the prostrate bodies of Charlie and Lee.

A lifetime of rage drove the pain from Andres' body. Pushing his right hand into the ground, he dragged his shattered limbs towards the lawn, and Lee.

Grant reached her first and swept up the rifle. Standing astride her body he took careful aim and pulled the trigger. A dry click. Empty! For an instant their eyes met. "Bastard." screamed Grant. "Filthy bastard," and taking two strides forward, smashed the heavy stock of the weapon into the still-calculating eyes. "Bastard," he screamed and brought the gun down again. "Bastard, bastard, bastard." He swung the rifle again and again.

5:37 PM – Day Four

For Jake and Sandra, the twenty-kilometre drive from Washago to the 9th concession and the white house Grant had described seemed to take forever. Alerted to trouble by a busy signal when they tried to phone after their own investigation turned up nothing more suspicious than an eighty-year-old widow, they had no idea what to expect, but with the busy signal droning on as Sandra continued to dial their number, they began to fear the worst.

They were not, however, prepared for the scene which confronted them when finally they wheeled into the laneway and skidded to a dusty halt.

The bullet-riddled, bloodstained car, Charlie's apparently lifeless body sprawled on the lawn, another body lying in a heap a few metres away and Grant, face swollen grotesquely and covered with blood, running towards them shouting, Lee cradled in his arms. It looked like the aftermath of a bomb blast and they sat stunned for a moment.

Sandra was the first to recover.

"Grant!" she cried. "Oh my God!" and threw open her door to help him get Lee onto the front seat while Jake dashed to the still form on the grass.

Despite his badly bloodied and broken face, she could tell that Grant was not critically injured, but Lee appeared to be very ill, moaning softly and gasping for breath.

"Charlie?" She shot the question at Grant.

"Dead I think, we've got to get Lee. . ."

She had the car up onto the lawn beside Charlie's body before he could finish his sentence. Jake had already begun to administer CPR.

"Quick, get him in the car," she shouted.

Jake shook his head. "Call an ambulance, I can't do this in a car, I. . ."

She cut him off.

"Jake, get him in the car now. An ambulance will never find this Godforsaken place. Not as quickly as we can get to a hospital. Do your best with CPR in the back seat."

In a moment they were speeding towards Orillia's Soldier's Memorial Hospital. Police, alerted by Sandra's phone call, spotted them at the edge of town and provided a siren escort. The emergency room staff was waiting for them.

Ottawa 6:43 PM – Day Four

The news trickled along the corridors of the Parliament Buildings, gathering momentum. Building volume and quickening its pace, it flowed from office to office, into the Centre Block, finally bursting into the spectator's gallery, cascading down over the member's benches, hurrying onto the floor of parliament itself.

The girl has been found. She's fighting for her life. At least one, maybe two others are dead, including, apparently, the man behind it all, was the information with some variations, which swirled about the Green Chamber with such vigour, that the speaker, in her flowing robes of office, had to call for order and finally when even her sternest admonition had no restraining effect on either the members in their seats, or the spectators in the packed galleries, she took the almost unprecedented step of calling for a brief recess.

The debate, until that point, had been one of the strangest in the history of the Canadian Parliament. Originally called into emergency session by the prime minister to deal with the crisis surrounding the kidnapping of Lee Henry and Quebec separation, parliament had quickly settled into, not a rancorous denunciation by the opposition of the government's decisions, as most had expected, but something quite different, a kind of requiem for a dying country.

Most members were only too well aware of the sentiments of their constituents. The letters, the phone calls, the faxes and the delegations from the home front had all been saying the same thing almost from the start of the Henry affair. The message was almost consensual, plain and simple, loud and clear: let Quebec go!

Most of the country's editorial writers and broadcasters, including many from Quebec, were, publicly at least, still maintaining opposition to separation, demanding that the government remain firm and not accede to what they described as intimidation from terrorists and kidnappers, but the message from the grass roots, from the men and women MPs would have to look to for votes during the next election, was much more visceral.

A sign carried by one of the ever-growing army of demonstrators gathering on the lawns of Parliament Hill read, "An ugly divorce beats war every time." It was a sentiment shared at that moment by the great majority of Canadians of all languages and cultures. Even residents of the Atlantic Provinces, while concerned about their fate, cut off from the rest of Canada, seemed to have accepted what they considered the inevitable.

It posed a tremendous dilemma for most members of parliament. Those who concurred with the majority of their constituents had no desire to be recorded by history as one of those responsible for the dissolution of a country, while those who believed that a united Canada was desirable and still possible, were reluctant to face the wrath of an aroused electorate.

Quebec members of the two federalist parties were in an especially delicate position. Independence would eliminate their jobs in the Canadian parliament, but create plenty of openings in the government of the new Republic of Quebec, so with their noses alertly pointed into the shifting political wind, and catching whiffs of new, and perhaps even deeper troughs from which to feed, most of their speeches were carefully structured to assure Quebeckers that while it was true they were now sitting as members of the government of Canada, they were only doing so out of a desire to best serve the interests of the Quebec people and would make whatever accommodations were necessary in order to continue doing so. They left little doubt in the minds of most that the campaign for election to the government of the world's newest country was well underway.

Marcel Picard, bright red and frantically licking his lips, was magnificent in his magnanimity.

"I for one," he said, pausing for a moment to locate the TV camera and gesturing dramatically into its eye, "have spent all of my political life in an attempt to serve my constituents, my country, and my province. If it is to be that my province becomes my country, as much as we will all mourn the loss, I am prepared to continue humbly serving my people. In fact," he peered intently into the camera, drew himself up as tall and stern as any great statesman, then continued. "If the need arises, I am quite prepared to make the ultimate sacrifice for my country and its people, whatever that country shall be called."

Stunned somewhat by the grandness of this idea and his own eloquence, he was about to soar off to new and greater heights when Jeanne Tremblay, with whom he'd been sweatily copulating only a few hours before, reached out, tugged sharply on his pant leg, and hissed at him.

"For Christ's sake, sit down and shut up."

Ordinarily, Marcel Picard could be rattled by the smallest of interruptions. Opposition members had long ago learned that shouting a phrase, even a single word into one of his long winded speeches in the commons was often sufficient to get him to lose his train of thought, the consequences of which could be quite spectacular. Not so this time! Inspiration struck him squarely between the eyes. Instead of sputtering into confused addledom as usually happened when he was distracted, Marcel Picard drew himself up even taller, cast a knowing but kindly eye about the house and said.

"Let the world know that Marcel Picard stands ready to answer to a higher power." He then sat down with great dignity. It was unquestionably his finest hour, although there were few in the house in a position to fully appreciate it.

The few members who out of principle spoke against Quebec independence found themselves loudly booed from the raucous spectators' gallery, and as the debate was being carried live on radio and television across the nation, those speaking in opposition to opening negotiations with Quebec on the terms of separation immediately found their parliamentary and constituency offices flooded with angry phone calls and faxes, sometimes even before they had settled back into their seats.

The offices of Employment Minister Sergio Hebert, (Lib, Blue Mountain, NB) who held the floor for more than half an hour with a plea for unity so impassioned it wrung tears from the eyes of many, received more than 400 phone calls and faxes from irate constituents within the next two hours. Several of the calls contained threats, taken so seriously by his staff that police were sent to guard his home. Security on Parliament Hill had already been substantially increased.

As the hours dragged on, the debate gradually settled into a strange kind of wake, sometimes silly, sometimes sad.

Several members of the federal separatist party, jubilant at what they sensed was impending victory, kept disappearing from their benches, only to return a few moments later afloat on acoholic clouds, until one of them, in attempting to catch the speaker's attention, tilted forward too far and, with a loud crash, fell across his desk on his face. Only a few titters fluttered up and down the benches at the incident which, had it occurred at another time under different circumstances, would have brought the house to a standstill with laughter and catcalls.

There was an embarrassed silence from his own ranks and a few angry cries from members of the opposition when Morley (Porky) Diedyk, (Reform, Quill Lake, SK) who had once publicly referred to French Canadians as a bunch of slippery frogs, rolled to his feet to claim among other things, that Quebec had always been one of his favourite places, inhabited by some of his best friends and losing it would cause him great pain. For the most part though, members refrained from name-calling and partisanship, preferring instead to play to the folks back home with artful displays of thoughtful sadness at a situation which they claimed had unfortunately reached a point where perhaps the only course to follow was a "careful and thoughtful examination of all the facts involved in the formation of a separate and independent Quebec."

That phrase and a multitude of mutations of it cropped up in almost every non-Quebec MPs speech, along with solemn assurances that he or she would make certain that any separation agreement was eminently fair to all parties concerned. Which, when spoken by those from non-Quebec ridings, roughly interpreted meant don't worry voters, Quebec will pay heavily through the nose for this.

Almost all of this oration was proceeded by a prolonged flag waving colloquy during which members from all provinces, including the separatists, tried to outdo each other in proclaiming their love of Canada.

As one press gallery wit wryly observed, "Sounds like one hell of a plot. Something like: Dear, I can't tell you how much I love you and all but, so sad, I'm going to have to hack about a third of you off. It may hurt a little bit, but don't worry your pretty little head about it because if you don't survive I'm going to make sure you get a very nice burial and rest assured I'll make sure your possessions are distributed fair and square."

The recess, which the speaker had planned to last no more than twenty minutes, stretched into more than an hour, during which the members, along with the rest of the country were brought up to date on the events which had taken place late that afternoon in Stephen Leacock's shocked little community on the shores of Lake Couchiching.

Police had now confirmed that two people were dead. One was identified as Constable Charles Dunn of the Ottawa City Police. The second was as yet unidentified, but believed to be the person responsible for the kidnapping of twelve-year-old Lee Henry as well as the shooting death of two Toronto police officers that morning in Union Station.

Lee Henry was listed in critical condition in Orillia's Soldier's Memorial Hospital, suffering from pneumonia and shock. Broadcaster Grant Henry, who had miraculously rescued his own daughter under very mysterious circumstances, had been injured but was in good condition in the same hospital. Police refused to speculate on what had occurred, or how Constable Dunn and the kidnapper had met their deaths. If they knew who the kidnapper was or anything of his motivation, they weren't saying.

When parliament finally resumed its emergency sitting, there was a brief flurry of speculation in the press gallery and enunciated on national TV by Charles Whitlaw, that these latest dramatic events might be sufficient to change the course of the debate. Adding some fuel to that speculation was the fact that the first speaker after the recess, Fisheries Minister Bud Williamson (Lib, North York, ON), delivered an impassioned plea that the session be adjourned until everyone had a chance to digest this new turn of events and the possible ramifications to the question of Quebec independence.

"We do not as yet know who this kidnapper is, or what motivated his actions," reasoned Williamson. "It could very well be that the kidnapping of Lee Henry and yes, even the murder of Georgette Courville in Ste Anne de Bellevue, had nothing to do with the separatist cause, but was simply the mad act of a single individual. We should at least wait to see what really happened in Orillia, and what is behind all this before parliament makes any decision on whether to begin negotiating the terms of Quebec independence. We may not know what we really have here."

His sentiments were shared by more than a few, but it was too late. The country's mind was made up.

When the vote was finally held, well into the early hours of the following morning, those in favour of entering into negotiations with the province of Quebec on the terms of separation outnumbered those who continued to hold out for a unified Canada by nearly two to one.

The vote, as several members were quick to point out, did not necessarily mean that Quebec would actually break away from Canada and form an independent nation. At least not immediately. What parliament decided was to enter into negotiations with the government of Quebec on the terms of a possible separation agreement, but few doubted that what had occurred was not a small step towards a divided Canada, but a quantum leap along that path.

A fundamental psychological barrier had been hurdled.

Canada had looked into the abyss and decided the leap across was requisite and survivable.

Montreal 6:56 PM – Day Four

His name was Bernard Baillot and he was ridiculously easy to find. There is, in Montreal, only a handful of people who own horse drawn calèches and the man who rented his earlier in the week to a tall dark-bearded man remembered the transaction very well.

"I mean after all come on eh," he sniggered in English, "how often does some guy come jumpin' out at you from a homo bar and offer you a couple hundred bucks to rent your horse and buggy for the afternoon? I mean it's not like I've got tomorrow's winner at Blue Bonnets Race Track here eh? Hey, hey, hey. Now if I had a stallion I might of had second thoughts about renting out to a guy like that eh? But old Harold here he's pretty safe eh? Hell he don't even have his nuts no more. Heh, heh, heh."

Phillipe Castonguay managed a small grimace of a smile in response.

The gay bar was *Les Trois Erables* and when assured that Phillipe's only interest was the pursuit of love (he claimed he'd spotted a tall, bearded stranger coming out of the bar earlier in the week and was immediately smitten), several habitues, from the description provided by Phillipe, were able to identify his quarry as an infrequent visitor to the bar, a man known to them only as Bernard.

When they discussed it among themselves, they were surprised to learn that none of them knew very much about him. Bernard apparently had been coming into the place only for about the last five or six weeks and usually kept pretty much to himself. Assured that the object of his affections showed up most nights around midnight, Phillipe snugged up to the bar, ordered a Blue Lite and prepared for what he sensed would not be an altogether unpleasant couple of hours. His presence was already causing a ripple of excitement in the room.

The head had barely settled in his glass when a stocky boy, not much more than eighteen, with beautiful shoulder length blond hair ambled over and sidled onto the seat next to him. Phillipe, anticipating a hustle, pretended not to notice him.

"He's in apartment twenty-seven at 478 St. Sulpice."

"Pardon."

"478 St. Sulpice, apartment twenty-seven." The boy flicked back his golden tresses with the palm of his hand and glanced at his watch, "but he's probably still sleeping right now."

"What's his full name?" asked Phillipe.

"Bernard Baillot, but I should tell you, you're too old for him."

For the first time, Phillipe turned to face the boy squarely.

"I'll take my chances. You know him well?"

The boy looked strangely at him.

"Of course."

"Why are you telling me where he lives then?" asked Phillipe.

The boy giggled softly.

"You're not too old for me. I'll be here when you get back." Without waiting for a reply he glided off his perch and was gone.

The blond boy had been right. Phillipe's knock on the St. Sulpice Street door, less than half an hour later, roused Bernard Baillot from a sound sleep and although he strongly resisted Phillipe's insistence that he accompany him to the Atwater Police Station, he seemed only slightly surprised and totally unconcerned when greeted there by Inspector Paul Boisvert.

"How nice to see you – again," said Boisvert, shooting his eyebrows to his hairline an "again". Turning to Castonguay he said pleasantly, "Phillipe, this has been an extremely busy night for you, why don't you take the rest of the evening off and let Mr. Baillot and me have a nice little chat here."

As Phillipe quietly shut the door behind him, the icy fingers of a sudden involuntary tremor ran up his spine. Without thinking, he crossed himself.

"Sit down, sit down Mr. . . what is it. . . ahh yes. . . Mr. Baillot. You look different then the last time we met. What is it? Yes. . . yes of course. The hat. . . that must be it. You're not wearing your hat. Too bad, it gave you a certain. . . what shall we say. . . flair? And of course the coat collar. It was all a bit. . . aahh. . . dramatic. . . don't you think? And that little scene in the calèche. What ever made you decide to rent one of those? I would certainly never want you working for me. You were so easy, so very easy to find. And of course your choice of, aahh, companionship." He shook his head and clucked his tongue several times. "I suspect even a rank amateur could have tracked you down. But please, please sit down, I am remiss." He pointed to a small straight-backed chair almost in the centre of the office. Rather reluctantly, Baillot settled himself into it, shifting about in a vain attempt to make himself comfortable. The situation was beginning to bore him and he glanced at his watch.

"My apologies," said Boisvert solicitously. "I assure you I do not intend to keep you long here, but I hope you can appreciate we do have a few things to discuss." As he talked, he casually strolled around behind his desk, slid open the top left drawer and surreptitiously pushed a small metal button, which locked the office door. Hardly pausing, Boisvert retraced his steps and halted directly in front of the seated man and stared down at him.

"Look," said Baillot, "what's this all about anyway? We have nothing to discuss. I told you be. . ."

The fist struck him directly below the heart with such force that, for an instant, his tall gangling frame and the chair in which it was seated were both propelled several centimetres into the air before they crashed back to the thickly carpeted floor.

Baillot was certain he was dying. Every breath of air had been driven from his body. His heart and lungs, convulsing in spasms of pain and shock, seemed incapable of ever functioning again. As he writhed on the floor, desperately trying to suck air back into his tortured lungs, Boisvert looked down at him, expressionless, and said, "Now Mr. Baillot, perhaps we understand each other a little better. Get back up here on this chair and tell me everything you know about the kidnapping of Lee Henry, the murder of Georgette Courville and anything else you think I might find interesting."

"You can't do this," gasped Baillot, finally forcing a dribble of air into his lungs, "I told you before, I was only the messenger, if they find out what you are doing here, I swear you'll wish that. . . aaahhh." His shriek was as much from shock and surprise as from pain, as Boisvert reached down and grasped his full beard with both hands and jerked him violently to his feet. Fingers still entwined, Boisvert pulled down hard until Baillot's eyes, watery pools of fright, were level with his.

"I doubt very much you are a brave man, or a foolish one," said Boisvert, his eyes slits of menace. "The fact is I can make you wish you had never been born and not leave a mark on you, or shed a drop of your faggot blood, and even if I did, who would believe my blows were not struck in defending myself against you. And as for those whose messages you bear, I assure you, once I know who they are, I will have nothing to fear from them, since my power will be as great as theirs." He pulled Baillot's face closer, his hands still buried in his beard. "And I assure you, before you leave this place, I will know everything you know."

Without warning, he pulled his hands apart with as much force as he could muster. The howl of pain and the ones which followed could not escape the soundproofed walls of Inspector Paul Boisvert's office.

DAY FIVE

Carol arrived during the night, having flown into Pearson International in Toronto and taxied north to Orillia. She looked terrible, her eyes swollen and red as she tried to shield her haggard face from the glare of the TV lights and the flashing strobes of the still cameras. She had to fight her way through a small army of reporters, TV crews and curious townsfolk which had assembled on the lawns of the hospital and was spilling over into the narrow street in front.

Escorted by police to Lee's room, her eyes shot wide with surprise as she spotted Grant's heavily bandaged head, but she'd already digested the reports of what happened, including the extent of Grant's injuries and it was towards the pale and shrunken figure on the bed that she hurried as Jake and Sandra quietly slipped from the room.

"Oh God," she cried, as she saw the snake-work of tubes attached to the frail little body. "Oh my God," and she began to tremble violently. "Lee, Lee. Oh Honey, what have they done to you? What have they done to you?" She turned to Grant, her hands clasping her face in anguish. "She hardly looks alive." Grant reached out to touch her shoulder gently.

"They think she's going to be okay," he said. "They have her temperature down to almost normal and they're getting the upper hand on the infection. She should be able to breath on her own within the next few hours. Thank God she's young and strong."

"Do they think there will be any after affects, any. . . any kind of lasting damage. . . with all that. . . ahh lack of oxygen what. . ."

"They're not positive," said Grant, responding to the unasked question, "but as best as they can tell right now, it doesn't appear there has been any permanent damage. . . anywhere. I think our little girl is going to be all right." He looked at her intently. "What about you Carol?" He raised his hand from her shoulder to her cheek.

She began to cry softly.

"I don't know Grant," she said, "I don't know, but if Lee is all right, does it really matter?"

"Yes," he said firmly, nodding towards the still form on the bed. "It certainly matters to her."

"And you?" she asked.

"It matters to me. You matter to me."

She had stopped crying and was staring intently at him.

"I never stopped loving you, you know," she said.

He nodded.

"I know. Nor I you."

"But things change," she said wistfully, "people change, we've changed, is that what you're saying?"

"It's time to move on," he whispered, looking at her steadily. "There is a part of me which will always love you, but we can't go back. You know it as well as I."

"You have someone else," she said sadly.

He looked away thoughtfully for a moment.

"Yes, perhaps."

There were tears in her eyes again.

"Good luck Grant."

She leaned forward, laid her hand on his forearm and kissed him lightly on the lips.

"You too," he said, his voice husky with emotion.

They regarded each other for a moment, each lost in their own thoughts, then with unspoken understanding they turned as one to the bed, and for the rest of the long night kept a silent vigil over their daughter.

The Old City, Montreal – Day Five

They began to arrive at dawn. A tiny trickle of twos and threes at first, then a steady stream pouring in from every direction, until by noon, thousands had jammed themselves into the streets surrounding the historic Montreal City Hall from whose balcony Charles De Gaulle had shouted his famous *"Vive le Quebec Libre."*

If asked, none of those now wandering aimlessly to and fro would have been able to explain why they had chosen to assemble there. No event was planned. Not until the streets of the Old City were already jammed had local radio and television begun to report the phenomenon. It was a spontaneous migration, prompted by the same need to share momentous occasions with others that drives people into the streets to celebrate the end of a war, to block a coup in Moscow, or defy tanks in Tianneman Square.

The umbilical cord was about to be cut. The first tentative breath of a newborn nation was only a heartbeat away. Those gathering were part of the birthing process, expectant, excited, anxious and uncertain.

The premier's aides, wary of the crowd's mood and uncertain of Charbonneau's ability to speak effectively with little preparation, advised him against making an appearance.

"Nonsense," he snorted, "Andre, start taking notes. Jean, advise the press I will be speaking from the balcony of City Hall at exactly twelve noon and make arrangements to get me there through the crowds in time."

He began to pace nervously back and forth across his office while dictating notes, then in the middle of a thought, stopped abruptly.

"What would you say the temper of the crowd is right now?" he inquired.

There was a pause as his aides reflected. Quiet, they agreed. Almost sombre, but not despondent. A bit uncertain perhaps about what lies ahead, a little confused about it all and yes, rather quiet for such a large number, was the consensus.

"Of course they would be quiet and reflective," said Charbonneau, more to himself than those about him, "they understand very well the significance of this moment. They know history is in the making and they are part of it. Sooo, let's make certain this will be a moment they will never forget."

His speech, at the outset, mirrored the crowd's feelings – quiet, reflective, almost sombre, then gradually he quickened the pace and the emotion, until at the finish he was electric with celebration and confidence and optimism and the crowd was roaring its approval.

"It was a masterpiece of a speech," wrote English Canada's best known political columnist the next morning. "The assembled throngs, though tremulous and more than a little dubious at first, would, at the conclusion of Charbonneau's address, have joyfully followed him through the gates of hell. Any lingering doubts the average Quebecker or the rest of this country may have had about the will of the province to forge ahead on its own must surely have been dispelled forever on that historic balcony.

Quebec independence is assured," continued the column. "It is now simply a formality, a foregone conclusion, a force which cannot be halted or even deflected. And we are all," he concluded, "much poorer and sadder for it."

The thousands in the streets who cheered their new premier till they were hoarse, many with tears streaming down their faces, and the millions more Quebeckers watching him on television and listening on radio, did not consider themselves any poorer or sadder for what was happening. Charbonneau's speech had left them euphoric. They had found the man to lead them into that brave new world which secession had always promised. Here was a man for the moment! A man who could surely work magic! A Montreal Messiah!

But he couldn't get rid of that pesky little Montreal detective Boisvert.

"He insists on seeing you right now," apologized an apprehensive assistant. "Claims it's really urgent. 'The fate of our new republic is at stake,' were his exact words."

Charbonneau, face glowing, eyes still ablaze from the wild cheering and outpouring of support and affection which had come surging up to him from the streets, was much more irritated than alarmed at the message.

"Yeah, yeah, sure, fate of the republic he says. I'll bet! Okay, let the ugly little bastard in, I'll see what he's got stuck across his ass."

Inspector Paul Boisvert's eyes were hard and cold.

"Alone," he snapped, "we'll meet alone." He gestured to the door. "There's a small private office just down the hall." He turned on his heel.

"Just a minute," said the premier, his voice rising. "What the hell is this all about? I have no intention of talking with you now, or ever."

Boisvert, whose back was completely turned to Charbonneau, stopped just short of the door and over his shoulder said coldly. "It concerns our mutual acquaintance Mr. Baillot." Without looking back, Boisvert opened the door and strode through it.

"Inspector Boisvert!" The premier's voice had the ring of authority to it, but Boisvert didn't pause in his march down the corridor.

"Okay, okay, all right, the goddamn office," shouted Charbonneau.

Boisvert stopped, backtracked a few metres and still without looking in Charbonneau's direction, entered a small office and closed the door behind him.

The premier found the little detective standing by the window staring out at the throngs of people happily jostling each other on the streets below. Small groups had begun to join hands and while he couldn't hear them, it was apparent they were singing.

"A very joyful occasion," said Boisvert. "You were magnificent on the balcony. Finally the love and affection you've always sought. Even your father never experienced anything like this!"

"What about this Baillot?" snapped Charbonneau. "Let's not play stupid games here. Agreed?"

"Certainly," replied Boisvert softly, still intently observing the crowd. "At your insistence I'll get right to the point. I know the whole story. I know about your man Derouin bugging poor old Jean Luc Menard's office and sending the tapes off to Grant Henry so he could start the ball rolling. I know about you hiring our Columbian drug friend Saurez and his team and by the way, that really was stupid trying to cheat him out of fifty thousand dollars. It's a good thing though, that you warned your friends in Orillia that Saurez would probably come after them, or we would have had a couple more deaths. I know all about the Notre Dame Cathedral rendezvous, the Ste Anne de Bellevue affair, the Union Station pay offs, the whole ball of sticky wax. I also know you fed me Larocque, thinking it would buy me off and stop me poking around too much. All very clever. You want Quebec independence with you as the big fish, something your daddy couldn't achieve, and you want to make the anglais pay for your wife's little escapade. I've got to hand it to you, you did a hell of a job. I am led to believe you even had a hand in the great Indian uprising at the Mercier. You and I will make a great team!"

Charbonneau, whose eyes had been boring into Boisvert's back, snorted loudly at this. "A team, you and I? Keep on dreaming my friend! You can't prove a goddamn thing. Not too many are going to believe the word of a faggot, furthermore I. . ."

"Oh, they'll believe him all right, at least enough to take some of that glow off your face," interrupted Boisvert, unperturbed. "I've got a signed statement from our gay bearded friend. What's more, I've got an hour or so of tape of him singing his little heart out. . . and. . ." Boisvert turned quickly away from the window and took a step closer, his eyes locking fiercely onto the premier's. "If that's not enough, let me ask you, have you been talking to Mr. Derouin today? Have you seen him around?"

Charbonneau went chalk white.

Boisvert became derisive.

"You can't seriously believe that Mr. Derouin carried out your instructions so diligently because of a simple desire to see the birth of a new nation here. You can't be that simple. I assure you Mr. Derouin has dreams and aspirations too, perhaps every bit as ambitious as yours and when confronted with some of the evidence I have accumulated, he very wisely agreed that in return for. . . ahh. . . certain considerations, he would compose a few brief sentences of his recollections of these past few days and make his little essay available to me.

"All these outpourings of confession are right now stored in a perfectly safe place and will not fall into hostile hands. . . unless of course, I should experience any kind of sudden accident or illness!"

A sudden burst of raucous laughter from directly below their window filtered into the room.

"What is it you want?" Charbonneau's voice was barely audible, resigned, weary.

"The same thing Mr. Derouin wants: considerations."

"What kind of considerations? Money?"

"Oh no, nothing like that."

"What is it you want then?"

"I've already told you. I want to be on your team!"

Epilogue

The late fall air was perfumed with the delicious fragrance of burning leaves. As far as Grant was concerned, it was one of the great pleasures of country living. Bureaucrats, desperate to create work and justify their existence, had long ago outlawed leaf burning in most urban communities, but here in the Gatineau Hills, leafy bonfires along with the morning trumpets of backyard roosters, were two of the simple pleasures of man which officialdom hadn't quite yet gotten around to banning, although there were rumblings. The more city folk moved to the country to escape city life, the more they agitated to turn the country into the city!

The biggest problem Grant was having this unseasonably warm and hazy late Indian summer afternoon, was keeping Lee and her new Samoyed puppy from demolishing the products of his labours. No sooner did he have a tidy little leaf mountain raked and ready for burning, than the two of them would plunge into it with shrieks and puppy-yips of joy. Sandra, from her vantage in the screened-in porch, was gleefully egging them on while he feigned gruff anger, when the phone rang.

She returned in a moment, a strange look on her face.

"It's Jake," she said, and handed him the cellular.

"What's up Jake?" laughed Grant, watching as Lee and the pup, who had mysteriously disappeared a moment ago, suddenly exploded from one of the piles, scattering his carefully raked leaves like wisps of smoke in a sudden breeze. "You should be up here today, this weather is just unbelievable, but it's not around for long, they're promising snow for tomorrow night if you can imagine. What say. . ."

"Grant, kee-rist are you not watching the news?" asked Jake.

"These days," said Grant, immediately subdued, "quite frankly I'd sooner not. If you want to know the truth, some of the things we're hearing from Charbonneau and that bunch since they won the referendum have almost got me convinced the time has come for us to get the hell out of this place. Sandra certainly thinks so. What they've already done to the country is bad enough, but some of the things they're hinting at now for Quebec are downright scary, especially for an anglophone. I. . ."

"Grant you haven't heard the half of it yet," interjected Jake disgustedly. "Listen to this and start packing your bags. Charbonneau has just announced he's picked his running mate for next month's election. . . Ready for it?"

"Geeze. Does it really matter?" asked Grant.

"Oh yes it matters," exclaimed Jake. "It matters one hell of a lot, because, unless the sky falls in, the first ever Vice President and Minister of Ethnic and Anglo Affairs of the brave new Republic of Quebec is going to be Mr. Chicken-Licken himself. . . Paul Boisvert!"

Chief Superintendent Marcel Charron's wife came in from the car with an arm full of groceries to find her husband staring at the television set, tears streaming down his face. She dropped the bags on the kitchen counter and hurried to him.

"Marcel!" she said, puzzled and a little frightened, "what is it? What's the matter?"

He pointed a finger at the flickering screen, but in his distress he couldn't seem to get all the words to come out right.

"Charbonneau," he spat between clenched teeth, "how could he?. . . what's he thinking about anyway?. . . that little weasel. . . with all the people he had to choose from?. . . Boisvert's got to be mixed up in the Henry thing. . . it's unbelievable. . . Charbonneau must know! I just can't. . . !"

The Chief Superintendent stopped abruptly and turned to stare at his wife, his eyes wide with sudden, shocked revelation.

"Oh my God." he moaned. "The two of them must have. . . ! Oh sweet Jesus, Maudie, what have we done? Oh my God, what have we done?"

ABOUT THE AUTHOR

Lowell Green is one of Canada's most experienced and controversial writers and broadcasters. His syndicated radio talk show is heard daily in seven Canadian cities and world-wide on the Internet. His articles and stories have appeared in a number of magazines, newspapers, and periodicals.

He has lived most of his life in Quebec and has two daughters, both of whom are fluently bilingual and one of whom still lives in the province. Lowell now lives with his wife Deborah and stepson Jeremy on a rural property on the outskirts of Ottawa, where he raises exotic chickens.

For more copies of

Death in October

send $18.95 plus $4.50 to cover
GST, shipping and handling to:

GENERAL STORE PUBLISHING HOUSE
1 Main Street, Burnstown, Ontario
K0J 1G0

Telephone 1-800-465-6072
Fax 613-432-7184